"Equal parts page-turning and thought-provoking, *Departures* is fantastic. It's grounded in the best kind of world-building—the kind that delights and disturbs and allows us to see our own world with brand new eyes."
Lance Rubin, New York Times Bestselling Author of
Denton Little's Deathdate **and** *Crying Laughing*

"*Departures* is a beautifully written, well-paced novel of two sisters' parallel paths of discovery of the tangle of lies woven by the Directorate, and the wonders and dangerous freedom of the world beyond its control. Evie and Gracelyn are delightfully nuanced characters--wrestling with the fears and insecurities that plague young adults amid a shifting world-view, yet their love for each other gives them courage to keep reaching for the other. Evie spices her perspective with wry humor, and is a heroine you'll be rooting for the entire way."
Jade Kerrion, USA Today Bestselling Author

"Wenstrom's masterful storytelling is on full display in *Departures*, with rising stakes, tense twists, and emotional resonance throughout."
Megan Lynch, Award-Winning Author

"Unputdownable from the very first page."
Natalie Cammaratta, Author of **Falling & Uprising**

Departures

E. J. Wenstrom

www.darkstroke.com

Discover us online:
www.darkstroke.com

Join us on instagram:
www.instagram.com/darkstrokebooks

Include **#darkstroke** in a photo of yourself
holding this book on Instagram and
something nice will happen.

For Rebecca and Sam

Acknowledgements

The journey this story has taken from concept to publication has been so winding that reflecting on it takes me back to different times and adventures. It dates back years and encompasses hundreds of drafts and correspondences. This book has truly taken a village.

First and foremost, love and gratitude to my spouse Chris, who has always taking this writing thing I do in the dark of early morning as seriously as our other careers. You've been a sounding board, a co-conspirator, and even on occasion an incredible author's assistant. I cannot express how grateful I am. I love scheming and dreaming with you.

Many thanks also to my family, who has supported me with matter-of-fact assumption of success from day one. Mom and Dad, Rebecca and Sam, Cheryl, it means everything to have you in my corner.

I have also been fortunate to have the support of many wise and talented authors, editors and beta readers, whose fingerprints are all over the text of this story. To my Athenas – Em, Femi and Megan – thank you for all the insights, perspectives and cheers. I'm in your corner for anything, forever.

Thank you also to Heather, whose insights and encouragement have been crucial to making this book its best, keeping it alive, and getting me through this journey's greatest plot twists. Thanks also to the City Owl flock who has kept rooting for me even as I set my sights in new directions. Thanks to Kristin for your thoughtful feedback, and the entire Alvarium Experiment for the support, sounding board and creativity. Thanks to Ralph for the feedback and cheers--and all of #5amwritersclub, the freaking best online writing community there is. And, thanks my critique partners at Capital Hill Writers Group for keeping me accountable and offering me new perspectives on these pages. Thanks to Florida Writers Association, who has built an incredible community and continued to offer me opportunities and support even after I left the region. Thanks to Bethesda Writers Center for the resources, friend and smarts.

And of course, many, many thanks to the lovely folks at Darkstroke Books who believed in this book enough to put it in your hands. Laurence and Sue, I'm so grateful for your expertise, guidance and partnership in making this book its very best and sharing it with the world.

About the Author

E. J. Wenstrom believes in complicated heroes, horrifying monsters, purple hair dye and standing to the right on escalators so the left side can walk. She writes dark speculative fiction for adults and teens, including *Departures* and the Royal Palm Literary Awards' Book of the Year, *Mud*, the first novel in her Chronicles of the Third Realm War series.

When she isn't writing fiction, E. J. Wenstrom is a regular contributor to DIY MFA and BookRiot, and co-hosts the Troped Out and FANTASY+GIRL podcasts.

Get bonus content and sneak peeks when you join E.J.'s newsletter at **EJWenstrom.com**

Departures

Chapter One

Evie

This is how I hope they remember me. Bathed in rainbow-bright lights, dotted in glitter, the tulle of my favorite dress swooshing around me as I bound through the pounding music on the dance floor. My cheeks flushed. Heart thudding. Alive.

That's the point, after all.

Tonight is my departure party.

We've finally gotten past the terrible, emotional departure rituals – the look back at my life's highlights, my speech of goodbyes. My final hours are passing too fast, but I'm relieved these rituals are behind me – I had to fill them out with fudged memories to draw out softened, saccharine sentiments, the edges sanded down. I had to stretch out my short life to fit the typical time frames. Most departure parties have to encompass a rich long life of a hundred years plus. Tonight, all I've got to cover is seventeen.

It's not enough.

But what do you do?

I know what you *don't* do. You don't sulk on your last night on this planet. Not when it won't do you any good and only devastate the few people you really care about. No chance. You take your remaining fun where you can get it. Or at least, you try not to ruin it for everyone else.

So I dance. I let the thudding bass roll over me and drown out my thoughts.

The lights of the Quad's event center are dimmed, transforming the great room and its arched white beams into splashes of moving colors. Rainbow-bright lights drift from floor to ceiling to windows, blocking out the Quad beyond, pink fading to purple, fading to blue, fading to green. The music turns up – never more than the maximum recommended volume, of course, careful to stay within Directorate recommendations for optimal health. My guests – neighbors, former teachers, my peers from across our Quad – stand from their tables on cue, and the dance floor begins to fill. Glitter drops over us like the night mist that keeps the plant life within the Quad dome green. Everyone smiles and bobs along to the beat. I mirror them, determined to keep my own smile in place, no matter what.

My little sister Gracelyn – the one person I actually want here right now – weaves through the shuffling crowd until she finds me. She smiles too, though her eyes glisten with a hint of tears at their edges. *No, don't cry.* That's what kills me the most about all this. I can't stand to see her hurting. I take her hand and squeeze it, pulling my smile even bigger, and twirl her around. When she turns back to me, the light is back in her eyes, even if a hint of tears still glistens in the corners. We jump and twist to the beat through the glitter raining from the ceiling, both of us determined to make the most of every minute I have left.

Too soon, curfew nears. The music turns down. The people settle down in response, and the Quad's mayor takes the mic.

"Thank you, Evalee Henders, for the gift of your presence in this Quad," she says, following the script of the ritual. As I take my place next to her on the stage, I look out at the event hall. Expressions have turned somber. "We have one last gift to you. May your passage be as peaceful and painless as your life."

She hands me a small white box. I open it and look at the translucent pill every citizen takes to trigger their departure, the serum sloshing inside it. A quake of fear washes over me, and I hope no one can tell. The whole point of departure is to avoid all that, the pain and struggle of whatever death would have waited for me around the next corner. Departure isn't the thing to be afraid of, I remind myself. *Not* departing is.

All the same, my heartbeat speeds up until everything starts to turn blurry. I blink hard, trying to push the panic down. Young as I am, this night will be talked about for years. The last thing I want is for something bad to be said about the way I went. I want to be remembered as strong. Brave.

I force my fear deep into my gut, nod in acknowledgment of the gift, and push it into my mouth before I can think anymore. Even as its sweetness dissolves on my tongue and the serum releases, a calming buzz quells my anxiety – the first taste of its promise to slowly pull me into a deep, everlasting sleep over the course of the night.

Hands raise in applause and everyone cheers, a final affirmation of my life. Then, the normal overhead lights switch on, and the magic of the color-bright dance floor dies. Like a spell has been lifted, my guests turn away, gathering their things and chitchatting politely as they file towards the exit.

After all, everyone else – whose lives will go on tomorrow – must get their full night of sleep to maintain optimal health and happiness.

Chapter Two

Evie

The guests filter out of the event hall and onto the waiting shuttlebuses, a line of rounded silver trolleys waiting in a line near the doors. They will deliver us to our assigned neighborhoods, which surround the Quad center in a carefully-designed ring for optimal flow. Already the Quad's white dome sky has started its fade to darkness as curfew approaches, and the usual soothing notes of the bedtime wind-down cue pipe in from the dome and into the vehicle. Mother yawns in response.

Gracelyn, Mother, Father and I get in line and step onto Shuttlebus Eleven, corresponding to our assigned neighborhood, find seats for the short ride home, and buckle in. A silence hangs heavy between us, leaving the usual stream of friendly announcements and warnings to fill the space in a warm, paternal voice: *"This is where you belong: Stay in your seat when the bus is moving... A healthy citizen is a happy friend. Be diligent in your daily fitness... Mind the step as you exit the shuttlebus, and always hold the handrail for safety... Notice something out of place? Be a friend and notify the nearest Directorate official."*

It is only minutes before the shuttlebus slows to a stop at the park of our neighborhood. Each neighborhood's park is in the center, a short trek from the identical manicured homes that surround it, each neatly framed with a sidewalk and tree. As my parents, Gracelyn and I make the walk, the silence between us grows thicker. A watchlizard's bulbous lens head tilts up at us as its electronic body whirs past our feet, its stubby tail waggling for balance, off to some new post. I stick out my tongue to whoever is watching the feed. An unnecessary act of reckless rebellion, but what does it matter, now?

As we approach the paneled door labeled "Henders," Father lifts his wrist to the laserscanner at its side to scan his digipad, and it slides open. It slides closed again behind us, and we all trudge up the stairs together. Tonight, the mellow beige of the walls, the auto-dim of the lights, and the calming low tones of bedtime music, reach me through a distorted filter of the serum in the pill from the ceremony, growing thicker in my veins.

At the top of the stairs, I turn for my room, but am pulled back by Mother. She wraps her arms around me tight for a final embrace. I echo her gesture, and then start to let her go, but she holds me tighter, refusing to release me, her thin fingers like eight little pressure points across my shoulders, and it feels like the weight of her sadness is leaking into me. We're not supposed to be sad. The Directorate handles everything to make sure of it. But her cheek presses against mine, and her breaths turn jagged and uneven, and she's still clinging to me tightly, until it starts to scare me, and finally I look to Father.

"Alright then, dear," he says, putting a strong hand around her forearm. "That's enough."

Father pulls her away and helps her to one of her small pills. Father echoes her movement, a rapid circle of his arms around me, and then he is gone, guiding Mother to their room at the far end of the hall. Her breaths are already starting to settle back into their normal, sedated rhythm. We go to our rooms without our usual "Good nights."

Caught up in the routine of life, I go into the bathroom. I unpin my hair from the fancy twists and curls Mother insisted on for tonight's party and let it loose. But then, my hand halfway to my toothbrush, I freeze. What's the point? The only ones who will see me tomorrow are the Departure Crew who'll come for my body. My arm drops back to my side. Not knowing what else to do, I return to my room.

The serum's soothing buzz makes the crisp white

comforter and two tidy pillows of my bed look even more inviting than usual, but I can't give into it yet. Not until I've talked to Gracelyn. I hear her shuffling in the bathroom, washing her face and brushing her hair. For her, tomorrow will come.

For several long moments, I stare at the calming blue walls, dazed. The serum is turning everything slightly blurry, even my thoughts. Idly, I wish I'd cleaned my room before the party. In the closet, a couple of shirts have fallen from their hangers and lie crumpled on the floor. The chair for my desk, the syncscreen mounted above it on the wall – everything is slightly out of place. Typical. Even though our standard-issue bedrooms are exactly the same, mine has never had the crisp, clean look Gracelyn's always does. But there was so much happening today I didn't think of it, and now I am sure that on the serum, I would only make it worse. The lamps on the desk and the nightstand, all the same rich brown of eco-friendly plastics modeled into faux wood grain, continue to dim, counting down to bedtime.

The bathroom door opens, then closes again, and I am about to go to Gracelyn's room when she taps lightly on my door. We've been doing this after our parents go to sleep for years. Basically our whole lives. I go to the door and let her in.

A few tears drop down her cheeks. Guilt tangles through my chest and into my gut. I've done this to her with my own stupidity and selfishness. The Directorate advised keeping us apart, from the day my parents found out Gracelyn was coming. It was better for her – for all of us – they said, to avoid letting us get close. It was unlucky enough, having one daughter with such an early departure date. It didn't have to impact the other one, too.

But when we were young, I didn't understand. And I was lonely. My life was pretty empty, with those numbers printed on my wrist for everyone to see. The other children weren't allowed to play with me; they didn't want that bond weighing them down later. My instructors didn't put any effort into teaching me. I had to do it all myself.

When I got older and began to understand, I tried to stop the bond growing between Gracelyn and me. I really did. But Gracelyn wouldn't give up. She kept sitting outside my bedroom door for hours every single night, ruining her rest metrics. Her medical advisor started getting concerned about her sleep count. Finally, I let her in.

She's only a year younger than me, but if there was one thing I've been good at, it's been protecting her. I've guarded her in dark nights when she used to get nightmares about the desolate world that lay beyond the Quad bubbles. I've helped her through the stress of her annual examinations. I've shielded her from Mother and Father when they got too intense about her future. But now, seeing the tears clouding her big brown eyes and making tracks down her pale cheeks, I can't help but face what I've let happen. I've hurt her. She's the one who will pay the price, for years and years after I'm gone.

"Don't do that." I whisper, wiping another tear away from her cheek. "Be happy. Always."

She shakes her head and presses the heels of her hands into her eyes. "I will. I promise. You don't have to worry about me."

When she pulls her hands away, her eyes are red from the rubbing, but dry.

"Here." I hand her a little box. Purple, her favorite color.

She opens it and pulls out the golden chain, with my favorite daisy pendant dangling from it.

"Oh," she sighs.

I've worn it every day since Mother and Father gave it to me – the day Gracelyn was born.

The tip of her mouth pulls into the hint of a smile, and she puts it on. Then she takes off her own necklace, a rose pendant, and stretches it out to me.

"Gracelyn?" I ask.

"Take it," she says.

"No way. That's stupid," I say, stepping back. "If you give it to me, it'll get…"

Her lip starts trembling. "Just take it, okay? It'll feel like you have a piece of me with you."

Anything to keep her from crying. I stretch my hand out and close it over hers. "Okay, okay. If that's what you want. I love it. I'll wear it. Always."

She nods and tips her palm open so the necklace falls into my hand. I put it on and pull at the collar of my dress to show her. "See?"

She smiles.

The serum's sedative is growing heavier, wrapping around me like a warm, fuzzy blanket, and the last thing I want is for Gracelyn to see me collapse into my final sleep.

I hug her, and she squeezes me so tight that my lungs strain. I almost say something, but really, at this point, what does it matter?

"You need to sleep," I scold her. "Go."

She squeezes me a moment longer. When she finally lets go, she turns away too fast, her shoulders shaking, and I know she is crying again.

I want to go after her, but the serum is taking over. I give in, flopping onto my bed and letting the blackness set in, unable to fight it any longer.

Chapter Three

Evie

Consciousness creeps in through a thick fog.

The first thing I'm aware of is the striking lack of citrus in the air, used by the Directorate to heighten alertness each morning. I tell myself I must have longer to sleep, but then, I realize sunlight is pushing in from the window behind my eyelids. Something is off, but my mind is too hazy for me to care. I groan, and my throat is scratchy and dry. My mouth tastes stale and mucky, and my body feels heavy, like if I ever moved again it would be too soon. All I want is to *rest*, to go on lying here forever, sunk into the comforting cushion of my bed.

But slowly, awareness creeps in like the sunlight, unwelcome and intrusive. When I finally realize why everything feels so off, I bolt upright.

There's no wake-up cues because I wasn't supposed to wake up.

Not today.

Not ever again.

My head sloshes in response to the sudden movement and the Directorate's serum, still thick in my blood. Despite it – because of it? – my heart races until I'm sure it will explode. The dread melts into my fingers, turning them shaky and numb. Then I'm falling, falling, falling, too fast to hang on, even as I cling to the sides of the bed.

Is this it – is this how I end? Did I wake up too soon?

I wait.

Brace myself.

For anything. For the nothingness sure to come any second

to relieve this attack on my senses. For my heart to burst, for my body to seize... I don't know.

My heart just goes on raging faster still, harder than it's ever gone, even in the stress tests during my medical exams. I wait for the corresponding alarm on my digipad to start, for the AI to tell me how to calm myself, to alert someone that I am still here, so they will come and fix this.

But it doesn't.

No one is monitoring my vitals anymore.

My labored breaths fill my ears, rising and falling far too fast.

I stare down at my hands, trying to calm myself. Trace a finger over the departure date inked into my right wrist.

The lettering is clear, and leaves no room for misinterpretation. Not that I could've gotten it wrong after seventeen years of fixating on it. And my parents. My instructors. Everyone.

It was the same thing every time. *Seventeen years?* they'd exclaim. *How? Why?* Parents would pull their children back from me as if they could catch it.

But what can you do? The Directorate doesn't decide when your departure date is. Its technology just provides the information. Makes sure you get as much life as you can before it becomes more pain than good. Then, it makes sure you don't suffer.

Everything always goes as planned. That's the Directorate's promise. Everything else out in the world beyond its domes may have turned toxic and wasted and ruined, but here in the Quads, everything is optimized and controlled and perfect.

I should do something.

The thought is mushy in my head through the serum's haze, and I can't quite get a grasp on it.

I stand, slowly, testing out my legs. The floor gives a *creak* in response.

I try to step forward.

Lose my balance.

Plop back onto the bed.

As I wait for my room to stop spinning, for any tiny part of this to start making sense, footsteps shuffle in the next room and I hear the door open. *Gracelyn's up.* She pauses in the hall.

Instinct forces me to keep still.

It's not until her steps fade down the stairs that the thought takes shape, through the fog of my mind, that maybe I should have called out to her.

No, no, no – I shake my head and try to get my thoughts straight. I could still depart at any moment. Last thing I want is for Gracelyn to see it happen. I'm not ruining a perfectly good life-long streak of looking out for her *now*.

The doorbell rings – the Departure Crew's here. No one else would dare come by today.

Another set of footsteps go downstairs and stumble towards the front door. The door opens. Low murmuring voices, professional and cool, offer condolences like reciting a script.

Then they start up the stairs.

My skin goes strange and prickly.

The steps stop outside my room. The doorknob shifts and twists. I freeze up as muscles I never knew I had, tense up.

Then, a pause.

I want to shout to them – *I'm here. I'm alive.* But my thoughts skid against the serum, out of balance, and I can't find a hold.

"Why don't you head to the kitchen? Get yourself some coffee?" The voice from the other side of the door is kind, though there's stiffness in it.

"Yes," Father's voice agrees. He's always raspy in the morning. "Yes, I think I will."

I wish he wouldn't sound so solemn. For Gracelyn's sake. He shuffles back down the stairs. Then the door opens. My hands squeeze into fists at my sides, cramming my fingers painfully into fistfuls of mattress.

What's going to happen to me? I'm not ready.

13

Chapter Four

Evie

A man and a woman stand in the doorway in standard Departure Crew jumpsuits, a crisp light blue. The woman has short dark hair that springs around her head in curls. The man is tall, with speckles of gray streaked through his sandy beard. Their nametags read *Ronni* and *Charles*.

As the door swings wide, Ronni leans into Charles, whispering. He smiles. Then they look to the bed and see me there, sitting up and very much alive.

Charles starts, knocking the fold-out stretcher out of Ronni's hand and creating a clatter of cheap metal against the hard floor of the hallway.

Ronni's face drains of color. "I'll be damned," she breathes.

My fingers ache, and I realize how tightly my fists are digging into the mattress. I loosen my grip and place my hands on my thighs, pressing my fingers over the fabric of my favorite blue dress. I was so exhausted after the departure party last night that I never took it off, and now it's horribly wrinkled. Mother's voice rises in my mind, scolding me for looking such a mess, and then I remember that right now this the least of my problems.

Ronni and Charles are still staring at me, wide-eyed and gaping.

From downstairs, the faint hum of the food printer drifts in. My stomach rumbles. I'd kill for something to eat right now.

Ronni glances towards the stairs, then shoves Charlie into my room and closes the door behind them.

Charles blinks. "A-Are you..." He looks at his chart. "Evalee Henders?"

I shrug and look down to my scrunched toes. "Evie."

Forming words is harder than normal. My lips are stiff and slow from the serum.

"Why...?" Ronni's expression shifts, her features sharpening into anger. "I don't know what you're playing at, but your time is *up* – "

"Shhhhhh!" Charles scolds, grabbing her arm. He nods towards the door.

Ronni shakes her arm away from him and continues, but her voice lowers to a hissing whisper. "Are you Licentia? You won't get away with this. We'll... we'll..."

She's looking around, maybe for something to use as a weapon, like she needs to defend herself against me.

Anger rumbles over me in quakes. *Licentia?* The terrorist cult isn't even real, nothing more than whispers people trade when something goes wrong so they have something to blame for it. How dare she compare my accidental alive-ness with the mass acts of intentional chaos that have become entangled with their legends?

Worse, somewhere deep under my anger I can feel my foundation crumbling – fear shaking itself loose. Because it is clear from the look in their eyes that Ronni and Charlie did not expect this, and that means there is no plan. The Directorate always has a plan. And everything stays perfectly in place because of it. It would be less scary if this *was* all some sort of Licentia plot.

Without a plan, everything falls apart.

I cling to the anger instinctively to fight back questions too big for me to deal with.

"I'm no *terrorist*!" I exclaim. "I took the pill. But here I am." I hear my words slurring, feel the world slipping, slipping, slipping, but can't make it stop.

"How can I know that?" Ronni steps closer to me, her face reddening. She shoves me. "What're you playing at? How'd you do it? Don't you know your place?"

My place? I don't have a place in this world anymore. I

never did, really.

"Hey now." Charles pulls Ronni back. "Something went wrong. But it's not her fault. Look at her."

It's not my fault. The phrase echoes through my head. My shoulders loosen, releasing painful tension all the way down my back. It still feels like the world is flying out of orbit, but it helps.

Ronni takes a deep breath. Shakes her head. "Okay," she says. "You're right. But Charlie, what the hell do we do?"

Charlie gives her a weak smile. "No idea."

And then they both stare at me.

I stare back.

I'm supposed to be departed. I'm realizing what it means on a new level now, the fact that I'm sitting up and breathing. It's like the ground is crumbling away from under me, but I can't move to get away. I press my arms over my middle, just to feel that my stomach's still there. But the anger takes over and forces my mind into action.

We have to figure out what went wrong, so I can get back to my life. So we can fix the plan. And clearly, they can't give me those answers here. Maybe this was some kind of weird inking glitch and I actually have another hundred years. Or maybe it was only off by a few days. I have to know before I just stroll out to the kitchen like it's any other morning.

"Don't you have... protocols?" I ask.

Charlie blinks. "Not for this."

"Protocol." Ronni purses her lips, then glances back to Charlie. "Right. Let's get her to the crem like usual, that's where she's supposed to be. Let the higher-ups figure out what to do about it."

"Right," Charlie responds. He's bolstering up a little too, following Ronni's lead.

"But how will we get her out of – oh!" Ronni bends over and lifts the body bag and folded-up stretcher. "It'll look like any other pickup."

"Seriously?" I pound a fist against my bed. "It's not enough that I'm supposed to be *dead* right now? You want

16

me to actually *act* like it?"

They jump at my profanity – we don't talk about *death* in the Directorate. Not outright like that. Their panicked reaction is satisfying, though. It's nice to see I'm not alone in being completely freaked out.

Ronni pulls herself together and unfolds the stretcher. "Have a better idea? This is all I got."

I wrack my brain. Nothing.

"Shit," I moan. Clinks of coffee cups and plates carry from downstairs, and I feel inexplicably homesick. "I'd kill for some coffee right now."

Ronni ignores me and lays out the bag between us on the floor. It's black, made out of some kind of thin but sturdy material. One of those optimized hybrids the Directorate uses to minimize waste. It looks scratchy and uncomfortable, but then I guess when you're departed that doesn't bother you.

I grimace. "How many corpses have been in this thing?"

"Lost count. Get in." Now that we have a plan, Ronni isn't playing games. She nods to it, her hands on her hips. Fear flares inside me, but underneath it, I have to admit I'm relieved someone is taking charge.

"Come on now. Think of your family," Charlie adds.

My hand drifts mindlessly to the rose pendant around my neck. I've never been more grateful for anything in my life. I need Gracelyn right now, even if this is as close as I can get.

I huff out a heavy breath and drop to the floor. I try to push down the panic rising through my chest and slip myself into the bag. It's made to fit much larger people, and as Charlie zips it closed, I feel as if I'm being swallowed into a crinkly void.

He pauses when he gets to my head. "Don't worry, kid. We got coffee on site."

Then the blackness zips over my face, and all the promises in the world wouldn't comfort me.

17

Chapter Five

Gracelyn

I wake up to a creak from the other side of the wall. I'm still half-asleep, and my first thought, the automatic thought, is that Evie is really getting a move on this morning. She is never up before me.

Then reality rushes back – last night's party, the final goodbyes, the tight squeeze of Evie's arms wrapped around me, and the tears crowding her green eyes before we went to our rooms at the end of it all. My hand drifts to my neck and traces over her daisy pendant.

Evie is not up. Evie is departed.

The Departure Crew must already be here. I glance to my digipad. 8.24. Guess they are the ones getting an early move on.

I get up and do the recommended full-body stretch routine, then press the button on the wall to raise the curtain. Light pours in through the branches of the large tree that stretches out between my room and Evie's, matching the gradually brightening lamps in my room.

Evie is departed.

I repeat it to myself to test it out. But all I feel is a terrible nothing. Though it has been a constant looming presence over my sixteen years, now that it is here, it doesn't feel real.

In the hallway everything is quiet; the only sound the smarthouse's electric hum rumbling within the clean, beige walls. Did Mother and Father let the Departure Crew in and then go back to bed? That seems odd. But then, how could I know what is normal, for a Departure Day? I pause by Evie's door, its crisp white color scuffed at the corners from

18

carelessness, then stumble down the stairs. In a daze of numbness, I pull one of our standard-issue white ecoplastic mugs from the cabinet and set it in place at the food printer. I scan my digipad, and select my first coffee. As the drip of steaming liquid fills it with a whirr, Father appears.

"Good morning."

He smiles, but it is not his normal smile. It seems heavy under his mustache, like the motion causes him pain. Usually this type of behavior would get a person reported to emotion management, but allowances are given for a departure. It is why we get this day off.

"Morning." I don't bother smiling back. "How long are they going to take up there?"

"Who's where?" Father yawns, pulling out his own cup and putting his digipad up to the sensor.

"The Crew." I can't bring myself to say Departure. "I didn't think it would take so long. Are they cleaning her entire room up there?" Evie's room is always a mess. Like a tornado got trapped in it.

Was. It *was* always a mess. Soon it will just be an extra empty space.

Father frowns and checks his digipad. "They won't be here for a few more minutes."

Goosebumps rise over my arms. "But... I heard someone up there."

"Maybe it was the tree's branches rustling."

The doorbell rings.

"There they are now," Father says. He heads to the door and lets them in.

A woman's voice greets Father at the door, gruff and businesslike, and while they exchange pleasantries, my mind struggles to reconcile what I heard and what is possible.

My thoughts drift to the idea of Evie's empty, limp body in her bed. I cringe and try to shake the image away. We do not think of such things. That is what the Departure Crew is for, after all. I redirect my mind to last night: the two of us dancing under rainbow lights and sparkles, Evie beautiful and alive, her hair all done up in elaborate swirls pinned back on her head, even though she hates that kind of thing.

Hated.

"Hello!"

Mother comes down the stairs as Father leads the Crew up. Her greeting has a strained chirpiness to it. They murmur a response and keep going.

Mother rounds the corner to the kitchen and goes right for the coffee. As she waits for it, she turns and smiles at me.

Her deep brown eyes are bloodshot and unfocused. Her usually tight curls are loose and messy, like she has just rolled out of bed, and her skin, usually bright with impeccable makeup, is pallid and wrinkled. I cannot believe she is downstairs like this, let alone that she let the Departure Crew see her.

Father returns. For a moment we all stare at the floor. Then the coffee drip stops, leaving behind a vacuum of silence.

"What are you two moping for?" Mother asks. Her voice feels over-animated and out of control. "I'm starved. Let's eat."

Somehow, I'd forgotten about breakfast.

We line up in front of the printer again and, one by one, we scan our digipads and take our meals. Then we sit around the table. I pick at the protein square and carbs, but can't seem to force it down. Across from me, Evie's seat is painfully empty. Mother and Father avoid looking at it.

Raised voices and a metallic clatter cut the quiet from upstairs.

I glance to Mother and Father.

Mother picks up the small pill that dispensed onto her plate with her meal and swallows it. Father focuses on his food, refusing to look up.

"That's weird. Right?" I say.

"Hmm…" Father's voice trails off.

It occurs to me that maybe they have not been present for a collection before. I have never asked. They have never said. It is not something that is discussed.

"I'm sure they know what they're doing." Mother nods. "They're professionals."

None of us want to go up there. We're not supposed to.

We eat. We wait. We go through the motions, pretending it is a normal morning. Evie's empty chair glares at me from across the table.

A few minutes later, the Departure Crew comes back down the stairs and shuffles through the front door.

It is a normal morning now. Exactly what every morning will be moving forward.

I stare into my square of carbs. Something feels off, and it's not just that Evie is gone. I heard something before the Departure Crew got here.

But I couldn't have. Right?

Chapter Six

Evie

It's like a dark mark, having a sky-blue Departure Crew van outside your home. Everyone knows what's happening.

Not that it's talked about. It would be rude to remind someone of their loss when they're supposed to be moving on. It's one of the things departure dates have given us: we get to say our goodbyes and let go, so we can move on without the baggage. Neat and tidy, like everything else about life in the Quads. So we can continue to thrive, by the official Directorate definition.

And that's good. I didn't want to be a source of pain for my family in an otherwise painless world. Even if the thought of them tucking memories of me away and moving on like healthy citizens makes me feel like something is tearing out my heart.

But maybe now that won't have to happen.

It's a bumpy ride out of the house and into the van, alone in the dark of the body bag. To keep myself quiet, I slowly – so as not to move visibly from outside the bag – tighten my fists and focus on the pressure of my nails digging into my palms.

Ronni and Charlie set me down gently – sort of – onto a hard surface, and then I hear a door pull down and fasten. The trunk. They dropped me in the *trunk*.

The van shifts as they settle into their seats, and the engine hums to life.

Ronni calls out, "Stay down back there. If anyone sees you through the windows they'll have a heart attack."

I poke my finger through at the zipper's end and work it

down around my face.

"Are you kidding? This thing reeks," I say. It does. Acidic and sharp, like the chemistry room after a lab day, and under that, I imagine I can smell the stench of all the corpses that were stored in here before me. I don't care if it's crazy. I smell it.

"Well. Unzip a little if you have to. But for the love of all that is good, stay out of sight."

Good? All we have here is a massive screw-up. I almost say it out loud, but Ronni's voice quivers with tension, and it reminds me too much of the fear still ringing at the back of my own mind.

As we pull onto the road, I stare at the van's ceiling. I breathe in, and my nose crinkles – it smells almost as bad in the van as it did inside the bag. Old. Kind of mildewy. Not at all in line with the Departure Crew vehicles' shiny, polished exteriors.

But what's it really matter? I'm in the back of an old van lying in a body bag on my way to the crem. Everyone I know believes I'm departed. I might as well *be* departed – I'm going through all the motions.

My mouth feels sticky and dry and stale. My stomach rumbles again.

Coffee. Charlie promised me coffee when we get there. Maybe he can get me something to eat, too.

Then my mind pulls back: This is what I'm worried about right now?

It's maybe about nine now. On a normal day, one where I'm *not* supposed to be departed, I would have eaten about two hours ago, and then gone to school.

No. In a *normal* life, one where I had a hundred years plus like everyone else, I'd have a career to go to, like Gracelyn will start tomorrow. But for me, all that training would've been a waste of Directorate resources.

Maybe I'll get a new departure date now, and a career assignment to go with it. I test the idea out. I can see myself returning. Gracelyn's eyes growing wide with amazement. Mother blinking back tears. Father standing and staring, unable to take it in. I'm so used to blocking myself off to any plans after this point, I have a hard time finding my own reaction. But I know I'd do anything for more time.

We slow down, and the rumble of trucks rises, passing around us in different directions. The van rolls over a series of bumps, tossing me within the bag. Then we stop and the engine turns off.

"Do we take her in with us?" Ronni asks.

"Hmm," Charlie muses.

I expect him to say more, but he doesn't.

"Don't *leave* me here!" My voice is high-pitched and scratchy, and I realize how scared I am.

"Okay, okay," Ronni says. "But we should take her in the bag again, don'tchya think, Charlie?"

"Mmm. Yeah."

I'm starting to feel Charlie's contributions to this whole thing are questionable at best.

I let out a loud huff. "Fine. Fine." I squirm around to pull the zipper back up over my head the best I can. "Let's *go*."

I swear I hear a snicker from Ronni in the front. "Geez, kid. Okay."

The front doors open and shut with a burst of rumbling vehicles, then the back pops open with a gust of ashy odor.

They lift me out, not bothering with the stretcher this time, and I try to give in to the slouch of the bag as they carry me.

A door slides shut behind us and we stop. They place me on a hard floor. A cheap bell *dinks*.

"Pickup van eight twenty-nine. We need to talk with Viv A.S.A.P." Ronni enunciates the letters, as if each is its own word.

A new voice, male but chirpy, responds. "Viv is pretty tied up this morning, but she could see you around two if you could – "

"You don't understand. We need to see Viv immediately. We've had… an irregularity. With our first pickup of the day. We can't go back out until we see her." Ronni's voice is getting tense. I imagine her face flushing with the frustration like it did in my room.

"An irregularity?" the man responds. "Well, um, yes... let me... I'll be right back." Desk chair wheels clatter, and then steps move briskly away.

Ronni sighs.

"There now," Charlie replies.

Fingers tap against a countertop. The air inside the body bag grows hot. As I start to sweat, the material sticks to my skin, creating a feeling of walls closing in. I slowly stretch out my fingers and flex my toes, fighting the impulse to rip myself free, while also wondering if maybe I should, because this is all so incredibly horrible and stupid. But you don't go against the Directorate. And I'm already going against the Directorate just by being alive. I know on a gut level that it's going to be better for me if I can avoid making a scene about it.

Footsteps come back towards us.

"Viv will see you now."

"Thank you *so much,*" Ronni says. They lift me off the ground.

"Oh," the assistant says. "Do you really need to take the bag? Let's put that – "

"Yes, we do *need* the bag." It's Charlie this time, with more bite in his voice than I'd have guessed him capable of.

"Of course," the other man says. "This way, please."

We trail behind a set of footsteps. The creak of a door, a turn, and I'm on the ground again.

"Viv will be in shortly."

The door closes, leaving behind an uncomfortable silence.

"Well?" Charlie asks.

"Yeah, I guess we can let her out," Ronni says.

The zipper tugs away and the bag falls open. Charlie stares down at me, a serious twitchiness about his mouth. I push myself up.

We're in a plain office. Ronni and Charlie are perched near a couple of chairs, shoulders tense and hands in pockets. Across from us is a desk, all in standard ecoplastic wood grain. The walls are a dull white-grey, and I wonder if they were painted that color or if they have faded over time from the ash in the air outside from the crem. Even in here, I'm sure I can smell it. The tail of a watchlizard scurries away under the crack of the door, and panic surges in my veins. *You haven't done anything wrong,* I remind myself. Ronni's eyes flit to the door's crack and then meet mine. She saw it, too.

The three of us stand there staring at one another, nothing to say, until the door flies open. A small woman bursts through it with short, wavy hair, streaked with gray. A suit jacket is thrust over her shoulders like it's struggling to keep up.

She starts talking before she is even through the door. "I've only got a few minutes, so let's get right to the – "

She turns to face us, and freezes as her eyes reach me, then drop to the bag and back again. A stunned look wraps over her face; she opens her mouth to say something but before she can, the door re-opens and the voice from the front desk cuts her off.

"I'm sorry, I forgot to ask if anyone would like any coffee or t – *oh!*" A lean young man with pale skin and delicate glasses pops in and jumps as he sees me.

If one more person reacts this way to simply seeing me breathing, I might scream.

But the man recovers and continues with a polite smile. "Anyone? Coffee? Tea? Water, too." His eyes only flit nervously back to me once. His white shirt is crisp and his hair meticulously gelled back. Unlike Viv, he looks like he belongs in an office. He can't be more than a couple years older than me.

"Coffee!" I exclaim. My stomach rumbles again. Coffee will at least hold me over better than the nothing I've got now. "Please," I tag on, regaining some degree of composure.

The rest of them shake their heads.

"Thank you, Tad," Viv says, dismissing him.

Tad nods and ducks out, closing the door behind him.

Viv settles into her desk, and her syncscreen rises from within it, a flat thin rectangle. "So," she says. She straightens out her face into something attempting normality. "I take it this is… um, your pickup…?"

"Yeah. She wasn't departed," Ronni responds, echoing

26

Viv's movement and settling into one of the chairs. Charlie follows suit. "We wanted to follow protocol as much as possible, but we figured taking her to the crem vault was not appropriate."

They *figured*? As if they really might have dropped me for cremation and gone on their way?

"Certainly," Viv agrees. "There's actually a..." She leans forward and taps madly at her screen. "...a contingency plan for this type of... no..." She taps again, then drags something else forward and searches more. "Ah! Okay."

So there *is* a protocol. My stomach churns, and I can't decide if this makes me feel better or worse. Has this happened before? How many times? Why haven't I ever heard about it?

The door pops open. It's Tad again, that dumb polite smile still matted to his face. "Your coffee, miss."

He hands me a white mug – same as we use at home, standard issue – the familiar welcoming smell steaming from it. I glance from him, to the three hovering over Viv's screen, and back again. I don't even think they noticed him come in.

"Thanks."

As I reach to take the cup, his hand lingers a moment too long. My fingers wrap over his, and he leaves behind a folded square of paper. I look to him, and his eyes widen ever so slightly. Enough to tell me that whatever is on that paper, it's important. I close my palm over it. He gives the slightest nod, then turns to leave.

"If you need anything else," he says to the room, "you know where to find me." He turns to give me a pointed look as he finishes. Then he leaves, closing the door behind him.

"Here we go," Viv says.

Ronni and Charlie peer at Viv's screen, all of them studying the information she's pulled up.

While they're distracted, I shift my hold on the cup to make sure the entire paper is covered with my hand.

"Okay... yes. Okay," Viv drags with both hands over the screen, enlarging the form. "Did any of the family see the departed individual alive, on or after the departure date?"

27

Ronni looks at me. I shake my head. "No."

"Are the family aware, by any other means, that the departure did not properly activate?"

"No," Ronni and Charlie say together.

"Is there any possibility that another party, such as a neighbor, passer-by, or other individual, besides Departure Crew professionals, witnessed the non-departed individual alive on the designated departure date, or after?"

"No," they repeat. Ronni adds, "We were extremely cautious. We brought her out, and then into the building, in the bag."

Viv glances to the body bag crumpled in the corner. "Very good."

She pauses, her eyes tracking down the screen as she scrolls with her finger.

"I need you both to complete a form about the incident by the end of the day. I'll forward it to you." She taps a few points on the screen, and Ronni and Charlie's digipads *ding* on their wrists. "But otherwise, I've got it from here. Surely it goes without saying that you do not speak of this, not even to each other, ever again. And that's it."

Viv nods. She's regaining her composure quickly, and I'm grateful for it. I'm starting to feel a little better, now that someone seems to have a real plan for what to do, and the process is so simple.

Ronni and Charlie move towards the door.

"Well... good luck, kid," Ronni says.

Charlie gives me a quiet smile.

"Don't worry," he says. "It'll all be set right."

He means it to be comforting, but it makes my stomach twist. Will it? I thought this would be over by now, not just starting. That I'd take some sort of quick medical test, get a new date, and be taken back home.

But what's going to happen to me now? Why the secrecy?

Ronni and Charlie leave, and I slip into one of the chairs. My hands clutch tightly to the cup, and the corners of Tad's folded up paper scratch against my palm. What could be so important, and so secret, that Front Desk Tad could have to tell me?

I've got to read it.

I peer at Viv. She's engrossed in her screen, perusing slowly, and everything settles into a quiet. I take a long, final chug of the coffee. It's already getting cool, and every sip is more bitter than the last. Then I set the cup on the desk and push it away, tucking the paper into my fist.

"Um…"

Viv whips her head up abruptly.

"Sorry. But I haven't been able to use a restroom yet today. Can I…"

"Oh! Certainly. Door's right behind you." Viv points, then turns back to her screen.

"Thanks."

The bathroom is bright white and uncomfortably quiet, the only sound the dripping faucet. I lock myself in and peel the paper from my sticky palm while I relieve myself. Then I open the note up and spread it out against my leg.

His writing is awful – thin scribbles, rushed and shaky. And who actually *writes* anymore? Where did he even get something to write *with*? MRRR, it says. Or MAAA? MAAR? MARA? MRAA? It is impossible to tell, and none of it means anything.

Thank you, Front Desk Tad. What a help.

I crumple the note into my hand to toss, and then on second thought, tear it into tiny pieces first. So much for that.

At least I got to pee.

I look at myself in the mirror as I wash my hands. The buzzing energy that's tingled over my skin ever since I woke up begins to fade, and I'm thinking a little clearer – clear enough that I realize that I still look like I've just rolled out of bed. This is at least one thing I have a little control over, and I claim it with a vengeance.

I use the wetness on my fingers to smooth down my disheveled blonde hair, then splash some water over my face. On second thought, I take another pump of soap and rub it into my face – the best I can do right now. I hate that waxy look my skin gets when I haven't washed it. It brings out the

29

stupid freckles that spatter across my cheeks and make me look like I'm still ten.

There. I turn off the faucet and look myself over. It's – well, it's a little better.

I push the door open and I step back into the room. Viv is gone. Then a hand grabs me and I almost cry out, but it's only Front Desk Tad again.

"Shit!" I pull my arm away. "What are you doing, hovering by the wall like that?"

"Sorry, sorry," he says. He wrings his hands and his eyes flicker towards the door. "Listen. If you go with them, you'll live. But life is totally different out there. It's not like in here."

In here? Out there? Them? I blink, trying to make sense of him. He stares at me, his eyes wide, like he is trying to bore the significance of his words into me.

"What?"

The office door opens and Viv returns. "Oh, Tad, there you are. There's some people at the front desk."

Tad jumps away from me, rearranging his face into his polite front, and disappears into the hall.

What was that?

I shake my head and replay his words, trying to make sense of them. I can't. Did it really happen? Maybe I misunderstood. Maybe the serum is still messing with me.

Viv is standing and hunched over her desk typing away, speaking into the delicate silver headpiece in her ear.

"Yes. She'll be ready." She glances my way and types another note. Then she hangs up.

"Specialists are on their way," Viv says. "It won't be long, sit tight."

She nods. And then she stands there a minute, her hands swinging. "Anything else you need, in the meantime?"

My stomach growls. "I haven't eaten anything yet."

"Oh." Viv frowns. "I guess it's been a strange morning for you."

You think, Viv? I hold back my sarcasm and smile at her, because I really, really want something to eat.

Viv pulls the corners of her mouth up, forcing them into a strange smile of her own.

"Well. I've got…" she makes a show of pulling back her sleeve to check her digipad, "Only a few minutes before I should catch up to a meeting. But I can show you to the food printer."

She leads me to the end of the hall. We turn a corner and step into an enclosed break space with a smooth eco-plastic counter, cabinets, and a food printer.

She gestures to me to go ahead. I scan my digipad to the sensor and wait.

The machine bleeps, and over the pad a message appears: *INVALID READING. TRY AGAIN.*

I try two more times, but we're both getting the picture.

Departed people don't eat.

Viv frowns. "Oh. Well. Here, I guess we can…" She sticks her wrist out, hesitates, then pushes it against the sensor. "Given the circumstances," she mutters.

I haven't liked Viv too much so far, but right now all I feel for her is gratitude.

We don't share food in the Directorate. It's not a rule, exactly, but we all know not to do it. Each person's diet is specifically configured to their own parameters, factoring in genetics, age, gender, daily demands, and other metrics. If you eat someone else's food, it messes up the whole program for both of you.

The machine hums, then spits out a small vegetable pallet.

"Well," Viv sighs, "Don't know if this is what you're used to, but…"

"Thank you," I say, taking it from the dispenser.

It is steaming and hot, and I am starving. My stomach rumbles. I take a bite and chew.

Viv shrugs.

As I eat, heavy footsteps tap from down the hall. Viv looks up to the source, and the mixture of relief and fear on her face makes me nervous all over again.

A stiff, deep voice calls to us as I take another large bite. "Is this the body?"

Chapter Seven

Evie

Two men in stiff dark suits stand behind me and Viv, blocking us off from the hallway. They're still wearing their sunglasses. One has graying hair and generous features, matching his sides, which heave over the top of his belt. The other is tall and lean, with a buzzed head and a thin mouth. Neither smiles.

"Yes," Viv replies.

I take another bite of the vegetable pallet, even though my mouth is still half full. Something tells me these guys aren't going to be big on letting me take it with me, wherever we're going. But hell if I'm not eating this entire thing.

"I'm sorry!" Tad huffs, coming into view behind them, half-jogging. "They didn't wait! I told them to wait while I buzzed you!"

Viv, to her credit, maintains a calm front. I can't tell if it's an act or not. "It's perfectly all right, Tad. I was expecting these gentlemen."

"Oh. Okay." He slows, his shoulders slumping. "I guess I'll be up front." He lingers though, staring at me until I look back. Then he nods pointedly to one of the Suits' lapels.

A shiny laminated badge is clipped to each of the Suits' chests, with a broad green stripe across the top. These guys are *Green Level*.

Oh shit.

Greens are an elite branch of the Life Quality Management Department with high-level clearance. Highly selective. The qualifications seem to be intelligence and a talent for keeping secrets. Father works there. Gracelyn probably will, too, after her basic LQM training.

Tad is still staring, like he expects something from me. I have no idea what, though, and his wide eyes are only making me more scared. I shrug back at him and take another bite of vegetable. Try to ignore the terrible tug in my gut.

There is no actual reason to be so scared right now. This is simply the next step. *Protocol.* Nothing ever goes wrong when you follow protocol.

Besides, the Suits are the only ones who seem to have any idea of what to do.

I take another giant bite, shoving the rest of the vegetable pallet into my mouth. When I look up, Tad has turned away and is shuffling back to the front desk. I look away and force down the rest of my food.

"Ma'am, come with us," the older one says. He doesn't move his head as he talks. With his sunglasses still on, it's impossible to tell who he's looking at. But it seems safe to assume it's me.

"Yeah, okay." I place the empty plate on the counter.

"Complete the protocol paperwork by the end of the day," the taller one says. To Viv, I assume. "You and the others will have a special session with your mental health managers tomorrow. After that, this will all be over for you."

Viv nods. She doesn't look at me.

The Suits close in at my sides and each drop a hand on my shoulders. I jump in response to the sudden weight. "Let's go," one of them says.

They guide me down the hall. The pressure of their grip makes me feel cagey, but I fight the compulsion to shake them off. *Show them you can go along, that you're not* trying *to cause trouble.* The Directorate does not tolerate troublemakers.

As we head outside and the door slides shut behind us, the ashy air fills my lungs, along with odors acrid and sweet, fatty and burnt, and the aggressive whir of ventilation fans floods my ears. I make the mistake of looking back and catch Tad's parting look. There's a well of emotion rippling over his face. A pang of guilt seizes in my stomach, as if I've betrayed him. But the tension in his eyes isn't anger. He looks afraid. For me.

The Departure Plant is the ugliest thing I have seen. A line of vans trail towards a flattened winding path through flattened dirt – none of the sidewalks or greenery that line the neighborhoods – towards a second building with tall smokestacks and dark clouds gathered over them.

"This way, please." The Suits push me into the back of a shiny black car, the windows too dark to see inside. I've never been in a real car before. Other than a few specialized services like the Departure Crews, we only have the automated shuttlebuses in the Quads. Cars are dangerous – only trained, qualified professionals use them. One of them opens the door to the back seat. "That's your place, right there."

They shut the door behind me, and I look around. More tinted glass separates me from the front seats, and the inside of the car doors are plain – no handles. I'm trapped back here until one of the Suits lets me out.

Protocol.

How many others have there been? Why haven't I heard of it? Even if it happened only once, surely this disruption of the system would have spread all over the Quads. Ronni and Charlie, even Viv, were sure shocked. But it must happen. So what happened to the others?

Pins and needles attack my lungs, and suddenly it's hard to breathe. A terrible but familiar feeling. It's happened since I was little – since the first time I realized what the number on my wrist meant. Every time it happens, I go back to that sinking panic, as if decades of my life were dropping away into nothing.

"Easy now, breathe," Father would say. Then he would start counting. "*In*, two, three, four, five," and he'd breathe in with me, slow and steady, "*Out,* two, three, four, five," and we'd deflate our lungs until they were completely empty.

I try it now. *In, two, three, four, five. Out, two, three, four, five. In... out... in... out...*

The car does not turn back towards the residential area, but out towards its border, into an empty stretch of the Quad I never knew was here. We pass a few clusters of unmarked buildings and continue all the way to the Quad's end, where the white walled bubble comes all the way down to the ground. I've never seen the edge of the Quad before. We all know the Quads are enclosed for our protection from the unstable elements of nature and remains of war beyond, but most of the time the brightness of the white dome feels like a broad, open sky. Staring at its edge, I suddenly feel stifled.

Still the car doesn't slow.

Where are we going? There's nowhere left *to* go. I press my forehead against the window, straining to look ahead, and see a piece of the wall pull up, opening into a tunnel.

We barrel towards the opening as if leaving the Quad were no big deal, as if these men zoom in and out of the Quad all the time. But that's crazy. No one leaves the Quads. There isn't anything beyond the Quads, only ruins from a destroyed world. I even heard once it rains actual acid from the sky. That's why we have Quads. But we zoom right out of the Quad through the opening anyway, and I catch myself holding my breath.

The tunnel is dark and tightly enclosed. As the wall seals tight behind us, I twist around and watch my world disappear.

Chapter Eight

Gracelyn

With nothing to do, we spend the day in the living room's overplush chairs, enveloped in the earthy greens of the walls and curtains. I pull one of the flat hand-held syncscreens from the dock on the wall, sync to my digipad and pull up the texts from my class – after missing today's LQM orientation, I will be behind tomorrow as it is.

I do not really need to brush up on the content for training. I only need to look at something once, and I can pull it up in my memory whenever I need it. But I do desperately need something to do.

Except that I cannot focus. The house is too quiet. The couch is too empty. Mother and Father are acting too strange. Or rather, they are acting too much like everything is normal.

There is nothing normal about this. Nothing is okay.

Evie's gone. It is like a crack spreading deeper into my heart each time I think it. The silence is like a wall, building up around me. I do not know that I have ever seen a crack in anything. If something cracks, it is fixed or replaced, almost before it has even happened. Why is no one fixing this? How has this been allowed to happen?

I slam my screen down on my lap and stomp as I stand up.

"Gracelyn," Mother chides, startled by the noise.

But the noise is the only thing that feels better.

"No. This is *bullshit*." That is not my word; that is an Evie word. But she is not here, and someone has to call this what it is. "What is wrong with you two, going around like it's any other day? Like it doesn't matter?"

My chest seizes and I know I am about to cry, so I turn

36

away and run, down the hall and up the stairs, slamming the door to my room behind me. I throw myself onto my bed face down and lie there, tears absorbing into my comforter, ashamed and surprised by my uncontrolled emotion.

Heavy footsteps follow me upstairs, and pause outside my door. There's a knock.

"Let me in, Gracelyn. Let's talk." It's Father.

"Fine."

Already regret and guilt are rushing through me. I don't make scenes. I don't argue. I am the good daughter, the one that follows orders and doesn't talk back. The one with the perfect recall and the bright future.

I roll onto my side and pull my legs in as he enters.

Father has always seemed larger than life, the way the glare of light blinks across his glasses and his mouth sets in a thin line under his mustache. It wasn't just because I was little. Everyone defers to him. I don't know what he does as a Green Level at LQM, but it is important, and it is secret. Maybe I will get to know more once I work there. But he is always gentle, his words always quiet. The gentleness of a man so confident in his power that he does not need to use it.

But right now he seems smaller than usual, his shoulders folded forward. He leans against the wall and tucks his hands behind him. I expect him to scold me, the way he does when Evie acts out. But when he speaks, his voice is calm as ever.

"Do you understand why we get this day to ourselves?" he says.

"It's a Departure Day."

"Yes, but, do you understand why Departure Days are days we stay home?"

Yes and no. I stare at the wall.

"Because we hurt."

Is he really admitting to pain? My eyes flit to him despite myself, too curious what he will say next.

"No matter what the Directorate does for us, it hurts when someone we love is suddenly gone. This is why we tried to keep you and Evie apart. We didn't want this hurt for you. But that is why we get this day. To acknowledge the pain."

They did try to spare me this. If Evie and I had followed the rules, I would be fine right now. But Evie needed someone. No one else was willing to attach themselves to her. And I needed her. I needed someone to remind me to stop taking everything so seriously every once in a while. Someone to show me it would okay if I let go on occasion, no matter what my instructors or our parents expect of me.

Who will do that for me now?

"But you can't give into it," Father continues. "You can't let it grow in you. That is a path to a life of pain. Today we let ourselves feel it, and then tomorrow we move on. You know this, Gracelyn. And I know you can do it."

I nod.

I mean to say more, but my words get choked on a swell of feeling, on the *pain* of it, and I know I have nothing to say today – at least, nothing fitting for the good daughter I should be, the good student, the good citizen.

I know without having felt it before: this is exactly what the Directorate works to keep from creeping into this society.

I feel ashamed, and the sting only makes everything worse. The only rule I've ever broken in my life, and now I'm paying the price. A tear escapes and drops to my comforter.

Father sighs. "Tuck this away, Gracelyn. Allowing pain inside yourself will only beget more pain."

Then he leaves.

Chapter Nine

Evie

We keep driving for a long time – every minute taking us farther and farther from the Quad, from home, from my life. We drive longer than I would have thought it possible for anything to go out beyond the Quads.

The tunnel is bolt-straight and lined in smooth metal arcs like a shell, hugging tightly around the vehicle, the only lighting coming from the car itself. Over the dull whirr of the engine, my heart is a rapid thudding in my ears. I do the only thing I can, clutching my hands tight into the sides of the seat cushion until my knuckles ache.

Finally the car slows down, and I press against the window to peer ahead past the end of the tunnel, catching the side view of a large block of a building. There's not a single window, just walls of concrete. My throat clenches. Whatever happens out here in this walled-up, hidden building, there's no way it's good.

Suits One and Two pull me out of the car and towards it, their hands tight around my arms in a way I'm sure will bruise. A defensive instinct kicks up in me and I almost snark at them for it, but then I remember I'm trying to be cooperative. To show I'm not *trying* to cause problems by being alive. To get back home.

The door is coated in beige paint that almost blends into the concrete wall, except for the chips and flakes at its edges. Suit Two holds his digipad to the scanner, and the door buzzes to let us in. Old-style screw-in electric bulbs swing on naked wires from the ceiling, spread far apart. The hallway is barely lit and our shadows stretch along the walls. I stumble as my eyes adjust, pushed by the forceful hands of Suits One and Two. Even in here, the Suits don't take off their sunglasses.

We pass an occasional door, rusted and shut tight. But the worst thing about this place is the quiet. The only sound is the echoing shuffles of our steps. The Suits guide me through a few turns in the halls before finally stopping in front of one of the doors. They thrust me inside. And then the door slams shut behind me.

A single light bulb leers down at me from the ceiling. Along the back wall is a banged-up med scanner, with a tray of tools on top of it. A flash of hope lights up in me – maybe they just need to check me out, and then they'll send me home. But then I realize: why would they bring me all the way out of the Quad to this creepy place, just for a checkup?

Damnit. Damnit, damnit, damnit. A threat of panic tightens down my spine, and I shiver to shake it off. I've got to get out of here. I look around the room again, scouring it for anything I might be able to use, but come up empty. I'm officially over this trying-to-cooperate thing.

I kick the door and scream at the top of my lungs, releasing the fear that's building in me with each syllable: "Let me out of here! Let me out! Let me *out*!"

I almost slam my fist into the door too, for good measure, but the idea of the pain calls me back to reason. Instead, I lean my forehead against the cool metal of the door and listen to my voice echo down the hall.

Nothing.

There's probably not even anyone out there.

I try the door handle, because what the hell. It's locked. Of course it is.

Desperation flattens me. I slump against the door and slide down until I'm on the ground, my elbows on my knees and my head buried between them, and let out a long, hollow whimper.

I don't know how long I sit there. With my digipad not working, time is impossible to tell in this dark, dingy place. After a long, long while, a tray slides through a flap in the

40

door, serving up an eco-plastic bowl of dry cereal, a stale roll, and a bottle of warm water. No protein. No vegetables. None of the neat squares of balanced nutrients the food printers serve up. There's a set of flatware on the tray too, but I don't bother with it, picking up pieces of cereal with my fingers instead.

Wait – I look again.

There's a knife on the tray, in a wrapped packet along with other flatware. Finally, something I can work with. It's plastic, but it could do some damage, maybe. If I poked it into an eye or something.

Ick.

I tear the package open and clench it in my fist close to my side. I have no idea if it'll work, but the idea of fighting back eases some of the painful tension in my shoulders.

I sit on the floor and wait, anticipation and rage surging through me.

And wait.

And wait.

Surely hours have passed. My stomach starts to grumble again. This is the most boring escape plan ever.

I pass the time scratching doodles into the plaster of the wall with the knife, chipping away the paint, the same way I scribble in the margins of my papers at school. But it's not long before my fingers hint at pain from the pressure, so I stop.

But I'm still bored.

I sprawl out on the floor and see how far I can roll my empty bowl across before it flops over onto its side. After a while I get pretty good at it. I roll a real nice one, evenly balanced and spinning fast, when the door flies open.

A woman strides in and shuts the door behind her, her mouth pulled tight. The door clangs into the rolling bowl, sending it flying against the leg of the med scanner before collapsing to the ground with a *clap*. The woman jumps, then looks back to me. She gives me such a startled glare that I jump too, and frown in return. Too late, I think to grab the knife, but the door is already shut again, and clicks as the lock fastens. My chest contracts – that was my chance.

The woman glances at the knife and raises an eyebrow.

"What was your plan, exactly?" She leans over and takes it out of my hand. "This would only get you outside to the hall, and that's if you're lucky. What then?"

I clench my now-empty fist. "I don't know. Seemed better than staying here." Anything would have to be better than here.

She sighs and opens the health scanner, tapping on its full-body tray.

"Up, please."

She checks my digipad for its account number and enters it into the machine. Its screen lights up as it restarts, and both machines *bleep* as they sync. The health scanner hums awake.

I start to go along out of sheer habit, but then my fear breaks free in a burst.

"No!" My nerves intensify until I have to clench my fists to keep my hands from shaking, but I'm getting desperate, fed up with the waiting and the secrets. "What's going on? Why am I trapped in here? Why won't anyone take me back home, where I belong?"

"Hush." She says it with urgency, fevered, under her breath. In her eyes there's steely determination and a hint of fear. Outside, footsteps pace the hall. The slow rhythm of their approach feels ominous, and I do as she says. As I press into the cool metal of the scanner, the steps continue down the hall, around the corner, and fade away.

She leans forward.

"I'm Mara," she whispers. "We can help you, if you want it. Do you wish to live?"

"What?" I exclaim. I'm so lost in this strange, upside-down day, so exhausted and confused, that part of me wishes to give up, to stop caring, to let the Directorate have its way – just so long as it all ends.

"Quiet," she mutters through a clenched jaw. "I can help you. Do you wish to live?" she repeats, the words pointed.

I blink, struggling to process.

"Yes." Despite how weary and disoriented I am, it comes out of me fierce and angry, an animal instinct. Yes, I want to live, I want to keep on for every second I can. I don't know why or what for at this point, but *yes,* under the anger and the fear and the confusion, *I wish to live.*

I hold Mara's gaze, my ears buzzing with adrenaline. She nods. Then she closes the lid to the scanner and it starts the familiar process of assessing my body.

In the quiet hum of the machine, my mind relaxes, and I have a flash of realization: MARA – that is what Tad wrote on the paper. Not an acronym. A name. At this hint of order returning into this strange day, I'm able to calm down, just a little bit.

The humming dies down. The lid lifts.

"You know Tad," I whisper.

She frowns. "How do *you* know Tad?"

I sit up and blink at her. My confusion balls up into a hot wad of anger.

"*Tad* was incredibly unhelpful, with his cryptic notes and his lack of directions."

"Notes?" She rolls her eyes. "Seriously, Tad."

The footsteps start coming back from down the hall.

She shakes her head. "There's no time. You need to listen to me."

She picks up a finger prick and reaches for my hand, but I shrug my hand away.

"Seriously?" I say.

"We have to go through the motions," she says. "Blow my cover and we'll both be departed."

Cover for what? But it's clear this is no time to demand explanations.

I sigh and stick out my hand. She collects the blood, and I feel a throbbing heartbeat in my fingertip. I hate this feeling. And doctors in general. Everyone in LQM is always trying to push me off like I'm a waste of their time, always pointing to my departure date and not letting me forget it. They poke and prod and make notes on their little tablets and make me feel so small and out of control.

Gracelyn's starting a track with LQM. She's so smart, already getting the high marks she'll need to get on the accelerated path. She could be a doctor, if she wants. And with her sweet temperament, she'd be the best doctor ever. Even I might not mind checkups so much if my doctors treated me the way Gracelyn treats people.

Mara cuts into my thoughts, talking low into my ear as she takes my blood pressure. "Listen, they're going to lead you into another room and give you a pill. *Do not swallow the pill.*"

"Why not?" I demand.

I'm not sure what I'm being so petulant. I just want to understand *one thing* about this day, and stop this feeling of being swept away in a current I'm not strong enough to fight against.

Mara ignores me, calmly turning to the monitor again. "I need you to calm down. Your numbers are through the roof." Then she pulls the Velcro apart and removes the band.

Calm? My heart pounds like it wants to break free of my chest, my breaths are shallow and stiff, and my stomach flips like I'm falling. Any chance of *calm* got left behind in my bedroom around the time I woke up this morning.

"Tell me why first!"

She looks me over, her expression tense and restrained, and sighs. "It is very similar to the one you took at your departure party last night." She cleans a spot on my forearm with a wet cotton ball. "Now. Really. Calm down."

Wait, this pill would *kill* me? I try to take a breath. But my mind is still wild with questions.

"What do they need all this for?" I ask.

"They're looking for patterns among people who... well, don't depart when they're scheduled to."

"Are there a lot of us?"

"A lot? No. But more than anyone feels comfortable with."

She studies the monitor, and starts typing.

"You asked me whether I wanted to live or not."

She glances to me. "Yes."

"Some people don't want to? Live?"

She pulls away from the keyboard and looks at me thoughtfully, studying my face before replying. "No. A lot of them, actually. And it's their right to choose that."

A right to choose? We don't choose anything for ourselves in the Directorate. The Directorate's algorithms already know what's best for us.

"But…" Why would anyone want to die? My mind floods with all the things I haven't gotten to do yet, all the things I was so angry I wouldn't live to reach – being selected for a profession, graduating into a career, seeing Gracelyn get married. Maybe apply for children someday. There is so much to do still. How can anyone turn down the chance for more?

"Most of them are much older than you. They have been conditioned for this. And it scares them, this idea that there's something else out there."

"Is there? Something else?" I hadn't thought about it yet, but if Mara's getting me *out* of here, where am I going? The question quivers through me.

"That is something we don't have time for. I'll have to leave that to Kinlee," she replies.

"Kinlee? Who's – "

Steps tap their way towards to us from down the hall, and Mara cuts me off. "Not now."

The door bursts open and I flinch in surprise. Mara picks up the tablet as if marking down something important.

A colossal figure enters – a heavily-muscled, very tall man with a shaved head. It's a wonder his shoulders don't burst through his uniform.

"Ready?" he asks Mara.

"Wrapping up," she says, making a few final marks on the tablet.

The man turns to me and hands me a teeny plastic baggy. Inside of it is a little white pill.

Mara glances to me. "That," she speaks in a detached, businesslike tone, "is the pill we discussed."

She steps away from the monitor and folds her arms.

"Right," I say. "I remember."

I stare down at it. I want to throw it across the room, shove my way past this giant of a man and run away. But it's like Mara said, I'd never even make it to the door. So for now, I take a deep breath and clench the little bag tight to keep my fingers from trembling. I have no choice but to trust her.

He turns to me with a startling grin that bares his teeth. "Follow me."

Then he heads down the hallway, leaving me to rush after him. Before I go, I turn back to Mara one last time, and she gives me a nod.

Chapter Ten

Evie

I hurry after this hulking soldier, our shadows scurrying around us with the dangling bald light bulbs. He is so large he almost knocks them with his head.

The hall is long, and my heart thuds rapidly, but finally we reach the end and turn, winding down a final stretch with metal walls and no doors until the very end.

Where the door's knob should be, there's only a large, dingy keypad – a *lock*. The really old kind. Are they trying to keep people out? Or *in*?

He pushes in a code with his thick finger, and the door clicks free. My fists clench.

It's thicker than any door I've ever seen – even my hulking escort has to strain to pull it open. When he's done, he turns to me with that misfit grin.

"You still got that pill?"

I loosen my fist and hold it out in my palm.

He nods. "Go ahead and take it."

I glance to the little white pill and hesitate, remembering Mara's warning. *I wish to live, I wish to live.*

But he presses, "Go on now."

He stands there, his hands on his hips, grinning. And watching.

Dread twists through me. Mara didn't warn me he would be watching to make sure I took it. And something tells me that even if he's smiling now, that maybe he won't stay so grinny for long if I don't do what he says.

I don't know what else to do, so I fumble at the little baggy and take out the pill. I place it on my tongue, trap it against the top of my mouth and take an exaggerated swallow. Then I tuck the pill under my tongue and wait.

"Good girl." He smiles. Cringe. "Now come have a seat in here. We're going to get this settled up, and then you'll be good to go. But it might take some time, and it's been a big day for you. So while you wait, try to rest, if you can."

I'll be good to go? My heart leaps and I almost think that all this anxiety was for nothing, that this was all stupid, and Mara and Tad are just a couple of conspiracy theory crazies.

Until I go into the room.

It is dark and enclosed and entirely metal, coated in clusters of black that can only be ash. Large vents line the sides. As the door shuts, the giant-man takes all the light with him, leaving me in darkness. The door locks shut.

Sit? Rest? Not a chance.

I spit the pill out right onto the floor. Then I wipe the residue off my tongue the best I can with my arm. Ugh.

Now what?

I hardly have time to think the question before the floor starts to clink and sputter, and hot blinding flames burst from between the large metal tiles. *It's a crem vault.*

Beads of sweat form on my forehead, and I grasp for anger to save me from my panic again – *this* is how they correct the mistake that was me waking up this morning? Everyone else gets a peaceful departure in their sleep, and I get to burn alive?

As I stare at the flames, more burst up in the cracks between the large metal tiles behind me. The smoke is growing so thick it catches in my throat. Maybe I won't burn to death, maybe I'll asphyxiate first. In fact, that might be better. Maybe I should breathe nice and deep and make sure I go unconscious before the flames close in around me. Maybe I was better off taking the pill after all.

As I try to talk myself into stepping towards the smoke and taking it in, a tinny rattling sound interrupts me. I whip towards it in time to see one of the metal tiles of the floor pop up and shove to the side.

A wild head of wavy dark hair pops up from the floor, a

wall of flames between us.

"Hey," a girl's voice calls out.

There's no time to question. "Help!"

"That's the whole idea," she says. "Come on."

Chapter Eleven

Evie

"You coming or not? It's hot in here."

The girl calls out over the hiss of the fire, a silhouette through the smoke.

I want to run to her, but a wall of flame separates us, bursting in a line through the floor's splits. I tell my body *go*, but I seem to be bolted to the spot.

"The flames," I start.

"Just do it," the girl says. "I got you."

Easy for her to say, she's not the one who has to leap over them. Fear chokes down my throat and tangles in my lungs. But I'm either burning to death trying, or I'm burning to death standing here like an idiot.

I press my hands against the skirt of my disheveled dress and launch myself forward. I land with a *thunk* against the metal floor, and am overtaken by a burst of sensation: the hiss of the fire, a sudden pain in my shoulder, a sharp burning smell. Then I'm dragged over the ledge and fall to a second floor below. As I fight a flood of coughing and gagging, the girl pounds at my back.

"Ow!"

"It's going to hurt a lot worse if I don't get these flames out," she says.

Then, she leans down into the dark of the lower level and drags something large towards the opening in the floor. She turns to me. "Help me lift."

"What?" I stare at her blankly, then force myself to get a grip. Now isn't the time for questions. "Sure."

I leap up and skid to her side. Her blue eyes are bright

with reflections of the fire and sparks around us, and she's grinning ear to ear.

"Grab a leg and pull it up," she says, nodding down to the thing in front of her. I look down and find a deer's furry leg and hoof.

"Shit!" I jump back. "Is that thing real?"

I've only ever seen them in children's books, where they're cute little characters which befriend squirrels or go on adventures with rabbits. This is not like that.

"Yeah," she says. "But it's dead. Grab a leg, we don't have time."

She's right. The flames are getting larger, and even from down here the heat is so intense that my skin feels like it could melt. I bend over and wrap my hands around a thin foreleg. The fur is rough and wiry – not at all like I expect.

"*Lift,*" she says. Her voice strains as she follows her own command. I obey, tugging as hard as I can. We shove the deer up and into the flames above, where it catches fire.

The girl sighs, and ducks back under the floor. I fall beside her. A dull thudding fills my head, and I can't tell if I am elated, or exhausted, or just *so damn relieved* not to be dead. I want to scream, and cry, and laugh hysterically.

Adrenaline. The Directorate talks about it like it's bad, and is always working to avoid triggering it, but it's got me lightheaded and pumped with giddiness. I feel good. No, I feel great. Fantastic, considering all that's happened to me today.

I try to focus. "What now?"

The girl pulls a thin metal screwdriver from her back pocket. "Now we gotta get this thing." She stabs the tool into my digipad where the fine lines of the plastic covering comes together and twists it apart.

"What are you – Hey! Stop!" I squeal. "You're going to set it off."

It's only then that I realize: the other girl doesn't have a digipad. In fact both of her wrists are completely bare – no departure number, either.

Sure enough, the digipad begins to warn us. "Caution," the

cool voice states. "Stop immediately. Caution."

But the girl keeps wrestling with it.

"They expect it to go off in the fire," she says.

It loosens and cracks apart under the pressure, and the girl pulls it off my arm. The hot air wraps around my newly-bare skin, freed for the first time in as far back as I can remember. It feels sensitive and vulnerable.

"Hey!" Before I can process what's happening, she has thrown my digipad back into the burning room. I reach after it, but I'm too slow.

"Are you kidding?" she says. "They can find you anywhere with that thing. Soon as they notice it's missing from up there, they'd activate it again and come for you. And the rest of us."

I freeze, processing her words. I know what she's saying makes sense. But how can I function without my digipad? My entire life is in there. My schedule, my health tracking, my meals. It catches fire amidst the flames, and as I watch it burn, a pang of homesickness seizes my stomach.

The girl pokes her head up, lifting the floor tile again.

"Last thing. We have to make sure it all burns up," she says. "They'll think it's pretty odd if your body leaves a hoof behind."

She grins at me, eyes wide. How can she joke right now?

She peeks out from under the floorboard for several more minutes, sweat dripping down her flushed cheeks.

I lean against the wall. Despite the adrenaline pulsing through me, no matter how great I feel, I also feel wildly out of control.

In, two, three, four, five. Out, two, three, four, five...

It helps. A little.

I look around. We're in some kind of tunnel. Wires line the walls in bundles, with stains of rust behind them. The floor is spotted with puddles, and the air smells dank with mold.

Smoke creeps through the opening and clogs up the air. The heat builds until my cheeks burn and I have to step farther from the vent. Still the girl hovers at the crack, peeking out.

Finally the fire dies down, and the girl leans forward, squinting out at the remains. Then she pops down and arranges the tile back into place. With it, all the light sucks out.

"Hold on," she says.

I try to, holding my breath against the terror building in me in the dark, and focusing on the shuffling of fabric coming from her direction. There's a *click*, and light bursts from a flashlight in her hands.

"Okay." She hatches a bolt lock over the tile, then pushes hair away from her face with a sigh. The sweat and ash from her forehead make it stick up in the front. "Follow me, and don't make any noise."

Then she turns and heads down the tunnel.

Chapter Twelve

Evie

I follow the strange girl down the tunnel as quietly as I can, as the wheels of the pallet she'd used to drag the deer over squeak softly behind us. As we round a corner, the door to the crem vault above us opens, and footsteps enter. Muffled voices follow. I hope that deer burned all the way... But then, whoever these people are, this doesn't seem like the first time they've pulled this off. We don't hang around to find out, and I am happy to put distance between me and this second near-death experience of the day.

It's dark and musty in here, crowded with the dense smell of the earth from the ground beneath us. As I adjust to the darkness, I notice a yellow line tracing the top of the otherwise naked white of the plaster wall.

"Where are we?" I ask.

"A tunnel," the girl says.

I roll my eyes. "Well, right. But where?"

She shrugs.

I blink. "Your face is covered in ash." It's even smudged into her hair, turning it even darker around her hairline and making the blue of her eyes spark brighter.

She tilts her head and grins. "What, you think you're immune?"

I swipe the back of my hand across my cheek. When I look down at it, it's smudged in black.

"Crap!" I do it again, and then realize I have nothing to clean my hand on. "Double crap."

The girl giggles. "Come on, this way."

Then she heads off deeper into the tunnels. I wipe the dirt

off my hands the best I can and rush after her.

"Where are we *going*?" My voice is getting that whiney tone I really hate, but I need answers. "Why am I even *here*?"

"Calm down," the girl says.

Calm down? Suddenly the weight of this day sinks into my gut with a burning anger.

"No. I won't *calm down*. I was supposed to depart last night, and no one will tell me why I didn't. I'm tired, and I'm hungry, and I haven't been given a proper meal or explanation all day long."

"Shhh, cool it," she says.

And I want to, I really do. But I am so far past cool. I lost *cool* about the time I woke up this morning. The shock is still fading, peeling away in phases, and now that I finally seem safe, all the confusion and terror of this awful day is clawing out against my will.

"Cool it? I've been carried around in body bags, been given cryptic, secret messages that make no sense, locked up in basically a dungeon, and set on fire. And now here I am, underground in some tunnel with some strange girl who doesn't even have a digipad." I turn on her and whisper-shout right into her face. "Who the hell even are you?"

The girl flinches at my volume and presses her finger to her lips. My eyes widen and I pop a hand over my mouth. She takes hold of my arm.

"I really need you to be quiet. Or it's both our asses," she says. "I'm Kinlee. Didn't Mara tell you?"

I blink. *Kinlee.* Mara did say something like that, now that I think about it.

"Maybe? Okay yes, but…" I shut my eyes and shake my head. "Your name isn't the point. What is all this? Where's your departure date? Where are you leading me?"

She glances up towards the room cautiously, but must decide the greater risk would be to wait and see if I explode again. "The short answer is that we're a group called the Alliance. We're a co-op of a few governments outside the Directorate who feel it's important to monitor them, among other things. That's why I don't have that number on my arm.

I'm not from there."

The words jam up in my head. "But that's not possible. There's nothing else out there. The Directorate's all that was left after the Final War."

Kinlee shrugs. "They lie to you guys. A lot. But we need to keep moving. I'm supposed to have you back before sunset, which is probably happening right now."

Kinlee leads us deeper into the tunnels. Eventually a blue line joins with the yellow line at the top of the wall, and then a green, and a red. We keep following it.

But my brain is still turned up with adrenaline, and it won't stop churning on the implications of what Kinlee said. I'm too exhausted and confused to keep my thoughts to myself. "But this Alliance you mentioned – if you're not hurting anyone, surely the Directorate wouldn't – "

"No, you don't get it." Kinlee whips around in front of me and blocks me like a wall. Under the smears of ash, her eyes are bright with intensity. "Remember the Massacre of 2197?"

"Well, not *remember*. I wasn't born. But yeah, I know about what happened. A group of violent rebels tried to overthrow the Directorate and dismantle our order. The Directorate protected us."

"I wasn't born then either, obviously, but that's not what happened. It wasn't some violent coup. It was a meeting of world leaders. A peaceful one. They were going to limit how much governments could regulate their citizens." She swats towards my forearm, and the inside of my wrist tingles where the ink marks it. "But the Directorate was so threatened by the mere idea of its control being limited that it tried to bomb us out of existence."

Kinlee huffs, nostrils flared.

But seriously. "Government conspiracies? Secret organizations? How stupid do I look?" I fold my arms, trying to press the date on my wrist against my body to hide it.

"Yes. And yes. And only moderately." She smirks.

I blink. I'm exhausted and confused and in no mood for this.

"So the Directorate's been blatantly lying to us about this

major historic event for fifty-six years? More than my entire life?"

"Yes."

"They took out an entire group of people, who weren't doing anything wrong, because they had some different ideas?"

"Well, it sounds dumb when you say it like that." She frowns, crossing her arms over her chest. "But yes. That's what happened."

It doesn't make sense. "Why would they do that? No one would be interested in a group like that anyway. It's inhumane to leave people to their own devices like that. People are happier being taken care of and protected. We have a good life in the Quads – everything is in order, and bad things like cancer and car crashes and heart attacks, they don't happen anymore. No one wants to disrupt that. No one would even listen."

"Are you sure about that?" Kinlee snaps. "Do you even get it, what the other countries were advocating for? There's no way you could."

She starts off, walking faster, so that her back is to me.

"Come on," she calls back, "You're not going to get it until you see."

I scoff. But I'm already following after her, more curious than I'd care to admit. After all, if the Directorate lied about the departures, what else have they lied about? It doesn't seem like so much of a stretch, really, after all I've seen today. And besides, where else am I going to go?

"By the way," she says. "What's *your* name?"

"Evalee," I say.

She laughs in such a sudden burst. Then she covers her mouth with her hand. "Sorry. That's a real, um, interesting name."

"Shut up." I agree, it's offensively girly. But I'm not about to let Kinlee know it. "Call me Evie."

"Whatever," she shrugs.

And then she leaps up into the air and grabs hold of a pipe overhead.

"Careful!" I exclaim.

She pauses for a moment, shifting her grip and kicks her legs out to swing. "Why?"

She kicks out to swing harder, lets go with one hand and flies forward to grab another.

"Stop! You're going to hurt yourself!"

"You Directees," she laughs.

She swings back and forth on the pipe, then releases, propelling herself forward to the ground. "So what? So what if I, say, fall and scratch my knee? Please. Tell me what happens."

She picks up the pulley for the pallet again and stares at me.

"You'd be *hurt*."

My heart is still pounding against my ribs from what she did. You don't *do* that, put yourself at unnecessary risk. In the Quads, we're careful with ourselves. The twice-yearly medical checkups, the elimination of individual vehicles, the carefully-prescribed fitness plans... the Directorate built everything around optimally preserving lives and preventing pain.

When someone departs before their date, in an accident or a fight or anything preventable, it's devastating. The entire Quad comes to a halt. It's only happened once in my lifetime, and once was enough. No one hardly even gets a paper cut in the Directorate.

But Kinlee stares at me blankly, like I've told her to stop breathing.

"Fine," I retort. "*Fine*."

To prove I'm no wuss, I jump up and reach for a pipe overhead, reaching to grab it like Kinlee did – it didn't look so hard. But my fingers barely brush against it, and then I fall away. Kinlee bursts into giggles. I land with a *thud*, my ankle turns over, and floods with piercing heat. I end up in a heap on the ground.

I choke on a gasp. So this is real pain. It's more intense than anything I have felt before. I press my lips together hard and try not look any weaker than I already do.

But as Kinlee runs to my side, even she looks rattled.

"Shit, shit, *shit*, they're never going to let me do a run alone again," she mutters, pushing her hair back from her face. "Does it hurt?"

"Umm. Yeah. It hurts." I try to play it cool, but the pain is thick and sharp and pulsing up my leg. It's the worst thing I've ever felt. I blink to fight back tears.

She gently moves my injured leg until it's stretched out in front of me, and I clench my fists to keep from gasping. As she rolls up the leg of my trousers, I glance down and immediately regret it – my ankle is horribly blue and purple and swelling.

"What is that bump!" I reach down to touch it but Kinlee pushes my arm away.

"Leave it alone." She frowns. "We need to get you to camp."

"You want me to *walk* on this? Hell no."

"We're almost there," Kinlee says. "You can ride the pallet. I'll help you on."

Before I understand what she means, she's wrapped one of my arms around her shoulders, and her own is tight around my waist. She lifts me to my feet.

"Don't put any weight on it," she says. "Lean on me."

I huff and wobble and cling to Kinlee for the love of all that is good and pain-free. For a flash, I have great love for the Directorate again, for protecting me from this all my life, even if it was a short one. And then, for the second time in one day, I find myself transported by a means generally reserved for the dead.

Finally Kinlee stops in front of a ladder, which leads us up a hatch in the ceiling.

"This might be tricky," she says, frowning up at it.

"You mean I have to go *up* that thing?" I exclaim. "No way."

"Oh, you can do it," she sighs. "Use your arms. Only step up with your good foot."

"That's not – " I cut myself off, unwilling to say the rest of it out loud: *That's not even the entire problem.* Me? Up a ladder? This is exactly the type of thing we avoid in the Quads. You could fall and hit your head, break a leg, snap your back, any number of things. And while already injured? Forget it. There are specialists for that, with safety equipment.

"Well. *Up* is where the help is. And the beds. And the food."

And then Kinlee turns away and climbs up the ladder like it's nothing. She pushes herself up over the ledge, and then her head pops back over and she calls down to me, "Come on!"

"I don't know…"

"It's the ladder or camping in the tunnel 'til your leg is healed up."

I sigh. Kinlee may be strange, but she has a point.

"Or you could follow the line down the tunnels. Leads back to the Directorate, if you follow it all the way back." She points to the blue line that traces the top of the tunnel wall. "I bet they'd *love* to see you right now."

I take a slow, steadying breath and place a hand on a rung. The metal is cool and slippery under my sweaty palm. I squeeze it tight and place my other hand on the next rung. Already my heart is trying to pound its way out of me.

"Stop thinking and get up here," Kinlee calls down. Then, she calls out beyond the tunnel, "Hoi! A little help? Medical help."

I shift my weight to place my good foot on the first rung, and a burst of pain swells around my bad ankle. I gasp and pull myself up to relieve the pressure. One down, I guess.

As I climb, I try to focus on placing my foot steadily, staring up at the rung ahead. I try to block out the pain, how high up I am, the way my hands and knees are shaking worse with each step. When I reach the top and pull myself out onto the floor, I've never been more grateful for flat ground. Much like the tunnels, the room at the top is metal. But this place is populated with desks and computers and chairs. I lay out and take a breath, relieved to be able to rest my leg.

A tall, lean woman kneels next to me. Her light brown hair

is tied back in a messy knot, and thin strands fall around her face. Her forehead is creased.

She looks at Kinlee. "You're late."

"Mom!" Kinlee exclaims, rolling her eyes. "Runners get an hour of leeway. Besides, injured dead girl here?"

Kinlee's mom raises her eyebrows at her, but then turns her attention to me. She takes a quick look at my outstretched ankle, then assesses my face.

"Okay. We got you, honey. Kin, get Sue. I'll get her up there."

Like Kinlee did, the woman wraps my arm over her shoulders and takes hold of me around the waist. She's stronger than she looks, and the relief – of the pain in my leg, and the anxiety buzzing through my head – is instant.

I lean onto her and let her guide me through another room, filled with long tables and large machinery, and then she talks me into going up another ladder. At this point, I'm too overwhelmed to think, overfull with the pain and the adrenaline and the disorientation, and I give in and just do what she tells me to. When I get to the top, I have to push away furious tears.

"I know, I know," Kinlee's mom says as she comes up the ladder behind me, and finds me sprawled out on the ground. "It's going to be okay. Promise."

Overhead, I don't find the usual blank dome of the Quads, but a dark stretch dotted with teeny lights and a fade of yellow light against a vast violet sky. Staring up at it, I get caught in vertigo, then gasp as I realize what I am looking at – *sky*. It's the actual, real-life sky, with stars and clouds and outer space.

"We're *outside*?" I thought the sky was supposed to be blue. What happened to it? No, I know what happened to it: the same thing that happened to everything else.

My chest tightens and I try not to breathe in. The Earth went *bad* ages ago. Pollution. Wars. Climate change. It all added up to a thinning ozone and heavy contamination. That's why the Directorate built the Quad domes in the first place.

"We are," she says. She is far too calm about it. "And we can get into the science of it all sometime if you like, but for now just know that you're safe. We breathe this air all the time."

All the time? This air is thick with sticky humidity, and I can feel its dampness pressing against my skin. This is far from okay. But I'm also far from prepared to deal with anything more right now. I take a breath and let her guide me through a string of randomly-placed trees.

Farther out, they cluster into a thick forest. Cabins are scattered through them. It's getting darker as the sun sets – the actual, UV-laced sun – and overhead a dusky navy-purple sky already reveals more stars than I've ever seen in my life. A way off, in a cleared-out circle, is the flickering glow of a large fire. Around it is a cluster of tables and benches.

Kinlee's mom leads me to it, and sets me down on one of the benches.

She squats down in front of me, smiling, but serious. "I'm Raina."

"Evie."

"Well, Evie, hang in there. We're gonna take care of you." She glances down to my swollen ankle, and her eyebrows crease together.

"What's this about a new Directee?" The voice is terse.

"Over here, Sue," Raina calls.

Sue squats by my feet and lifts the injured one onto her knee. She runs her fingers firmly over the swelling. Then she presses into it, and I flinch.

"Ow!"

"Hmmm," she says, raising an eyebrow as she assesses. "Good news. Looks like only a sprain."

This throbbing pain isn't *only* anything, but I don't dare argue. It's embarrassing enough to have this bustle of attention over me, and all for a stupid klutz moment. I don't want them to think this girl they saved is more trouble than she's worth.

And after this particular day, I'm nowhere near ready to let my guard down around anyone. Who are these people, anyway? They behave completely differently from anyone I've ever met, and all I really know about them is that they're some kind of alliance of woods-people who are against letting me burn to death. Good start, but still.

Kinlee rushes back carrying a thick translucent cuff. Raina takes it and wraps it around my ankle until it clicks into place. It's frozen.

"Now sit tight for a bit," Sue says, standing up. "Let that ice do its work. Then I'll come back and wrap it for you."

Sue nods and both women turn and leave. Kinlee hops onto the log and perches next to me.

"You might wanna get the ice away from the fire," she says. "Ice isn't as effective when it melts."

I take the point and slide my leg to the side as much as I can.

"Why am I even doing this?" I ask.

"Seriously?" Kinlee asks. "Ice helps with the swelling."

"Oh."

My ankle *is* starting to feel some relief, now that I think about it. Kind of numb. Which is a nice break from the pain.

A voice comes from behind us. "The dead keep getting younger."

I twist around to take a look, causing a pinch in my leg. A boy about the same age as Kinlee and me is standing there, arms crossed over his chest and a goofy grin on his face.

"Shouldn't you be, like, feeding a cow or something?" Kinlee says.

"A cow? There's real cows here?" I exclaim.

"Did that already," he says, playfully pushing Kinlee out of his way as he wiggles onto the log between us.

Kinlee sighs. "Yeah, there's cows. This is Connor. Connor, Evie."

"And chickens," Connor adds. He's tall and gangly, his build slight. His hair is wavy and disheveled, curling in loose swooshes all over his head and at the nape of his neck, and falling into his eyes. Once he settles onto the log, he looks at me. There is a directness in his gaze that makes me uncomfortable.

63

"Why would they kill you?" he says. "You're our age."

A pang of anger flashes through me, and followed by exhaustion.

"The Directorate doesn't *kill* us," I snap. "They just have the technology to tell us when our quality of life is going to decline, so we can live our lives accordingly and go peacefully and painlessly."

Connor and Kinlee exchange a look.

"But, um…" He glances back to me. "If that's true, why aren't you in some kind of pain?"

"I am, actually." I point to my ankle.

"Yeah but, the Directorate couldn't predict a hurt ankle from genomics."

"What do you mean?" As soon as I say it, my stomach twists, and I realize I'm not sure I want to understand him.

"I'm just saying," he stretches his arms out. "If the Directorate knows exactly when you're going to decline, and that time was this morning, and their thing didn't work… how are you not suffering? With their amazing-genius science-predicting, wouldn't this awful thing be setting in about now? But here you are. So my question is, if the Directorate is as good at this as they say they are, how are you not 'declining' yet?"

It's a question I hadn't gotten to yet, and it's a terrible one. A chill runs over me, and the blood drains from my face.

"Shit, Connor," Kinlee mutters.

"What do you – but – that's not even close to what they do. It's not – "

The smartass smirk on his face, like he knows everything there is to know, has me so furious I can't think straight. This boy talks too fast, says too much. We don't talk to each other like this in the Quads. We're polite.

"Why are you so mean? Has anyone solved that great mystery of science yet?"

Kinlee snorts. "I like her."

Connor's eyes go wide, and then the light behind them falters. Something warm and satisfied pulses through me.

He turns to Kinlee and they exchange another look. Like

they're parents deciding whether to tell a kid there's no Santa Claus. Kinlee shakes her head. Only slightly, but I still see it.

"Um, yeah." Kinlee pushes off the log and stands up. "I've got some things I'm supposed to do before I'm done for the day. You okay here, Evie? My mom's gonna be back for you any minute."

She's leaving me? With this boy? My stomach drops, like when I stop paying attention and miss a step on the stairs. But I don't want her to think I'm any more of a wuss than I've already proven myself to be.

"Sure, I'm fine."

"Okay, good. Connor has to go too, don't you?" she says pointedly.

Connor gets up. "I've got those cows to see to, I guess."

My stomach lurches again – I wasn't exactly enjoying his company, but I don't want to be alone out here, either.

"Bye, then." I try not to care.

The fire crackles, and somewhere out there, a choir of crickets chirp. It's not so bad, actually, except that now that I'm alone, in the quiet, all the thoughts I didn't have time for today rush in at once. I'm supposed to be departed. I *am* departed, as far as anyone I love is concerned. Mom and Dad and Gracelyn are probably eating dinner about now. I can almost see it, as if I'm hovering over them at the table: the strange quietness looming over them all as they eat, the empty clinking of the silverware against the plates.

Or maybe they're fine. It's not like they didn't prepare for it. And they still have their good daughter, the one with the perfect recall, the even temper, and a hundred and forty years of promising future. The one they've poured everything into. At the thought, my stomach aches and I feel hollow and fragile, like I could implode from the weight of this day and disappear.

I try to stop my thoughts by studying my surroundings. It is not at all the wasteland I imagined the outside world would look like. Trees rustle in the brisk breeze overhead. Birds chirp. There's an occasional voice from somewhere through the trees. Because everywhere – *everywhere* – there's tons of trees. I didn't think there was anything green left out here at all.

There's a few cabins strewn about, and their placement seems as random as the trees. How can they live like this, so disordered?

A tinge of panic itches under my skin. My breaths grow harder, drawing the awful humidity into my lungs, which reminds me of all the toxins the air is surely full of, no matter what Raina says. I try to stop, but that's impossible of course, and it's too late for that anyway.

In the Quads, everything was always right, always orderly. Trees were carefully placed in systemic lines in the grid, evenly spaced along clean, even walkways. People didn't run or jump or leap around like crazy people. They walked in a calm, orderly fashion. It protected us – made sure we had safe, pleasant lives until our departure dates. That we didn't do stupid things and sprain our ankles and cause ourselves unnecessary pain.

"Oh honey. It's okay to cry. It's a lot to take in." I was so deep in thought I didn't notice Raina returning. I jump, and a bolt of pain shoots from my ankle. Sue is trailing not far behind her.

Cry? Who's crying? I ball my hands into fists and press them against my eyes.

Then I look up at Raina, hoping my eyes aren't red. "I'm fine."

"Yes, you are," she says with solemn reassurance.

Sue joins us and sets down her supplies. "Let's get you patched up."

Chapter Thirteen

Evie

A girl in my class – Harper – tripped once, a few years ago. She fell all the way down the stairs, and by the time she hit the bottom, her arm was twisted completely out of place.

I wasn't there, but I heard all about it at school the next day (along with everyone else) from Cynthia, who *was* there, and said she had never seen anything so horrible in all her life.

Emergency Care rushed to the house in one of their special white vans, the lights on top flashing. They injected some Instaheal into her arm and set it, and by school the next morning, she was loopy from the painkillers they put her on, but her arm was as good as new.

Ever since, Harper's gone extra slow on the stairs.

But that was in the Quads, where the Directorate looked out for us. Out here, it's me, Raina and Sue, and a cuff of ice. Sue removes it to study my ankle, then begins wrapping it in a bandage.

"We're going to put a splint on it and get you some crutches. You'll be fine again in a week or two," Raina says.

"Splint? *Crutches?*" It's like she's making words up. "A full *week?*"

"Or two." Sue approaches from behind and sets a pair of long wooden poles next to me, the top part wider and wrapped in cushioning. "Here. So you can get around without using your leg while it heals."

"You're not going to heal it now?"

That whiny tone is creeping back into my voice. This time, I'm so tired and hurting and confused, I don't care anymore.

"Sorry," Raina says. "We don't have the Directorate's budget. Instaheal is for life-threatening injuries only. You'll have to do it the old-fashioned way."

I half-sigh, half-pout.

"Here," Sue says, demonstrating how to use the crutches. Then she thrusts them at me. "Got it?"

"Sure." I pull on the handles and stand up.

"That's the idea." For the first time, Sue smiles a little. "Okay, well, you're good to go."

Something about her carelessness makes me feel a little better. Like it's not such a big deal.

"All right then," Raina says. She nods to me, and I get up to hobble after her. The crutches may help me avoid some pain, but they're definitely not graceful.

"Where are we going now?" I ask. As my ankle thaws out from the ice, it begins to throb again.

"We're getting you settled into your new place," Raina says. "You'll be with me and Kinlee."

She leads me through the scattered trees. Cabins are scattered through them, some close, some farther out, all wooden and small and plain.

"How do you keep them straight?" They all look the same to me, and there's no order to them at all.

"Don't worry," she says. "Wait and see, you'll know your way around here before you know it. Give it a few weeks."

Settle in? A few weeks?

"Oh no, no, no, no, no…" My chest clenches. "I can't *live* here."

"Evie, now listen – " She reaches out, but I shrug away.

"No! You can't make me stay out here and… and… *live in the woods*. With all the environmental contamination."

I do my best to storm off, but the crutches make it difficult. She catches up.

"A place like this must be scary after living in a Quad your whole life. But it really will be okay. You're going to adjust."

I huff and pant, trying to go faster, as fast as it takes to get away from her.

"I will never adjust to *this*," I whine. I miss home so badly

68

I feel hollow.

"There's nowhere else for you to go, honey, at least for now. I'm sorry."

Raina pauses as if waiting for me to speak, but emotions swell within me that are too powerful for words. I shut my eyes tight to keep my panic from spilling out in uncontrollable tears.

She continues. "You know you can't go back, right? They'll kill you. But it's not just that. If that were all, we'd let you make your own choice and that would be that. But the Directorate is trying to keep all this a secret, and they'll protect it at any cost. Your parents. Your siblings. Your friends. Whoever you were to go to. They'll kill them too. It's the only way they could protect their secret."

I stagger to a halt, the crutches digging into the dirt. Would the Directorate really do that? I don't want to believe it, but after this particular day, it's not so hard to imagine. What's going to happen to Charlie, Ronni, and Viv in those mental health meetings tomorrow?

"And," Raina goes on, "They'd know we're out here. They wouldn't stop searching until they found us. Honestly, it probably wouldn't even take that long, once they were looking for us."

Anger wells up in my chest in hot bursting bubbles. "Obviously I can't go back. I never said – I wasn't going to…"

But I am drowning in my overwhelm and I am out of words. I scream. A loud, angry, awful scream that reaches past the trees and into the sky. A horrid sound that would never be tolerated in the Quads. It's been building inside me all day, and relief replaces the pressure as I let it out.

It's funny. My parents, they drove me nuts. So protective. So careful. Model citizens. I hated them sometimes, for how they fawned over Gracelyn and left me behind. But I understood it. All things aside, all the anger and loneliness, I still miss them now.

Raina puts a hand on my back. "Here," she says. "The cabin is this way."

We walk the rest of the way in grudging silence.

She opens the door to the cabin and stands aside to let me in. Inside is dark and musty. My nose crinkles.

"Yeah, it's not the best for ventilation," Raina says. "You'll get used to it, though. It's not so bad."

Get used to it? I hope not. But then, what else I can I do?

I push myself into the room and look around. Two sets of bunk beds are shoved against the back wall, and a third against the far side wall. The closer wall, next to the door, holds a couple of dressers.

I reach out and touch one – it's wood. Not the eco-plastic wooden pattern of the Directorate, but *real* wood. And from the looks of it, they're pretty old.

"I know, it's not what you're used to. But it's a safe place to sleep, for as long as you choose to stay here." Raina smiles weakly.

"For as long as I choose?" My heart does a flip. "But you said I can't go back?"

"There's a whole world out there, Evie. We're under a transit freeze right now for security, but once that's lifted, if you want to, you're free to go and explore it."

Right now, the world's already far too big for me. In contrast, the tight space of the cabin feels almost comforting.

"You can take that bunk," Raina says, pointing to the one on the far wall. "Go ahead and settle in. Rest up. You've got maybe an hour before dinner. We'll come and get you when it's time to eat."

"Okay," I reply. "And Raina? Thanks."

I hope she can't tell how grudging I am about it. I try to force a smile but I think it ends up just pulling the corners of my mouth outward.

All the same, she smiles back at me. "It's going to be okay, Evie. Give it some time."

And then she turns and leaves the cabin, closing the door behind her.

I hobble across the room on my crutches and plop onto the bed, letting my crutches drop to the ground.

I gingerly pull up my wrapped foot and spread out on the

bed. My ankle throbs, a pain that starts in my heel and stretches up my shin. My head rushes with all the strange things about this day that I have yet to take in. The stiffness of the bed presses into my back, pushing pressure against my spine.

But somehow in spite of it all, I crash into quiet darkness.

Chapter Fourteen

Gracelyn

Today I remember from the start that Evie is gone. As I lie in bed, I listen through the wall, but there is nothing to hear. Father is right – what I heard yesterday morning must have been branches on the window. To think anything else would be ridiculous. To think anything else would be treasonous.

Evie is gone, and that is the way it should be. It is better for her this way. We all know what happened to people before departures – slow, painful, ugly deaths. I would never wish that on Evie.

The alarm on my digipad is still buzzing. A spritz of citrus settles into the air to waken my senses, but when I lift my arm out to tap the snooze, a deep tiredness permeates through my muscles. I groan. I wish I could lie here all day – pull the covers over my head and stare at the inside of the blank white comforter. The thought only feels good for a moment before it is chased with guilt. That is not the thought of a good Directorate citizen.

We weren't supposed to be close, I scold myself.

They all knew that being close with Evie would only lead to pain for me. That it would feel like this.

But it is hard, when it is your sister. Especially when your sister is Evie. She was different. Goofy, and messy – everything we're taught not to be. And angry. She deserved more than her short life.

Seventeen years. It is no wonder she was angry. I would be too.

I *am* angry. I wasn't before, but this morning, buried beneath the layers of exhaustion, there it is. *My sister is gone.*

But I had my day to let Evie go. Like Father said. Now it is time to move on and get back to normal. Whatever normal is, now.

This system always seemed so tidy from the outside. From my bed this morning, it feels impossible.

I force myself up.

The bathroom mirror shows me dull freckled skin, with dark circles under bloodshot brown eyes. I push back my dirty blonde hair and try smiling, to see if I can hide it. It helps, but not enough. Then I get in the shower.

Yesterday at this time, Evie's body was still in her bed. How does it happen? Does life leave you right at midnight like a switch? Does it fade away slowly like a dying battery?

I shake my head and push it under the shower flow, staring at the blank white tiles at my feet.

"Pressure up," I say.

"Water pressure increasing," the shower confirms.

I let the sound of the intensifying water flow drown out my thoughts.

It is unlike me to let my mind wander to these dark places. Mother would say I am making things harder for myself. *Think of something happy, dear.*

At breakfast, Mother wears the same manic smile as yesterday and clings to her mug. Father studies me as I push the food around my plate.

"All of that from yesterday – it's behind us now, right? Like we talked about," he prompts.

I force a bite down my throat. "Right."

It is selfish to be sad now. We all knew it was coming, and we had plenty of time to prepare. Letting Evie go is the best way to honor her. Even if she did deserve so much more time.

"Aren't you *excited*, Gracelyn?" Mother's voice cuts through my thoughts, shrill with forced enthusiasm. "Oh, I remember my first day of career training."

Actually, career training started yesterday. I've looked forward to this transition for as long as I can remember. But since the start date was set last quarter, that excitement became tangled up with my dread of Evie's departure. Today, it doesn't feel like it matters at all. What good is a career without Evie to share my accomplishments and triumphs with? I don't know if I can get through the stress of LQM's competitive program without her here to talk me down when I need it.

I push my face into what feels like a smile and hope it doesn't look as forced as Mother's. If people start to worry about me, the Directorate will step in. They will assign pills to improve my mood, or even to forget. I don't ever want to forget.

Working for LQM is a prestigious posting. After all, this is the department that keeps us living painlessly and departing on schedule. *Like Evie.* I shake the thought out of my head and refocus. If I can get past this and do as well as everyone expects of me, maybe someday I'll be Green Level like Father.

I'll have a lot of catching up to do, but I barely feel up to finishing my breakfast. How am I going to go there, to that department, and not think of Evie?

It's going to be a long day.

Outside, it is a perfect morning like every other. The smell of fresh, damp grass remains from the nightly misting, and overhead the Quad dome is completing its transition to white daylight.

The shuttlebus pulls up to the small park at the center of my Quad, and I step on.

The Quad's soothing notes of meditative morning music lowers as I step on, layering with muted tones are the usual safety reminders: "*Watch out for the watchlizards – keeping an eye on your safety and happiness…*"

A hand pops up from the back – it's my classmate Hanna, who lives in Neighborhood Ten, right next to mine, waving at me. She was assigned to LQM, too.

We've done almost everything together. We're the same birth year, same IQ level, and the same departure class – she'll pass on two years before me. She even shares my perfect recall. We're the lucky ones, the top two percent across not just the Quad, but the entire Directorate.

I force myself to smile and walk down the aisle. She pulls her bag off the seat next to her and I plop into it, quickly securing my seatbelt.

Hanna is usually talkative, but as the shuttlebus rolls forward, she stares down at her lap. I know what she is thinking. There is nothing to say. Not after a departure. An inexplicable urge to shout Evie's name rises in me – something, anything, to stop pretending everything is fine. To make Hanna look at me and acknowledge what has happened. But that is not how things are done.

"How was the first day of training?" I ask.

Hanna brightens and turns to me, her eyes widening. "*Oh. It was very interesting.*"

She launches into a breakdown of everything that happened, how our classmates handled it, and who isn't going to make the cut at the end of the year.

"We're starting in the Prevention Division – routine health scans, managing the Quad's life protection systems, continued optimization to ensure citizens have safe and pain-free lives all the way to their departure date."

"Mhm." I know what Prevention is. Everyone does. But once Hanna starts prattling, she turns into an encyclopedia. Which works for me right now. The more she talks, the less I have to.

She keeps going until the shuttlebus glides to a stop at the Quad center, and even as she leads me down the crowded sidewalks to the LQM office building.

"I came *three times* last week to practice the walk," she says. "This way."

I probably would have done the same if I hadn't been so busy with Evie's departure preparations. Knowing your way around means less stress, and less stress means a clearer head.

I stay close to Hanna as she weaves through the crowds to a particularly large building. It stretches an entire block. The sensor on the sliding doors only allow one person in at a time, checking our digipads for access credentials.

On the other side, security greets me. "Oh-eight-seven-three-two-two-eight-one. Gracelyn Henders?"

"Yes."

"You were not here yesterday."

"Correct."

I wait for the guard to say more, to acknowledge the reason why, recognize my loss in some small way. She doesn't.

She prints an ID badge for me. Across the top runs a yellow band – Prevention Division. Below it runs a thinner band of blue.

Hanna points to it. "It's for intern."

The lobby is crisp white. The far wall projects a floor-to-ceiling screen of slowly swirling earth tones: brown, then clay-red, then moss-green, and more. Hanna leads me across it to the elevator and shows me how to swipe the badge on the elevator to go to our floor.

The elevator slows to a stop, and a calm female voice announces we've arrived. "Floor Eight."

The office is like the lobby: white, crisp and calm, filled with a light herbal scent of rosemary, for focus, like our classrooms always were. I breathe it in, centering myself in the comfort of the familiar.

I follow Hanna past the lobby and down a hallway, into a separate section of the office. It's filled with a series of long white eco-plastic tables, each lined with syncscreens and matching ergonomic chairs. The ambient background notes settle my mind, and some employees are already getting to work. A watchlizard crawls across the broad ceiling. I have always liked the watchlizards – it is a comfort, to know the Directorate is always watching, always looking out for us.

"We're over here," Hanna says as she leads me down a few rows. "I made sure we were together."

Hanna and I have always been each other's biggest competition. She likes to keep me close. All the same, I feel a swell of relief. Hers is a familiar face, and familiar is scarce right now.

As we pass the other first-years, classmates I have learned with and competed against every year of our lives, they don't bother hiding their stares. I can hear the whispers that follow. Why won't anyone just say it? My sister departed. At least

Hanna has the decency, if she doesn't want to talk about it, to pretend it never happened at all. I straighten my shoulders and fix my eyes on Hanna's swinging ponytail ahead of me. I also need to pretend nothing has happened, if I am going to make it through this day.

Hanna stops at a chair mid-row and gestures for me to take the one next to her. I adjust the holding pod for the syncscreen, place my new ID card into the side where Hanna shows me – an extra security precaution for DMD access – and sync it to my digipad. A quiet settles over the office as we all get to work, reviewing the introductory documentation pushed to our account feeds that are only accessible when we're logged in on-site, for security. Which means that while we're in one of the most competitive placements, we're only able to prepare for the exams at the end of the year while we're in the office.

Career training starts off more academic in nature, like a particularly intense course. The real work starts gradually. Too much change at once causes cortisol to increase beyond the recommended levels.

"This must be our girl?"

The voice is melodic, breaking the silence that has filled the office all morning. It's a young woman, perhaps a few years older than me. But she seems tall, seems so *adult*, with her sharp suit and casual composure, as she perches against the table. Her looks are striking: brilliant red hair in tight curls and a complexion so pale she almost glows, framed by a crooked smile. Her eyes are an unearthly shade of light gray.

Hanna straightens.

"Yes, this is Gracelyn," she says. "Gracelyn, this is Quinn, the professional we are shadowing this year."

I bolt to my feet. "Nice to meet you."

She takes my hand and squeezes it. "I'm so sorry about your sister."

A shudder overcomes me, followed by relief. Finally, someone is acknowledging what happened.

I hold her hand tight. Her touch wakes me up, as if an electric shock passed between us.

"Thank you."

I peer up at her to see if she feels it too, but her expression is impenetrable.

She pulls her hand away. "We're glad to have you. Your file indicates great potential."

We follow Quinn to a conference room on the other side of the floor. Quinn takes a seat at the table. A few other students timidly sit in a second ring of chairs against the wall, with their hands in their lap, and we join them, behind Quinn. A few others join and settle in.

Just as the meeting is about to begin, the door opens, and the room abruptly falls to order. I look up and find Father settling in at the head of the table. Unlike at breakfast where he was stoic and stiff, here he smiles ear to ear. As they get into the business at hand, he even jokes with others. He *laughs*.

A confused heat floods through me. Father and Mother and I, we were in this together. We were the only ones that would remember Evie and keep her here. But just like Hanna, just like my classmates, just like everyone else today, Father is acting as if nothing happened at all.

All through the meeting my emotions burn, and afterwards I escape as quickly as I can into the hallway. I lean against the wall and shut my eyes, trying to sort through the thoughts rushing my mind. Maybe he's only pretending, but how can he even pretend such cheer so soon after Evie's departure?

A tear escapes, trickling down my cheek.

I rush to wipe it away, but it's too late. Father catches my eye as he speaks to a colleague from the end of the hall, and shoots me a harsh glare. Then he turns away, so fast that I am not sure what has happened.

Throughout the rest of the day, the weight of Evie's departure creeps back into me. It follows me through the cafeteria and sits with me in the lecture hall. It adds weight to my fitness hour and rides home with me on the shuttlebus.

As I walk in the front door at home, the smell of fresh paint hits me. I still expect to see Evie's shoes haphazardly dropped in the closet, her jacket on the hanger next to mine, her backpack on its hook on the wall. It's all gone. Even the hook has been removed, and the hole in the wall patched up and covered with mellow beige to match the rest of the house.

Cover up. Remove. Forget. It's better this way, they say. Like she was never here.

But she *was* here. Even though her coat is gone, her chair at the table, her favorite cup with the little chip on the bottom. With each little way I notice she has been removed from the house, the hole in my heart expands. I wonder if Mother or Father feels like this. If they do, neither of them shows any sign, and it makes me want to scream. Someone should react, someone should protect Evie's memory. But I swallow my impulse and trace over the daisy pendant around my neck, one piece of her they can't take away from me. Remind myself to remain compliant.

At dinner, Father is gentle and somber like he was at breakfast, as if he has flipped back a switch to become the Father I know again. Which version of him is the true one? The Father at home or the Father at work? One has to be a lie.

After eating, I excuse myself to my room, close the door behind me and collapse into bed. I pull the covers over my head, and allow the gaping hole I have ignored all day to swallow me up.

Will it always be like this? Part of me wishes to let go of Evie and be done with this pain. It is what I am supposed to do. But I have a feeling this kernel of her will remain ingrained, a part of me, for the rest of my long life. And I want to hold on to her.

A hundred and twenty-four years to go.

I listen to the silence through the wall. There is no scratching of branches, no wind, no creaking of the house. I heard something yesterday morning, and there is only one thing it could have been.

No matter what Father or anyone else says, deep in my gut, I know what I heard.

Chapter Fifteen

Evie

"Hey! Evie!" A voice jolts me awake.

"Uuuuuuuugh." I roll onto my side, my eyes still shut, and curl up into a ball. As I do, I knock into the edge of the bunk, and it all comes back – I'm not in my bed at home. I'm in some camp in the middle of the forest. Back at home, they all think I'm departed.

"Wake uuuuuuup." The voice is right next to my cot now. I squint my eyes open. Kinlee is hovering over me.

"Why?"

I'd really just as soon never move again.

"Cuz," she says, "Breakfast. The foods. Om nom nom."

She gesticulates wildly as she talks, as if shoving food into her mouth.

I moan. My muscles and bones ache.

But now that she mentions it, my stomach is feeling terribly empty. It growls in protest.

"Fiiine."

"Don't want to miss it," Kinlee says. "Most important meal of the day."

"Aren't they all important?" They were in the Directorate. Everything we did was important. If it wasn't important, it was eliminated.

I push myself up, stretch my arms and shake my head, trying to get the sleepiness out. I guess it works. A little.

"Shit."

"That's what you said last night. We let you sleep through dinner. Mom said you needed the rest. Now she says you need routine."

My stomach rumbles again.

"I'm starving." Last thing I ate was that dry cereal while waiting for Mara. I pull myself up and tilt my wrist to check my digipad, and am reminded that I don't have one anymore. "This has been the *most* messed-up twenty-four hours."

The door opens and Raina comes in.

"I got you some clothes," she says. "Just a few pairs of Alliance regulations, but at least you'll be warm and comfortable."

She hands me three full outfits of gray and navy; sweatshirt, tee, joggers, everything.

"Thanks." I take them from her. I hadn't had a chance to think about it yet, but I can't keep wearing my crumpled party dress everywhere. These look like gym uniforms – ugly, boring gray and navy ones – but it's a kind gesture, and really, at this point, what does it matter? I force a smile, hoping it shows how grateful I am, and change into a pair of the soft cotton sweats and a loose t-shirt.

"Be good to those. From now on you're going to have to buy your clothes yourself from what you earn," Raina says.

"Earn?" I ask.

"Yes, everyone has a job here," Raina says. "And that includes you. But first you'll try out a few different areas, like all the teens do when they start. So you can learn, and we can see what your skills are."

Skills? Oh no.

"What if I don't have any?"

"Don't be ridiculous," Raina says. "What did you do in the Directorate?"

I shake my head. "Nothing."

Raina raises her eyebrows.

"Really," I say. "With my departure date... they pushed me through education with the others, but why train me for something I wouldn't be around to actually do? I didn't even take the aptitudes test."

My arm prickles where the numbers are inked into it.

Raina blinks at me. "So what *did* you do? After school was over?"

I shrug. "I helped a bit at home. And I prepared for the departure rituals. Final visits to extended family, gave my special things away to loved ones, planned my departure party."

"Well, this should be fun, then," Raina says. "A chance for you to discover something about yourself."

I'm not so sure. "And if I'm not good at anything?"

Raina laughs. "Don't be silly. Everyone's good at something."

What am I good at? I really have no idea. I was a pretty good sister, I think. That's all I ever really was.

And I'm good at not departing, I guess. I don't think that counts.

"You deserve to know what you're capable of, Evie. And now that you don't have a clock counting down your time, you can plan on a long life of contributing. Find your place in the world."

Can I?

Connor's question from last night – about why I haven't started 'declining' – nags at me. The departure dates aren't random. They're supposed to let us live as long a life as we can, before something kicks in and our quality of life begins to drop.

Whatever that something is for me, it's still *there*. Maybe it's already started, and I just haven't noticed yet.

"Come on, I'm *starving*." Kinlee herds us towards the door.

Outside, morning sunlight stretches through the branches with a too-bright glare, and birds are chirping. The humidity is even worse this morning, pressing against my skin and beading on the back of my neck.

Kinlee leads me – hobbling on my crutches, of course – through the trees and back to near the fire pit and scattered tables. Clusters of people are all over the place, standing and sitting in groups, chatting and laughing as they eat. Right out in the open, under the strange violet sky.

As we get close, I hesitate, struggling to take it all in. In the Quads, breakfast was a quiet event at home, at a clean orderly table, our meals predetermined by Directorate scientists.

Kinlee nudges me. "This way."

I do my best to keep up as Kinlee dodges through clusters of people and towards a group of teens – some standing, some sitting – around the wooden table. She leaps into the air as she gets close, and pounces onto the shoulders of a guy with his back to us.

The boy yelps, and I tense up, anticipating conflict – this type of behavior would never be tolerated in the Quads. But he twists around and, amazingly, he's grinning. He grabs Kinlee and tosses her forward over his shoulder. I gasp and my chest tightens, but when he puts her down, she is giggling. As they settle, he rests one arm comfortably over her shoulders.

Then Kinlee twists back and points at me. "That's the new girl," she says. "From the Directorate. Come on, Evie, whatchya waiting for?"

I hobble closer, suddenly self-conscious about my regulation clothes. No one else is wearing them – or at least, not the way they come. They've all modified them in some way, cutting the sleeves short, or tying up the sides, so that they might all be wearing the same thing, but they all look different.

"And Evie, this is everyone," Kinlee continues.

Their grins fade as their expressions shift to curiosity.

I wish I didn't have these damn crutches. They don't help my awkwardness at all, and I am sure I look like an idiot.

"Actual names would probably be good." Connor walks up and stops next to me. His hair is even messier than it was yesterday. Is this something he does on purpose?

He points as he goes around the circle, starting at my other side and ending at the guy with Kinlee. "Lucas, Sam, Ginnie, Joel, Meredith, Dave."

"Like she's going to remember all that." Kinlee rolls her eyes.

She's got a point. Half of them are already slipping my mind. There's too much going on, too fast. The crutches, and the noise, and I still feel lost and woozy from all that happened yesterday.

"Yeah?" Connor raises his eyebrows. "Bet she learns them a lot faster if we actually tell them to her in the first place."

Kinlee sticks out her tongue. "Whatever."

This casual interaction, completely devoid of etiquette, both shocks and fascinates me. In the Directorate, such behavior got you sent right to your mental health manager for adjustments. But no one here seems to think it's a big deal. The adults nearby don't even bother to notice.

Large baskets of different foods begin to pass around, and the group reassembles around the table, plopping onto the benches. As I join them, I am careful to keep my arms away from the worn wood of the table – we don't have real wood in the Directorate for a reason: splinters. And this table's weathered old panels look like they're made of nothing but. But before I can say anything, I am distracted by warm wafts of proteins and carbs filling the air. My stomach grumbles.

"So... you're from the Directorate?" one of the girls asks, looking at me. Her hair is dark and her eyes a deep brown. Ginnie, I think.

"Huh? Oh. Yeah." What I wouldn't give to be back there now, eating my assigned meal, in the quiet of my own home with my family. Not to mention near *real* medical help.

"What's it like in there?" she asks. She opens a basket and pulls something flat and brown and delicious-smelling onto her plate.

I've never really thought about it before. It's just what it is. It's *normal,* what life is supposed to be. "It was... nice. Everything was organized. Everything was taken care of. Predictable."

Their eyes are all on me, somber and curious. I try not to think about Gracelyn, or my parents. I refuse to cry again, at least not in front of them.

"Right. *Organized*," Connor says. He stabs at some food on his plate. The way he says it, it's like it's a bad word. "More like *controlled.*"

His brows pull together and his cheeks flush. It makes me

want to back away. "Controlled?" I echo.

Kinlee nudges me, holding out one of the baskets. But I'm too distracted by Connor's glare. She proceeds to spoon something onto my plate.

"Yeah," Connor says. "As in, they control everything about your life and don't let you make any of your own choices."

"It's not like that," I snap. It comes out harsher than I mean it to, but what's he doing? This is what he was doing last night. As if the Directorate was trapping us in there, rather than protecting us. "They keep us safe. They make sure we live optimally to our departure date, happy and healthy."

Kinlee has taken my plate and seems to be pulling over all the baskets that have passed our way.

"Right. Like they kept *you* safe. 'Til your departure date," Connor snaps back. "And what then?"

My mind goes blank, and it's like the floor's dropped out from under me. People didn't talk like this in the Quad.

"Food time! Everyone shut up and eat." Kinlee glares at Connor and shoves my plate back to me.

I look down at it, and find it overfilled with piles of foods that look strange and malformed. I'm supposed to eat this stuff?

One brown-ish pile seems somewhat like some of the carbs we eat in the Quads, except it's not in a neat square. It's all sort of cut up into a pile.

I pick up some of the mush with my fork. "What is this stuff?"

"Are you serious?" Kinlee asks. "It's potatoes. Hash browns."

"I've never seen food look like *this* before."

I scrutinize the rest of what Kinlee has put on my plate.

"Okay. Right." Kinlee glances across the table at Connor, who stares blankly back. "So this is eggs. Bacon. Toast. You've really never seen any of this before?"

Sure, in theory, I always got it – the proteins come from animals; fruits and vegetables are grown from the ground. But this egg is a strange yellow, all broken into weird squiggly pieces. The bacon isn't much better. In the Quads, the food printers offer up our meals in tidy squares.

But everyone else is eating, and my stomach is growling fiercely. I shut my eyes and take a bite.

And whoa.

The food in the Quad was always fine. But we didn't eat it for the flavor, we ate it to optimize our bodies. These hash browns explode with flavors, crispy and savory and crazy delicious. I devour the rest of my plate, taking samples from everything Kinlee passes my way, then handing each basket on to Connor and down the table.

But when I pass the bacon, he pulls away and hands it quickly over to Ginnie.

"No bacon? But it's so good," I say. I take another bite and savor it, warm and salty.

He crinkles his nose. "I have a strict policy of not eating animals I know."

I frown. It never occurred to me to think about where my food came from before – I didn't have to, it just came from the printers, rearranging the molecules from the nutrient packs it was loaded with. And it never tasted like *this*. I shrug it off and savor the flavors.

When I'm done, I want more.

"How do you know how much?"

"What?" Kinlee replies, chewing.

"How do you know? How much you're allowed to eat?"

"*Allowed* to eat?" She blinks at me. "Are you hungry or full?"

My eyes wander to the baskets sitting on the table. It all smells so good. "Hungry."

"Okay then."

Kinlee picks up the closest basket and hands it to me. The biscuits inside emanate a bready, buttery aroma. She doesn't have to tell me twice.

Meanwhile, Kinlee and the others are rambunctious – joking, laughing, shoving each other around and shouting with mouths half-full. Don't they worry about choking? About falling off the benches? There's not even a back to them as a safeguard.

They don't wait and make sure everyone is keeping up. They don't check in or take turns to share about their day. They're reckless, somehow bigger than these worries. I shrink back behind their wild gestures.

As they finish eating, people start to get up and leave.

"All right, Ellie. You're starting with me."

I turn around to the familiar voice to find myself face to face with Sue, the stern lady from the Med cabin who wrapped my ankle last night.

Oh no. I bite on my lip to keep from saying it out loud. I'm starting my job rounds with her?

"It's *Evie*. With a V."

She looks like a Sue. As in, *so sue me.* One of those funny old phrases the Directorate made irrelevant and you don't hear anymore except in those old video feeds they used to make, movies. I don't really know what it means, something about courts, back before the Directorate put order to everything. But the gist is, you don't give a shit.

And that's what Sue's face says right now. Her expression is hard and tense, her eyes wary. She raises an eyebrow.

"Fine then, Evie-with-a-V. Let's go."

Then she heads off towards the Med cabin, expecting me to keep up, crutches and all.

I huff after her. Of all the people I've met so far at this camp, I can't believe I'm stuck with *her* all day.

A loud giggle from the table makes me look back. Kinlee is leaning forward, making a goofy face, and the others are playing along and laughing hysterically. Except Connor. He's twisted around and staring at me still, his frown softened into something more pensive.

On impulse, I frown back, but the intense way he's studying me makes the back of my neck tingle. Something I've never felt before tugs at me, something I don't know what to do with. Then I realize we're both staring, my cheeks flood with heat, and I turn away to follow Sue.

Chapter Sixteen

Evie

Sue leads me to one of the other cabins. I push in through the door, and am met by more hideous, old wooden furniture – a desk in the middle of the room at the front, a series of shelves full of overstuffed stacked boxes of supplies along the side walls, and two beds and another desk flattened against the back of the room. But everything inside it is tidy, scented of powder and antiseptic.

From the side, a man steps forward from a partially-loaded cart.

"I'm Noah," he says, stretching out his hand. "Boy are we glad to have you here. We could really use the help."

He is warm and friendly, the opposite of Sue. More like people in the Quad. A big smile breaks through his scruffy beard.

I shift awkwardly on my crutches to shake his hand.

"Yeah?" It's impossible not to smile back at him. It's taking the edge off my anxiety already. "I hope I can help."

He turns back to continue loading the cart. On the other side of the cabin, Sue is marking up some papers on a clipboard. On actual paper. With an actual pen. Before Tad, I'd only read about this in history texts. But then, without digipads, I guess you have to do your own writing sometimes. I still don't feel quite complete without mine.

When they're done with the cart, Noah and Sue step towards me.

"Well Ev, this is the Med cabin," Noah says, throwing his arms wide. "It's our home base, of sorts. Where the equipment and medications live. And it's where we start and end each day. But we don't spend the whole day cooped up in here. We do a lot of cabin visits and check-ins."

Ev? No one has ever called me *Ev.* It's hardly even a full sound, let alone a proper name.

He slaps the cart he's been loading up since I got here. "That's what this is for. Sue is about to go out on rounds. And you're going with her."

"What?"

Sue looks as displeased about this as I am. But she stands behind Noah's proclamation.

"You need to get a quick understanding of how things work around here," she says. "And we need you to be able to help fast. Perhaps you have noticed that you're the only one your age here right now. We can't force anyone to work in medicine, and the sick aren't as cute as the sheep."

"You can't?" In the Quads, positions are always assigned. The Directorate makes sure we go where we're needed. "Why not?"

"Because *here* we believe in choice." Sue's voice is sharp. "And that everyone is better off when they have free will."

I can't imagine anyone volunteering for this work, where other people's lives are in your hands. It's too much risk, too much responsibility. Especially without Instaheal.

Sue stares at me, seeming to dare me to say anything else.

I can't help myself.

"Did you say there's sheep here? *Real* sheep?" Didn't Connor say something about chickens last night? I was so overwhelmed by everything that it's only now coming back to me.

"Yes." Sue rolls her eyes. "This place was designed this place to be as self-sustaining as possible, off the grid. That includes keeping shipments into the camp minimal for things like food and clothing. Now let's go."

Sue takes the cart and heads out of the door.

She doesn't check to see if I am keeping up on my crutches, but even with the cart's wide wheels she has to move slowly to get across the uneven ground outside. We weave through the trees, past the campfire and tables where we ate breakfast, past several cabins, and approach one of the doors.

Sue parks the cart against the outside of the cabin. "Come here," she says.

I hobble to her side. "What can I do?"

I *do* want to help, if I can actually do anything. I might not be happy about the situation, but these people did save my life. Only, I've never been all that helpful. With such an early departure date, I wasn't expected to be.

"Take these," Sue says. "Don't drop them."

She puts some supplies into a bag – some pills, a needle wrapped in plastic, a bottle of a strong-smelling liquid, thick cotton pads, and a large roll of the same canvas-y wrapping they used for my ankle – and hands the bag to me.

She starts for the door, then hesitates and turns back to me.

"Now look," she says. "This man is injured. He is in pain. And I know, pain is not something you encounter in the Quads. He also has dementia, and some of what he says may not make sense. Don't argue with him. I need you to handle yourself and do as I say. If you don't think you can do that, don't come in at all. Got it?"

What am I about to walk into? My gut squirms. I want to run away, far into the woods, and never come back. But then I remember Kinlee's fearlessness, and the carefree attitude of all the others.

Surely, I can at least stand in the same room with someone *else* in pain. "Got it."

Sue opens the door, and I brace myself. A whiff of thick odor wafts out, dense and sour.

"Morning, Sue," a voice calls as she steps in ahead of me. It's not the grizzled voice I expected. A woman sits in a chair close to the bunk on the opposite wall. She looks tired, her hair limp.

"Hi Carla," Sue replies. "How's my favorite guy today?"

The abrupt change in Sue's voice makes me look at her. She's different all of a sudden, holding up a front of cheeriness. Except – it's not a front. It's more as if the opposite has happened, as if a defensive layer has peeled away and suddenly the real Sue is coming through. This is a Sue with purpose, and even some kind of cheer that I'd have never expected.

"We're having a pretty good morning," Carla responds.

A figure shuffles in the bed. "Who's there?"

"It's me, Frank. It's Sue." Sue walks towards him so he can see her.

The man props himself up on wobbly elbows and squints. "Sue?"

"That's right," Sue says. "And I've brought someone with me." She snaps her fingers at me and gestures for me to come closer. I hobble over as quickly as I can, and she takes my arm, pulling me closer into Frank's view. "This is Ellie."

"Evie!" I cut in.

She continues without acknowledging me. "She's helping in Med for the next few weeks."

She pauses, to let Frank take in this information. He stares at the foot of his bed without any response. Can't he hear us? My throat constricts, and I can feel the thick wheezing in my breaths that comes before an attack. I want to shake off Sue's hand from my arm, run away from this strange man and take in some fresh air.

Sue's grip tightens, as if she can read my thoughts. She continues talking to Frank. "Evie is from the Directorate, Frank. Like you."

"Directorate…" For a moment Frank's eyes seem to sharpen with focus, and then it fades again. The expression on his face shifts, and suddenly he's in a panic. "I've got to get out. We've all got to get out," he says.

"You're safe, Frank. We've got you," Carla replies. She takes his hand. "You understand, Frank? You're safe."

"No!" he shouts. "They want us dead, all of us." He lurches upwards in the bunk, then seizes, gasps, and collapses back to the mattress, clutching his side.

"Take it easy, Frank," Sue says. "I know, it hurts. That's why we're here. We're going to help you get better."

She looks over to me. "He fell and broke his hip a month after we got him out."

Shit. The sprain in my ankle was bad enough … but an actual break? And in a hip, too. Why are they allowing him to suffer like this? He doesn't even know where he is.

"Okay, Frank, let's have a look at this, shall we?" Sue pulls up a chair next to the bed. "Right here," she says to me, patting it.

Oh no. A whooshing noise floods my ears. A front-row seat to this old man's debilitating injury is the last thing I want.

But Sue casts me a sharp look, and I do as I'm told.

Sue turns to Carla. "Now's a good time for you to step outside if you'd like. You deserve a break. Get some air. We'll be here an hour or so."

A whole hour of this?

"Sounds good." Carla leans over to Frank so she can see his face. "You hear that Frank? I'll be back real soon. Sue and Evie are going to take good care of you."

Then she leaves.

Sue takes a pair of latex gloves from the box in my bag. "Get the supplies out of the bag and put them on the tray. And grab a pair of gloves."

I do it. The gloves smell like rubber and are powdery against my skin.

Sue has me spray down a wash cloth with soapy water, and she washes him from head to toe. His wrinkly skin rolls around his upper arms, at his waist, and on the insides of his legs. Under the bandages, his hip is a swollen mess of purple and black, and rusty stains of blood run along the seams of his stitches. His limbs hang limp in Sue's strong hands. He mumbles occasionally, moving in response to Sue's prompts and nodding along as she chats with him.

My cheeks flush hot and I feel I should look away, but I can't stop watching. My eyes keep drifting back to the bloody stitches over the skin of his hips and the swollen bruises around it. How does he bear it?

When Sue is finished, I help her get Frank into clean clothes, and then she sits him up on the edge of the bunk.

"Frank? It's time to stand up," Sue urges.

What? She wants him to use that swollen, bandaged hip?

Suddenly my palms feel cold and slick.

Frank's eyes go wide. "Stand up! No, no, no." His face scrunches, as if he might cry. His hand trembles in mine, clenching to me tightly. My heart softens – he's so scared.

"Come, now, Frank, what's all this?" Sue's voice holds sympathy.

He shakes his head side to side.

"Frank? Why won't you stand up? It will help you get strong again."

"F-f-fall. I'm going to fall."

"We're not going to let you fall again. That's exactly why we've got to get you up. So you get strong and don't fall."

Frank nods.

"We got you, Frank. Up you go."

Sue somehow coaxes him onto his feet. He clings to my hand with a grip stronger than I would've guessed him capable of, and we get him a full ten steps across the cabin before Sue pulls a chair behind him to rest. Then, the real work begins. Sue coaches him through a series of leg lifts and pushes and other exercises.

All through it, Frank grimaces and whimpers. I feel so helpless, so angry, faced with his pain – why are they putting him through all this? He should've been allowed to depart. He should never have lived to be weak enough to fall in the first place. But Sue coaxes and cheers him through it all, and Frank keeps on. Turns out he was hiding a lot of fight under all that hesitation.

Carla comes back, and I can't believe the time is gone already. When it's time to walk back to the bed, Frank is as resistant to lie down as he was to stand up. We leave him sitting in a chair near the bed, with Carla.

"Not bad," Sue says as we push the cart away from the cabin. She gives me a stern half-frown, like she is studying me. "For someone from the Directorate. You all get so squeamish around illness. But you did just fine."

I have a feeling this is as much praise as I can ever expect from Sue. But she's got one thing right – it was unsettling to see a person so broken and vulnerable.

She continues. "I gotta give the Directorate credit for one thing – they take great care of their citizens, physically. For his age, Frank is in great condition. He's strong. He'll be walking again in no time. Maybe with a walker this time, but he'll get around fine."

"And the dementia?"

"He'll have that the rest of his life. It's almost certainly the reason Frank is here right now, and not in the Directorate." She shakes her head. "They used to look for cures, you know. For dementia, for a lot of things. Now the Directorate's the only ones left with the resources to do it, and they're too busy optimizing the lucky ones to bother helping the others."

The old lines the Directorate repeated to us over and over in school come to my lips.

"But people suffered, that way. What they do now – so much is eliminated with the right diet and exercise, by eliminating pollution and stress. We'll never be able to eliminate every cause of suffering, but we can eliminate the suffering."

Sue studies me, raising an eyebrow. "Tell that to all those who the Directorate killed over the past seventy-five years, without any say on whether that's what they wanted or not. Or even how they lived."

I have no response for this, and Sue doesn't wait for one. She pushes ahead, and we're quickly at another cabin, another patient in need of Sue's energetic care. A cancer patient this time.

"So she's departing?" I ask.

"No!" Sue grabs my shirt. "She is *not* dying. If you go in that room and mention death or in any way imply it, I will personally drag you back to the Directorate, and I don't care what they do to you once we get there. Do you understand me?"

Her anger catches me off guard, giving me a jolt like an electric shock. But it's not Sue's words that get to me. Even Sue, gruff as she is, wouldn't really turn me over to the Directorate, I'm sure of it. It's her eyes. They ignite with anger, as if we were heading into some kind of battle. There's something different about this patient.

"Okay, okay. Just trying to understand. Got it, *not departing*."

Sue shoves the supply bag at me and heads inside, leaving me to catch the door behind her with my crutch.

Sue immediately shatters the quiet, her voice packed with energy and a smile plastered to her face. "Rosie! Still in bed? It's past ten!"

The woman in the bed looks so depleted I almost panic. Her head is entirely bald, with hardly enough fuzz to call eyebrows framing a face that is sunken and pale.

She lifts her head slowly, as if dragging herself out of a dream. But I don't think she was asleep.

"Only ten, huh? I got more time to kick back than I thought."

A slow grin spreads on her face. It looks half-hearted to me, like maybe she's only playing along for Sue. But if Sue notices, she ignores it and goes on about her business. She unhooks an IV bag from behind the bed and grabs a new one from the supplies.

"This is Evie, she's new. Directorate."

Rosie glances towards me. "You're so young." I don't know what to say to that, so I shrug. She continues. "Quite an adjustment, huh?"

My eyes trace over her hollowed cheeks and her bald head. I can't believe she's alive, with all that her body is going through. "Adjustment. Yeah."

Rosie laughs, glancing at Sue, who smirks back at her. As if they've shared some kind of inside joke. "Oh, you don't know the half of it. You've been here, what, a few days?"

"One."

"Yeah. Don't worry, you'll get used to it."

"Get used to what?" I ask.

"Being around pain," she responds. "It's not easy, at first."

I glance to Sue. Her eyes brim with sadness, and the lines of her face are strained. Something tells me it never gets easy to be around pain, not the kind Sue has been showing me this morning.

Sue parks me in the chair next to Rosie's bed with the clipboard, and I update her vitals on the chart as Sue gives her a full checkup.

It takes a while. Sitting still, I suddenly realize how strained my body is from all the moving around on the crutches. My arms and neck are sore from the movement, and my muscles are tired. But in the lull of the beeping machines, I start to relax – for a moment.

"What's that?" Sue demands, peering over my shoulder at the clipboard.

"Nothing." I impulsively move my hand to cover up the tree I started sketching in the corner of the page. "Sorry."

I've always drawn little doodles like this, when my mind starts to wander. And it's always gotten me into trouble. I used to draw in the margins of my syncscreens in class with my stylus. I tried to pay attention, but my mind would drift off, and next thing I knew there was half a sketch covering the page and the instructor was frowning over my shoulder.

But Sue doesn't scold. She studies it a moment, then cocks an eyebrow. "Not bad." Then she points to the chart. "Heart rate. Forty-eight bpm."

She turns away to get back to Rosie. I write down the number and try to pay attention.

When we're about to leave, Sue leans over the bed, presses their heads together and whispers to Rosie, and then they share a kiss. Goosebumps shoot down my arms – *oh*. No wonder Sue got so angry at me for saying Rosie was dying.

Sue turns away without so much as looking at me, her eyes fixed on the floor.

As we walk back towards the Med cabin, I can't help but wonder how much pain Rosie is really in. If she told the truth, if Sue wasn't there determinedly telling her she was going to make it, if the camp didn't expect her to fight through it... if she could go back and let herself slip away in her sleep on her intended departure date, would she do it? Does she really want to live if it means suffering through all this? The Directorate would never stand for all this torture.

We move on to more patients. A broken leg, and then an

older lady who we have to make sure eats something.

Each time, a panic tries to climb into my chest, and each time, I dig my fingers into the handles of my crutches and force it down. But as we walk between cabins, I can't fight it anymore. The panic takes over, choking my breaths and strangling my lungs. Blackness edges in on my vision, and I have to stop and lean forward keep my head from rushing.

In, two, three, four, five. Out, two, three, four, five. In, two, three, four, five. I fight to get my breaths back under control.

"What on Earth are you doing?" Sue demands. Her voice feels far away. I want to answer her, to explain. I'm sure I look ridiculous hunched over with my crutches sprawled out. But I can hardly get air in and out, and I have none to spare for talking.

"I'm dying." It's all I can get out, half-shock, half-whine.

"Don't be ridiculous. You're not dying. You're panicking. Slow down your breaths."

"Not now," I gasp. "But soon. I'll be like the rest of them. My date's already passed. It's probably happening right now."

"Oh." Sue sighs. "I probably should have expected this."

A hand runs back and forth over my back. "Take it easy, now, breathe," she coaxes. She's gone into doctor mode, strong and caring, kneeling beside me.

"And listen. Just because the Directorate says your time is up, that doesn't mean that's what's going to happen. They set departures for all kinds of reasons, and not all of them are actually terminal. People can live long lives after the Directorate writes them off. Happy ones. Healthy ones, even. You'll see. For now, I need you to breathe, and to not give up on yourself so easily. You might have a battle to fight. You might experience some pain. But your time is far from up."

Her strength is soothing, and as she speaks, my breaths slow back down to normal. There's a determination in her voice, and it makes me think of Rosie.

"But is a life in pain really a life?" I whimper.

Sue's eyes flicker with anger. "Does pain stop you from loving, or thinking, or feeling? The Directorate has it all wrong. Out here, with the pain, there's *more* life, not less. A life dedicated to just avoiding the bad, that's not a life at all. Now, are you all right? You look better."

She gets up. I follow her lead and stand, too.

"Yeah." I'm more confused and scared than ever, and my head is still rushing with the fear of what the Directorate was trying to protect me from. But my breathing is back to normal. "But can I go back to my cabin and rest?"

She looks at me, frowning as she considers. "No. And I know you think I'm being a hardass. But lying around is the worst thing for you right now. Staying busy. Acclimating. This is what you need. So, compromise: I'll take you back to the Med cabin, and you'll take inventory the rest of the day. Any injuries that come in, you'll observe and assist Noah."

She raises her eyebrows, waiting for my consent.

No one has ever sought my consent before. The Directorate's always told us what's best. If I really insisted, I actually think Sue would actually let me go hide in my cabin right now.

But even though she's gruff and snippy and can barely remember my name, even though I'm terrified and every instinct is telling me to run and hide, I want to prove to her, to all of them, that they didn't waste their effort by saving me.

"Okay," I say. I try to smile but I'm not sure it comes out well.

Sue nods. "Atta girl."

As we head back to the cabin, I try to focus on my steps to stay calm, but under the surface, fear still simmers and bubbles. *I'm dying.*

I'm dying.

I'm dying.

And I have no idea from what.

Chapter Seventeen

Evie

When we get to the Med cabin, Noah is waiting for us with a big smile and even bigger sandwiches.

"Breakfast and dinner, we all come together," he says. "But lunch, it's more grab-and-go. We're a people on the move, Ev! No time to stop and eat."

He actually winks.

The bread is thick and filled with all kinds of seeds and grains, and between the slices are brightly-colored tomatoes, lettuce, beansprouts, and thick cuts of meat. It looks like a weird, malformed mess. But after breakfast, I'll try anything they give me. I take a bite, and an explosion of juicy flavors fills my mouth. I've consumed the rest of it before Noah can hand me a napkin.

Sue takes a couple bites from her sandwich and puts it back down.

"She's seen enough for a first day. I'm heading back out."

She doesn't mention my freak-out. My heart floods with gratitude.

After lunch, Noah sets me up along the wall next to the overstuffed shelves, each box filled with different supplies. I spend the next few hours counting. Counting cotton swabs. Counting bottles of pills. Counting rolls of bandages. Counting sheets. It helps.

It is a boring afternoon, and in the quiet, I start to feel almost normal again.

Then the door bursts open with a boom, and three people covered in camouflage and dirt rush in, carrying something between them.

A voice calls out. "Soldier down, soldier down."

They rush in and drop their cargo on the medical table.

Noah shifts gears, suddenly a whirl of tense motion as he rushes to the table. I follow, too confused by the commotion to think, and then reel from shock. They weren't carrying a thing, they were carrying a *person*. The man is covered in blood and shrapnel, writhing in such great pain his cries are rendered silent as they twist over his face.

I freeze in panic.

Thankfully, Noah doesn't.

"Everyone step back," he orders. As he starts checking the man over, he barks a series of questions. "Did you see the hit? Did he say anything about where the pain is worst?"

"Leg," one of the soldiers replies. "He was reaching for his leg."

"Gloves." Noah stretches out his hand to me. "Scissors."

I stare and blink, unable to process. Noah doesn't wait, turning instead to pull the supplies cart to him and does it himself, then cuts away the man's uniform.

"We've got work to do," Noah says. He doesn't look up from the man on the table. "You all need to go."

One of the soldiers leans over the man on the operating table. "Stay strong, Benjamin."

Then they reluctantly head for the door. My pounding heart wishes I could follow them, but panic has my feet glued to the floor.

Noah sets to work, applying a tourniquet and giving the man a shot that sedates him, then performing surgery on his leg to remove the shrapnel and correct the damage.

I stand terrified and stunned in the corner, watching the blood pulse out of his body.

Once the worst is addressed, Noah starts talking to me while he works.

"Evie?"

I can't find my voice to respond.

"It's okay, Evie."

Nothing about this is okay.

"He's... he's going to be all right?" I can't imagine how

that could be possible.

"Yes. He won't be going back to the front lines, and his leg will always give him some pain, but he'll live."

Always in pain? What kind of life is that?

"What happened to him?"

"Well…" He clears his throat. "Did you know the Directorate protects its borders along the surface with bombs?"

"No," I whisper. This was the Directorate?

"They're powerful and quite effective, unfortunately. Designed to inflict as much pain as possible, without killing, and keep soldiers from returning to battle. The camp is losing support from our ally countries. Some are starting to fear the Directorate more, others are just giving up. Intel & Recon has been working on ways to defuse the bombs so we can develop more effective attacks on them. Benjamin, and the other brave soldiers who brought him in, are testing out those methods."

Understanding creeps into me. The Directorate *knows* other people are out here. And they're hurting them as much as they can, to keep them away. I stare at the man on the table, pale from blood loss. How can they lie to us so completely?

"But look," Noah continues. "It's dinner time. Sue will be here any minute. Go eat, Evie. You don't need to keep watching this."

I nod, and then leave. I feel guilty leaving him there, but I also know I can't take anymore, not today.

Chapter Eighteen

Evie

I was in such a rush to get out of the Med cabin I forgot that I don't know how to get back to where they eat. Thick clouds have overtaken the sky since lunch, making the woods darker. I almost turn back, but then I hear voices, and they lead me to where everyone is gathering. As I reach them, the horror from the Med cabin disperses a little in the open air and wafts of delicious smells.

Kinlee is standing on of one of the tables – actually *on top* of it – as I approach, and she waves to me, jumping up and down to make sure I see her. As if it's even possible not to.

"It's Evie!" she announces when I get there. She jumps down and sits, so she's perched on the table with her feet on the bench, facing me.

"So! How was it in Med?"

"It was…" How could I explain the fear that choked me this afternoon – to *her* of all people? The horror of the soldier, sprawled unconscious on the table and covered in blood? This isn't how things happen in the Directorate. But even if they did, they wouldn't be talked about. "It was a lot."

Kinlee nods. "Yeah. You'll get the hang of it."

And that should have been the end of it. Next, I would ask Kinlee what she did today, and we would move on as etiquette dictates. But before I can, a voice pops in out of nowhere.

"Get the hang of what? Actual work?"

I whip around to find Connor has slid onto the bench next to me.

"What's *that* supposed to mean?"

In an instant, my ears are thudding with my racing heartbeat. How does he do this, how does he make me a thousand times angrier than I've ever been in my life, just by showing up? After yesterday, today was the worst day of my life. Benjamin's writhing is still fresh in my head.

He shrugs. He's so calm, and it only makes me angrier. "The Directorate doesn't exactly prioritize strenuous work."

That's *it*.

The entire horrible day comes to a head and bursts out of me.

"Like you would even know," I snap. "Growing up in the *woods*. Like some kind of…" I realize too late, I don't know where I'm going with this. "… of… of… squirrel."

Kinlee snorts with laughter from behind me. I ignore her and keep going.

"Not that you would know, or care, or have any reason to even bring it up," I stand up, fumbling with my crutches, so that I'm yelling down at his forehead. All the anger and fear and confusion of my day crackle through me in a burst. "But we actually spend most of our time in the Quads working in some form or another."

Hearing my own voice raised to such a volume surprises me. But it's also freeing, releasing everything that built up inside me all day.

Connor leans back on the table so he's looking up at me. His eyes are sparkling. Ugh, he's *enjoying* this. Now it doesn't feel so good. Does he think this is some kind of game?

"Sure. 'Work.' Like your carefully-scheduled classes and your carefully-organized homework, all designed to stimulate without stressing? Or when you go to your carefully-constructed gyms to perform your mathematically-determined, low-impact workouts?" He smirks, his words flying fast and cocky, calm in a way that bites. "You don't even know what real work is. It's not your fault. It's just the truth."

Overhead, the clouds release a rumbling groan, echoing the anger that's welling in my chest. How can he talk like that? In the Quads we talk slowly, respectfully. There's no need to raise heart rates or upset someone. It only adds unnecessary stressors.

"You don't know anything. You think I've been sheltered my whole life, in the Quads? At least I was part of the world, and not hidden away where I can hate everything without having to bother understanding any of it."

I don't know what I'm saying anymore. Words are flying out of me, my mind grasping at anything I think might hurt him. I pause with a gasp of breath and realize I'm about to hyperventilate for the second time today. And that's one thing I can't afford for Connor to see, so I get up and do my best attempt at storming off on my crutches into the trees.

It's not long before I can hardly see my own hand in front of me in the growing darkness, and the fear of exposing my weakness to Connor hits up against the fear of being by myself in the woods in the dark. I slump onto the ground against a tree and try to steady my breath.

Within minutes, the smell of bread and meat and seasonings floats out, and I realize how dumb I am for leaving before I could grab some dinner. My stomach growls, but it's too late now. There'll be another meal in the morning, and I remind myself, I can eat however much I want.

Breathe. *In, two, three, four, five… out, two, three, four, five…*

As my breaths begin to quiet, I hear the crunch of footsteps over leaves and twigs.

I really want to be alone right now.

"Don't worry about me, Kinlee. Go eat."

The footsteps stop. "Actually, it's me."

"Connor?" Shit. The last thing I want is to go another round with him. "Can you just *not*."

"I'm not here to argue," he says. "I've got food."

I really don't have anything more to say to him. But my stomach rumbles.

"If it makes you feel any better, Kin completely laid into me after you left. She really let me have it."

"I don't need Kinlee fighting my battles for me."

"No. You really don't."

Is that respect I hear in his voice?

"She called me 'squirrel' the whole time, too."

I can't help it, a laugh slips out. He steps a little closer and I can see his face. He really does look penitent.

"Look, I know I can be somewhat…"

"Annoying?" I volunteer. "Pushy? Stupid?"

"Thank you, Thesaurus," he teases. But his voice is friendlier now, not the combative tone he threw at me before. "And yeah. All of those. And I'm… I'm…" He sighs. "I'm *sorry.*"

Wow, that was really hard for him. He looks down to his feet, his wild waves of hair falling over his face. For a moment I'm almost softened by how cute it is, but my stubbornness kicks in and protects me.

"Kinlee made you do that."

"Well. Yeah. But I am. And if I go back with this plate still full, she's gonna kill me."

He raises his eyebrows, pleading, his hand tapping against the side of his leg.

My stomach growls again. My resistance melts. Real food is an indulgence I'm not used to, and I like it, a lot.

"Fine." I pat a spot on the ground next to me. He plops down and pushes the plate into my hands. I dig right in.

While I eat, he talks.

"I don't mean to be so difficult," he says. "I really don't. It has nothing to do with you."

"So then why are you?" I ask, mouth full.

He sighs, and his resistance is almost tangible between us. I take another bite and wait.

"I've lived in the camp my whole life. That's unusual. Most of the people here, they're either from the Directorate, or they're activists from ally nations who can't sit by and do nothing."

The mention of other countries catches my imagination – what else is out there in the world beyond the Quads? But I let him keep going.

"My mother was one of those. When she came here she

105

was just out of school. She only planned to be here a few years, to learn, so she could go back and tell others what's really going on inside the Directorate."

He looks away and stares down at his fidgeting hands.

"But she ended up staying and working with Intel & Recon. Then she met my dad. My dad was like you; he lived in the Quads, and the serum the Directorate uses for departures didn't work on him. The Alliance got him out. And, well, he was my dad, so he and my mom got together. And they had me."

"He chose for himself who to be with?"

I've heard of people trying to do this, but it never works out. The stories get passed around; every once in a while, rumors from other Quads. A person who believes she's found a mate on her own – at work maybe, or someone she knew in school. I've even heard stories where perfect strangers meet on a shuttle, and that's it, they're hooked.

They say it feels so good at first; that you don't you think it's going to happen to you. That all the bad things they warn you about, when a person casts aside the Directorate's careful matching assessments, won't happen this time. But they always do.

Because even if they're not matched to someone when they meet, they will be soon. And then what? It always ends in pain. And I don't just mean heartsickness – sometimes it ends in injuries, or even deaths, when people get really desperate and start making reckless choices.

People used to choose mates for themselves, but it had to stop. The anxiety of trying to find a good mate, the depression when it didn't work out, the divorce rates and upheaval to their children. It was a huge mess of emotional trauma for everyone – like a drug that people couldn't stop themselves from craving, no matter how much damage it did.

The Directorate uses all the best technology and research to pair us comfortably, optimized for compatibility and genetic potential. How could anyone think they could do better on their own, based solely on the people they happen to meet, from a fleeting first impression?

106

But now, my parents' lackluster coexistence comes to mind. They never struck me as liking each other particularly well. But it was normal. It was peaceful.

"Yeah, they chose each other," Connor continues. "I mean, that's what most people do, outside of Directorate. But my dad thought it was really special. He thought everything about our freedoms here were special. He told me everything he could about the Quads, so I would understand all I have, living out here."

What you have is a world of pain and chaos, I think. *A life of hiding in the woods.* But I don't want to argue again. So all I say is, "He sounds really great."

"Yeah. He was." Connor shrugs. "Then he died."

"Oh."

I should have guessed. That's why we have departure dates. But then – he had time before it happened, too. And look how much he did with that time. "What happened?"

"Cancer. In his brain."

"That's awful." It seems like such an empty word for it, but it's the best one I've got.

"We can save a lot of the people who come to us from the Quads. But not that, it was too fast. We were glad the Directorate was off by so many years, that we had the time with him that we did."

I think of Rosie. I can't imagine facing her day after day, that sunken, exhausted face, the terrible IV and blipping machine, and know that I could only make the pain a little less, that I couldn't do anything real for her.

"You know what kills me, though?" Connor's voice is all bitterness. "The Directorate, they have all that technology and advancement and funds. If they'd put it all to work towards saving people, maybe they could have done something for him. But instead they have become so obsessed with avoiding any discomfort, they'd rather kill him."

That biting bitterness he threw at me earlier is back, raw and crackling in his voice.

"I don't mean to take it all out on you. The Directorate just makes me so angry."

I stop eating for a moment and think. He's right, about what the Directorate does. It's no secret, that's the whole idea. We've got the technology to make it possible for people to live for two hundred, maybe three hundred years if we kept working at it. But with the treatments and surgeries it would take to prolong lives to that point, it's putting the number of years in a life over everything else.

Who wants to live in a preservation chamber, unable to interact with the world, just to keep on going? Who wants to undergo three, or four, heart transplants? But left to our own devices we would, it's just instinct – we *did*, for most of history. So the Directorate made the choice we couldn't and gave us the departure dates instead. We all accepted it.

But now that Connor puts it this way, it's impossible not to see it. It sounds like Connor's dad got a lot out of those extra years. Hell, if he hadn't gotten them, Connor wouldn't even exist. The idea makes me sad, even if he is infuriating. We sit there for a while. I chew my dinner and pretend I don't see him rubbing at his eyes.

Overhead the sky grumbles again, and then a wet drop falls from the sky onto my cheek. I reach up to touch it, then look at the wetness on my fingers.

"Oh no!" By the time I have wiped it off, two more have fallen on me. "We have to get out of here."

Connor cracks a smile. "It's just a little rain. A sprinkle, really." He tilts his head back as if he is enjoying it.

"But it's *poisonous*," I shriek.

Connor tilts his head and raises his eyebrows.

I pause, waiting for the water to burn into my skin or... I realize I don't know what. I look up to the sky and squint. "Isn't it?"

The Directorate always said so. But then, so much else that they have told me has been wrong. Lies.

"I mean. I wouldn't *drink* it without a filter." Connor shrugs. "But it's fine."

"Oh." I relax back onto the ground. Another drop hits me. Even if it's not poisonous, I *am* still getting all wet. I'm not sure I like it. "Does this just happen randomly all the time?"

"Yeah, well, you know," Connor says. "Nature. Climate change. Etcetera. So yeah, the weather tends to shift pretty fast. Though I mean, those clouds have been gathering all day. We had a little warning."

The rain comes down harder, soaking into my hair and matting it against my head. My face scrunches with distaste. Connor laughs, then hands me his sweatshirt to shield myself from it.

"Wanna get inside?"

"Yes please."

He helps me hobble onto my crutches, takes my plate, and leads me back to Raina and Kinlee's cabin. A bright bolt flashes over the sky. He laughs when I flinch in response, but it's not like before, this time it makes me feel better, like there's nothing to be afraid of. When we get to the door, we pause.

"How long ago was all that? With your dad?" I hand his sweatshirt back to him.

He balls it up in the crook of his arm and stares down at it. "About ten years now. I was only six when he died."

No wonder he's so angry.

"And your mom? What does she do here?"

His eyes flicker. "She's gone too. After Dad, she started getting... well... She joined the squads working on the bombs at the Directorate's border. One of them went off while she was too close a few years ago."

He's all alone?

It's like a punch in the gut, and for a moment I'm so struck I can't speak. I stutter to catch back up. "And... you stayed anyway? Here with the Alliance?"

He shrugs. "I've lived here my whole life. And I don't exactly have anywhere else to go. Raina's my guardian now, so I'm here until I turn eighteen, unless she and Kinlee decide to leave. Though when I do, I've got some big plans. Go see the world. All of it." His entire body lifts with energy as he says it.

I don't know what to say. How can someone the same age

109

as me already have so much pain in his life? How can he still find so much to look forward to? But I don't need to say anything. In the quiet that passes between us in that moment, with thunder rumbling and rain pattering over us, something shifts between Connor and me. Our eyes meet and I hold his gaze too long. Something in me tugs to lean into him. But lightning flashes again, I flinch, and the moment is gone.

"Well," he nods, "See you." Then he heads back out in the rain to his own cabin.

Chapter Nineteen

Gracelyn

I think I'm going to like working for LQM.

I think I'm going to be *good* at it.

All day long they throw information at us, and we do our best to keep up. In the mornings, we shadow Quinn, absorbing as much as we can, watching her in meetings and discussing ongoing projects. In the afternoons, there are lectures on department history, the foundational science behind enhancing painless lives, organizational policies and protocols.

It is a deluge, and I throw myself into it. It is exactly what I need right now – the perfect distraction to block out my thoughts about Evie, and what I heard that morning. There is nothing I can do about that anyway, and it is a relief to stuff my mind with so many other bits and pieces.

It feels good to contribute to the Quads, too. Once I am past training, I will make a real, quantifiable difference, helping to hone food plans, assign marriage pairings, or something else to *optimize well-being throughout each citizen's span of life*, as described in the LQM Handbook.

But for now, we follow Quinn around and take notes.

Everywhere we go, there are two layers of chairs around conference tables. One for the employees, and one for the trainees. Our ring is usually sparse, Quinn's audiences typically being supervisors and directors who far outrank her in years.

The unspoken implication is that Hanna and I are expected to out-perform our peers, too. We have done it everywhere else in life so far, edging each other out for top placement.

But here, everything seems so big and unknown, and I cannot imagine ever pacing these halls with Quinn's cool confidence.

At meetings, she pulls forward, her bright eyes focused and those red curls framing her face. When she speaks, she does so with clarity and efficiency, delivering pointed thoughts in short, crisp sentences through red lips and a crooked smile. She is only a few years older than Hanna and me. But it seems like she is from a completely different world.

Sometimes I get so caught up in her I forget to listen to what she is saying.

Hanna is not so enamored as I am. In fact if she were allowed to apply for another mentor, I am certain she would. She starts venting about Quinn as soon as we are out of the building in the evening and doesn't stop until I get off the shuttlebus.

"Can you believe she told that deputy chief his idea wouldn't work today? Flat-out said it. Like they were equals.

"Mhm," I reply.

She shakes her head, still offended.

I stare out of the shuttle window, turned away so Hanna can't see my face. On the matter of Quinn's behavior, she and I could not disagree more, and I am not about to let her know it.

***

As I wrap up my studying to go to lunch, I catch a voice from across the room.

"Hey Phil, are you looped in on that Code Twenty-Seven from oh-eight-oh-three?

That date. It is a date I know all too well. It is Evie's departure date. Hearing it sends a prickling jolt down my spine.

Stop it, I scold myself. I shake out my shoulders and try to calm down. Plenty of other things happened on that date. Plenty of other departures, even. If it were, somehow, about Evie, I still should not have a reaction to it – it has been almost two weeks since her departure. Life is moving on. *I'm moving on.* If I keep telling myself that, I am sure I can make it true.

But.

What is a Code Twenty-Seven?

I have been studying the department codes and terms since I got here, but I don't remember a Code Twenty-Seven. And I remember everything.

I stare down at my syncscreen and pretend to study, listening for more hints. But Phil rushes over to the other man, and they keep their voices low.

"Ready to go?" Hanna chirps from behind me.

I jump, startled, and choke back the urge to hush her. Then, I force a smile.

"Sure."

As we cross the open office space, I glance back to the men, taking in all that I can about them. The first one has steely gray hair clipped tightly around his head and deep wrinkles around his mouth. This first name is too small for me to read from here, but the last name is Gunders. The other – Phil – is starting to bald, with a blond mustache. Last name Johnston. A green stripe runs across the bottom – Green Level. Under it is a dark blue line for his subdivision. I strain to remember what that correlates to, but there is no dark blue subdivision. Not in the Handbook, at least.

The elevator dings, and Hanna and I step in. As the door is closing, a hand sticks in to open it again, and Johnston and Gunders join us. I can't believe my luck.

"… still can't identify what causes the anomaly," Phil mutters as they step in. He looks at Hanna and me, then leans towards Gunders and mutters in a lowered voice. "They're talking about wiping the whole initiative if they don't get some answers."

The two look at each other, eyes steely with the implied significance of this. Gunders shakes his head.

Anomaly?

Later, as Hanna makes her regular complaints on the shuttlebus home, the word is still on my mind. I chide myself to stay out of it. *No point in putting your entire future on the line for someone who's already departed and gone.* That's what Evie would say.

I go home, eat dinner, have a normal evening and go to bed. But through all of it, the conversation I overheard nags at me.

Chapter Twenty

Evie

Maybe I have skills after all. Against all odds, I seem to have become actually useful to Sue and Noah. I know where all the supplies are now, and even know how to use a lot of them. Caught up in it all, the days pass faster than I can blink, and I can't believe I have to leave Medical soon and find something else to try.

Even better, the humidity has cleared out, and the weather has settled into a crisp coolness that isn't so bad. At least, so long as I don't forget my sweatshirt, which I do constantly. I've never needed extra layers before.

Maybe it's going to be okay. Maybe this can turn into a life.

We've just wrapped up with Frank, and I can't believe how far he's come since I first came here. He is getting so strong our only struggle is getting him to rest again when we leave. His physical therapy is almost done, and it feels good knowing I played a part in his recovery.

As we make our way to our next patient, Sue slows her pace.

"Hold up a moment, Ev," Sue says. "I have to talk to you about something."

Sue's got that grim, unreadable expression on her face, lips pursed. This can't be good. I replay the session we just had with Frank. Was it something I said? Did I handle him wrong? I wasn't particularly patient today.

I brace myself. "Did I do something wrong?"

"Not at all. Actually, you're great with Frank," she says. "This is about you. We don't have the Directorate's tech here – heck, we don't even have the tech most other countries have – but there's still a lot we can do. In fact we're particularly well outfitted for departure diagnosis."

"Departure…" The word sets my heart racing.

"Evie, the Directorate assigned your departure date for a reason. If you have something life-threatening, we can fight it. But we need to know what it is."

I step back, shaking my head. My insides are tangling up in knots.

Sue pushes again. "I know you're touchy about the whole dying thing, but you've got to get over it. What if it's something we can treat? We need to know as soon as we can. Or what if it's something trivial you don't need to worry about at all?"

I flinch at the word *dying* – touchy, yes, that's one way to put it. Why is she bringing up this ugliness? This isn't how things are done. In the Quads, we politely keep conversation to pleasant, easy matters.

I know she's right. I may have escaped my departure date, but whatever the Directorate saw coming when they set those numbers on my wrist, it's still there, in my body, maybe already developing. Thinking about it makes my skin buzz like a thousand pins are scrawling over it. Which is why I *haven't* thought about it, not since my panic with Sue on my first day.

And I don't want to think about it now. It's too much. Like the walls are closing in – no, like they're falling *out*, leaving me unprotected and exposed. Anger flares through me. How can she ask me to go through such pain? What is wrong with these people?

I wrap my arms around my body and clutch my elbows.

"I thought the whole *point* of this place was that I don't *have* to do anything."

I'm not talking about this with Sue. I'm not. I'd rather sprain my ankle again.

She looks me over carefully, and I try to look tough.

"You don't have to," she says. "It's your choice. That's why we're talking about it and not just doing it to you. But you do *need* to do this. Without a diagnosis, we might not be able to help you."

"No!" My hands ball into fists and throw to my sides. "Nothing is happening to me!"

"Evie, calm down – "

"Calm down, *Sue?*" I say her name like it's a dirty word. I'm so angry at her right now it feels like one. "What the hell do you know, *Sue?* Who put you in charge of my life choices? My *death* choices?"

I realize too late that the d-word doesn't hold the same impact with Sue as it did in the Quad. She doesn't react to the h-word, either. But she sure cares that I am refusing her advice.

"Now one minute," she snaps. "This is sound and experienced medical advice, and you've learned enough by now to recognize that. You've got to be brave, Evie. I know it's hard, but you've got to. You're wasting critical time – time that could be the difference between life and death. How are you going to handle it if you start showing symptoms? How will you even know they're symptoms?"

She pauses and stares at me, her brows pulled together tight. Anger burns through me and my cheeks grow hot. But I can't think of anything to argue back to her.

She pushes again. "Evie, this is nuts. You gotta know. It could be something you can easily live with and will never actually cause you harm. Something we can help you live with better. I've seen all sorts of things from the Directorate. They dispense of people like they're yesterday's used napkins. And Evie, if it's something like that, don't you want to know? So you can stop being afraid of it?"

She closes the gap between us, and lays a hand on my shoulder.

"And what if it's not? What if it's – " For the first time she hesitates, clearing her throat and averting her eyes. "What if it's something like Rosie? We could fight it with everything we've got. Even something like that doesn't have to be the end. Not out here."

She pauses, and her quiet forces me to think. It all knots together in my stomach, too big and impossible to untangle, and something in me bursts. I can't. I can't think about this.

117

"What do you know?" I yell. "You just want a new pet project."

"Evie!" she calls.

But I'm already running away into the woods, my hands trembling and my face twisting with tears I know I can't hold back for long. When I'm far enough away to be hidden, I slump to the ground and let it out.

I miss my room. I miss my home. I miss my Quad. The rules were tight, but they were clear and simple, and everything moved together in predictable sync. I miss Gracelyn, the only person I can stand to talk to when I feel like this.

What would my life be like there right now, if it weren't for my departure date? I try to imagine it. Last year, I would have been assessed and assigned a career. I would have spent all of last year and this one learning and observing. Next year I'd be working full-time. Contributing to the Quad in some way. I'd have been assigned my own housing dorm for the next two years in the Young Adults Building, and finally be away from my parents.

I wonder what my career would have been. I'm not a genius like Gracelyn, but I think I'm smart enough to avoid the more menial jobs, like cleanup or maintenance. I got good grades, before I understood my departure date and stopped caring.

Who would they have paired me with for a marital partner? Would it have been like my parents' mechanical life? Would we have filed a request for children? Who knows. It's a bottomless well of possibilities that will never be tapped. I sit and dream about what my life should have been, until the sun begins to set and I'm sure the splotchiness of tears is completely gone from my face.

***

The next morning I'm almost too afraid of Sue to go to Med.

I left my assigned position in the middle of shift. I shouted at her. I *swore* – and at an *adult*.

118

"What's up with you?" Kinlee nudges me in the side with her elbow. "You're hardly eating."

I can't bring myself to tell her. Just thinking about it makes my hands shake with fear again. I pull them into fists.

"Sue. She's..." I don't know what to say. Instead, I sigh.

"Don't let Sue get to you. She's all bluster. What could she really do to you?"

I shrug. That's part of the problem, I have no idea. I'm still shocked that I've gotten away with yesterday's outburst for so long. In the Quad, there would have been a penalty notification on my digipad in minutes, along with an order for a mental health management appointment. Maybe mood-stabilizing medication. Whatever it took to keep the peace. Waiting to know how it works out here in the camp is almost worse.

"Eat!" Kinlee insists, her own mouth half-stuffed with eggs.

I sigh and press my forehead into the table. "Ugh."

Soon everyone else is leaving and I can't put it off any longer. I head to the Med cabin and brace myself as I open the door.

Sure enough, Sue is standing on the other side, waiting. Her forehead is crinkled with a frown and her eyes are sharp – I shrink back as I meet them, disintegrating into a ball of nerves.

"You're late. Let's go." She nods to the supply cart and walks out of the door.

That's it? I stare after her as she heads off towards Frank's, and then grab the cart and follow.

Sue doesn't bring up the testing again – in fact, it's as if yesterday never happened at all. Eventually, I relax into it and we do our work.

The only hard part is a follow-up visit to Benjamin, the soldier who was bloody and unconscious on Noah's operating table. When we enter, a crew of soldiers is standing around his bed. They step back to let us work. I try not to look too carefully at the wound as I supply Sue with the tools she needs, and listen to the other soldiers.

119

"It's gotten worse out there, Sue," the first one says. "They must have an idea of what we're up to, because we go out and assess a site one day, then the next we go back to give defusing a try, and it's gone."

"It's not just that they're gone, though," the woman next to him adds. "They're moving the bombs to other places. They're changing how they place them. They're usually right up against the border walls, but yesterday, there was one out in the woods. We never saw it coming. Sheer luck no one was seriously injured."

Sue's mouth tightens into a grim line. "You fools are going to lead them right to us," she says.

"They aren't gonna find the camp, not as long as we stay on transit freeze. But there probably will be a lot more of this coming," the first one says, nodding to Benjamin's wound.

So that's why they're on a freeze. They're expecting more of these injuries? And they're still going out there? My stomach twists. How can they do it?

When we get back to the cabin, Noah is unpacking a series of heavy-duty storage containers.

"Rations day," he says. "They let me into storage to pull what we need for the next month. We'll have to update the inventory tomorrow."

"Sure." I edge past the boxes to place my clipboard on the desk before leaving, and find something resting on the desk already: a small tin of pencils and a bound pad of paper. I frown and pull back the cover, curious.

"Had a talk with Raina. Now you have something to draw on that's not my charts," Sue says, hovering behind me.

"This is for me?" I can hardly believe it. I run my hand over the page and take in the paper's pulpy texture. "Thank you."

Sue has already turned back to the business of unpacking, but Noah smiles and gives me a wink. Maybe Sue's not so bad.

After work, I take my new supplies and run off to my cabin. I splay out on the floor, open to the first page – a full page to draw on, and no one to scold me for it – and test out my new pencils.

My fingers tingle as they work across the page. The pencils smell like ash and freshly-cut wood, and the graphite smudges across the side of my hand. Hours slip away as I dissolve into the faint sound of the pencil against the page, and my focus narrows down to the lines and shadows forming under my hand.

The Directorate would never allow it. It's heaven.

Chapter Twenty-One

Gracelyn

It's like Gunders and Johnston don't even exist.

I haven't seen them again, and they aren't in the LQM Directory. There isn't even a subdivision listed in DMD that uses the dark blue stripe.

After the Directory, I turned to the DMD section of my guidebook. But upon closer review, the section reveals shockingly little about what they do. Jargon. A few lines about order, integrity, managing the dignity of life. How did I fail to notice before how empty this content is? I glanced through the rest of the division descriptions, and they're all like this.

When that didn't get me anywhere, I pored over every word of the introductory materials we're able to access from home and don't need the on-site servers for, in the late hours in my room at night after everyone else was asleep.

Still nothing.

I should have stopped there. That was all the information at LQM that I have been given permission to access. No one has told me *not* to access other LQM's files, but no one says *no* in the Directorate. It's just understood.

I tried to let it go. I went about my life, focused on my work, minded my own business.

But Evie *is* my business. My mind kept replaying that haunting shuffle that came from her room that morning. The morning of *oh-eight-oh-three*.

If she didn't depart the way she was supposed to, if anything 'anomalous' took place that day...

I consider asking Father about it. But every time, a deep shame spills into my veins, and I remember the expression on his face when he caught my tear in the hall.

***

I know I should let it go and forget all about it, but the idea of Evie keeps nagging at me, the guilt pinching within my chest: *She would do it, if it were the other way around.* Evie wasn't afraid of anything, as far as I could tell. How could I let fear stop me from doing the same for her? Don't I owe her that much?

So one morning, I slip into the office early. Five minutes. Enough to give me a little space to see if there is anything worth looking into, without anyone else around to see what is on my syncscreen, but hopefully not enough to raise suspicions. The Quads run like clockwork – no one is ever late, and no one is early.

But I have to know, I have to understand.

I take a breath, my heart already pounding, and open up the DMD folder. Then I pause.

For what, I don't know exactly – an alarm to sound? My screen to crash? But nothing happens. Everything is fine. A wave of relief washes over me. Part of me can't believe I've gotten this far, and I realize I didn't truly expect to, because now that I'm in folders, I have absolutely no plan for what to do. What exactly am I looking for?

But my pulse throbs in my neck, and I need to do *something* to take advantage of this chance. So I click on anything that looks like it might be connected.

All it does is lead to more folders, and more, and more. I click through them like turns through a maze, hardly knowing where I'm going or how to turn back. My hands turn clammy with anxiety, leaving smudges on the screen as I tap through the options.

"What are you doing?"

I jump at the unexpected voice, a bolt of panic shooting through me.

It's Hanna.

Her brow crinkles, but she looks more defensive than suspicious.

"Nothing. Reviewing yesterday's lecture."

123

I tap to close the screen before she can get a good look, my fingers shaking. Last thing I need is Hanna turning me in so she can get ahead.

What a waste of effort.

Let it go, an anxious voice in my head urges. *This is too much. Too far.*

And I know the voice is right.

But another piece of me feels the burden of what I owe Evie, especially now that I know I can access the files. I hate the way she is slipping away. Already the new routines are replacing the old, filling up the space where Evie used to fit into my life. It's not right. She can't evaporate into thin air.

I still do not know if this Code Twenty-Seven has anything to do with Evie, but I have to find out.

***

I am in the office early again the very next morning.

I'm setting myself up to get caught, an inner voice warns.

It would be safer, less likely to attract attention, if I left it alone for a few days. Or, at least, it would look less like an obvious trend and more like an isolated incident if someone were to catch me – something I might be able to pretend was an innocent mistake.

But I am afraid that if I do not do it now, I will never do it at all. It's not like I am truly losing my way, like the terrible stories that spread when someone disappears from the Quad, or the warning tales of Licentia – people who start rejecting Directorate guidance and turn against the Quad. Not that anyone *really* gets as bad as that, but they are warnings for a reason. I am not straying like that. I just need to understand. I just need to know what happened to Evie. Then everything will go back to normal.

This time I know to expect the thudding rise of my pulse as I open up the DMD division and start exploring the subfolders. This time I look through them systematically, reviewing each folder and subfolder in order.

Most of it is dead ends, lacking in context and too filled

with jargon to understand.

Finally, buried several layers deep into the folders, I find one labeled only with a color – dark blue, like Gunder and Johnston's tags. One of the documents inside the folder is labeled *Directory*.

My fingertip tingles as it hovers over it on the screen. A separate, hidden directory? No wonder I couldn't find them in the main listings. I tap to open it, and my breath catches in my throat. But instead of opening, a box pops up, prompting me for a password I do not have.

No.

A password? For a list of names and contacts?

No, no, no.

Helpless frustration flares through my chest. What are they doing in this top-secret dark blue division, and why do they have to hide who's doing it?

The rustle of employees trickling in brings me back to myself. My time is up. I have no choice but to close out before Hanna sneaks up behind me again.

Is it possible that I have stumbled onto something much bigger than how much I miss Evie? If anyone finds out what I've uncovered, what will happen to me?

Chapter Twenty-Two

Gracelyn

The next day, when I step off the shuttlebus into the Quad center, I pass the LQM buildings and enter the Citizen Care campus, then head all the way up to the mental health facilities. It's my first appointment without Mother and Evie.

The waiting room is empty except for the rows of cream chairs and the deep earth-toned walls. I sit. In the normal checkups, Dr Little asks me a few questions about my thoughts and stress level, and then I'm on my way. But I have no idea what a post-departure check-in is like. I hate this feeling of not knowing what to expect, how to prepare. These are the safe, clear boundaries of the Directorate that guide just about everything else I do and show me how to succeed.

My digipad vibrates with an alert: *Your appointment begins in ten seconds. Please enter.*

I stare at it a moment as the seconds count down and then head through the doors. On the other side, Dr Little waits for me.

"Have a seat, Gracelyn." Her voice is chirpy and slow, like a robin just waking up. As a child I found it soothing. Today, it makes my shoulders tense. But I settle into the plush chair facing her across the table. Her eyes watch me, shaped into the hollow expression of sympathy.

"Hello, Dr Little."

"You are practically an adult now. Why don't you call me Joyce."

"Okay."

I prop myself up on the chair's arms, my hands squishing into the soft padding.

"Your first loved one's departure."

Joyce pauses, gazing at me with a vacant smile.

I shift, feeling as though I am expected to say something. "Yes."

"How have you been sleeping?" Joyce asks.

"Fine."

I realize as the lie leaves my lips that I do not want to tell her anything.

She narrows her eyes, studying me. My stomach knots – I said it too fast. I straighten up and try to project more positive energy.

"How much sleep did you get last night?" she prompts.

Oh no. Anything specific I say she can compare to my digipad readings.

"Last night?"

None. I got no sleep at all last night. I spent the time poring over my LQM files, and as soon as she checks my digipad's data, she will know it. I pause, hoping it looks like I am trying to remember, like I had not given it any thought. "I tossed and turned, I guess. I'm not sure exactly."

Joyce nods. "Have you experienced any dreams?"

I don't know what the right answer is to this one. I shrug. "Sometimes."

She nods, her stiff smile never budging. Her eyes look hungry.

"What do you dream about?"

I look down and smooth out my skirt, try to act as natural as I can.

"Placements. End of year rankings."

The hunger in her eyes dims, and I am sure I got it right – nothing for her to read into there about Evie's departure. *Yes, get the conversation away from Evie.*

"There is so much to learn. I don't want anyone to be disappointed in me. I keep dreaming I rank too low to go on, and get reassigned to a Depart – " I choke on it mid-sentence, realizing my mistake.

Joyce straightens up.

I started saying it because it always seemed like the worst

127

career to be assigned. But now we're back to Evie again.

"A...?" Joyce prompts.

My mind races for a substitute, but I can't think of anything fast enough.

"A Departure Crew."

The idle music fills the dead air and we study each other. I press my lips together, determined not to say anything more.

Joyce sighs.

"Gracelyn. We already established you're not a kid anymore. So I'm going to level with you." Her eyes swim in disengaged sympathy. "I've helped a lot of people through their first departures. And I have to tell you, after reviewing your metrics, I'm concerned. You do not appear to be coping with the situation."

She leans forward. I fight the urge to back away.

"Want to know a secret, Gracelyn? Despite everything the Directorate does to keep us happy and optimized, it's human nature to feel sad after a departure. It's called 'grieving.'"

She pauses, letting it sink in. *Grieving.* What an ugly word. An ugly word for an ugly thing.

"I can help you stop feeling it. I can even help you forget your sister altogether, if that's what you need."

She means she can give me pills.

"But only if you acknowledge what you are feeling. You're a good girl, Gracelyn. You always follow Directorate guidelines, and you have thrived because of it. So understand, feeling these things will not make you bad. You need to feel them, and you need to tell me about them, so we can move you past them, together. Otherwise..." She shakes her head. "I've seen some truly tragic situations. And I don't only mean sadness and pain. I mean dropped grades, skipped lectures, sullen attitudes. Things that could put your career in jeopardy. If you don't let me help you, you may begin to sabotage this bright future you have worked so hard for."

I try to listen with a blank, slightly concerned expression – and to hide the prick of alarm spreading through me as I realize her warning fits all too well with what I have been feeling.

"I'm not – "

"Maybe not yet, Gracelyn," she says. "But you will. Unless you start talking to me, so we can address it."

She sits, waits another moment. I say nothing.

She sighs. "You've always been compliant with me in the past, Gracelyn. So here is what we are going to do. I'm going to write this up as a successful visit – a free pass. But I want to see you again in two weeks. That's a little time for you to think about what we've talked about today. Then we'll try again."

She pushes a button on the desk, and the door slides open.

I have to do this again? I nod and slowly stand up. I have never had trouble doing what was expected of me before.

When I get to work, I let Hanna's gossip from a meeting I missed dominate my attention, because my fingers long to dig deeper into the DMD folders, and that would be sure to get me into even more trouble. Now that I am flagged as a problem, it is no time to be reckless. Now I am going to have to be even more careful.

Compliant. I can't seem to manage it anymore. I've got to find out what happened to Evie. I'll just have to be smart about it.

Chapter Twenty-Three

Evie

Every day is so busy and different, the time is starting to blur. The routines here are hardly a routine at all, the weather changes every few days – sometimes a few times in one day – and a few days ago I left Med duty for my new rotation. But despite it all, the Alliance camp is starting to feel like a place I could belong. Maybe.

"Pssst. Come on."

The voice whispers from the dark a few feet away. It's Connor. And it's too damn early.

From Medical, they moved me to farm duty. Which means getting up before the sun. Which means this is how I wake up now, at least for a few weeks, until I change rotation again.

Waking up is some kind of superpower Connor has. He says he's been on farm duty long enough that it's second nature. But no one should be this energetic, this early.

"Nnnmmm." I roll over to my stomach and stretch.

I've never done real physical labor before. I know this now, because my body has never felt like this. My muscles are tight and achy, including several I didn't even know I had.

The first day it happened, I panicked – I thought this was it, this was my departure starting. But when Connor finally got me to confess what was wrong, he laughed so hard he doubled over. This is normal, apparently, when your muscles are adjusting to something new and hard.

Even if it was a false alarm, the panic made it harder to ignore that nagging feeling that I should have listened to Sue about departure testing. But the idea is still too big, too terrifying. I shove it away into the back of my mind.

I stumble out of bed and follow Connor, out of the cabin, trying not to wake up Kinlee or Raina. I've started sleeping in my clothes for the next morning. It saves me some stumbling around in the dark. I can hardly put one foot in front of the other this early, so forget finding a sweatshirt in a drawer in total darkness.

It doesn't matter if I'm kind of grungy. There's no point in getting clean before doing all this physical labor. We're outside all morning. In the real, unpredictable weather. And the real, UV-laced sun. I've been rained on twice so far this week, and even with the cream Connor swears protects my skin from the sun's rays, my skin is darkening with the exposure. I can practically feel the cancer seeping into me. I told Connor so, and he laughed.

"You're fine," he said. As if saying it made it true.

After my first day, my face turned bright as a strawberry and hurt to touch. It was only after that Connor remembered to share his sunscreen with me. It's getting better now, but the skin is peeling away in thin layers. Another thing he had insisted was normal. I hadn't realized before how pale I was compared to the others in the camp.

Connor hands me a canteen of coffee and a thick slice of bread with cheese. I munch on it gratefully, its rich flavors filling my mouth. He learned pretty fast not to start prattling away at me until I had something in my stomach.

And then there's the animals. In the Quads, a cow was about as mythical as a unicorn. But now I'm milking them every day. And feeding the chickens, pigs, and sheep.

This is why the food tastes so good here. It's coming from real plants and real animals, not the genetically-engineered compounds the Directorate creates for the printing dispensers. I try not to think about that part. It's only been a few days but I already love these little guys, especially the cows. Working here makes enjoying the food harder. Connor told me to stop naming them.

I'm done eating by the time we get to the barn. I take a long sip of the coffee before grabbing a pail. As we start

131

milking the cows, Connor talks. I don't know how he has so much to say all the time. What does he do when he's working alone? Does he talk to himself? The guy's got about ten different thoughts bouncing through his head at any given time, and it propels out of him with such momentum I'm not sure how much control he has over it.

I take hold of Maybelle's udders and get to work.

As the sun rises, we move on to feed the chickens and pigs, and then round up the sheep and take them out to a nearby clearing to graze. Each day they graze here for hours, and they have to be watched. Which means that for hours, Connor and I are sprawled on the grass, keeping an eye on them.

This job really isn't bad, other than the befriending-your-food problem.

Connor drove me nuts the first couple of days, with all the nonstop chatter. But, well, I got used to it. And the thing about Connor is, he's as eager to hear what you have to say as he is to share his own thoughts. And to please and amuse whoever's around him.

Besides, I learned how to tune him out when I need a break from all the talking.

Growing up here in the camp, books have taken him all the places he couldn't go yet. I don't know how he's managed to learn so much – he's an encyclopedia of random facts about almost anything, and it's amazing all the details he can hold in his head. I've had far more formal schooling, but outside of the Quads, the things I was taught don't hold much value. Things like Directorate Rules and Directorate History – or, as I'm learning more and more, Directorate lies.

Today we lie in the grass on our stomachs, and he talks about the weather. Not the typical pleasantries you exchange with other people on the Quad shuttlebus. Like for real, how weather is made in nature, and how it came to change too quickly. Warm and cool fronts. Wind patterns. Condensation. Nuclear wars and global warming. Today, the heat is blistering, the sun so intense it shimmers in waves at the edges.

132

"In the Quads we made our own weather," I shrug.

"What?" He twists and stares at me incredulously. "But how?"

"I don't know exactly. But the Quads are giant domes. Everything is controlled in there. Everything."

His head tilts, and I can see the wheels turning in his mind behind his eyes. "That is… I have to give it to them. That's pretty impressive."

"It's how we do things. On the inside."

On the inside. It's a joke Connor made on my first day about being from the Quads. Something about old jail lingo. It made sense when he explained it.

He leans in until our bodies are touching, nudging me with his shoulder. His touch sends a burst of flutters through me.

"Whatchya doing there?" he asks.

"Oh, um, nothing, really." I try to lean forward to hide the sketch of the sheep I've been scribbling out while he talked. "I doodle sometimes. I know it looks like I wasn't listening, but I was, I swear. It kind of helps, actually."

Helps me listen, helps me process, helps me keep my mind off the departure that's still looming vaguely in my future.

Connor leans in so close his cheek is resting against my shoulder. I hold my breath, scared to move because it might make him pull away.

"That is not doodling," he says. "That's pretty good."

"Really?"

"Absolutely."

I duck my head down, hoping the hair that falls over my face will hide my blushing.

His stomach rumbles. Mine echoes the sound a moment later. We laugh. That's our cue to head back for lunch – the schedule for the farming crew is pretty loose. Besides, the sun is already high in the violet sky (a result of smog particles and thinning ozone, Connor says – I *knew* it was supposed to be blue). We herd up the sheep and get them back to their pen, and then head towards camp.

Usually we're early for lunch – because we start the day so early – but today everyone seems to be showing up around the same time. The adults all seem tense, taking seats without much discussion. The table where we usually pick up our sandwiches is empty.

"Umm," I start.

Connor is already nodding in agreement. "Looks like an emergency all hands," he says.

Emergency? I don't like the sound of that.

Connor and I head to the teens' usual table and wait for the others to get there. We sit together so that we're shoulder to shoulder, until I look around the empty table and realize how weird it probably is that we're squished right next to each other when the whole table is open. I scoot an inch away.

"Oh good, they got word to you up in the seventeenth century," Kinlee says as she approaches.

"No, they didn't," I reply. "What is all this?"

"Oh, oops. They'll start soon," she says.

We wait for her to go on, but she doesn't. She's usually eager to share, but when it comes to things related to her work with Intel & Recon, she's more tight-lipped.

My chest tightens, and I look to Connor. The crease between his eyebrows deepens.

"Anyone say anything to you?" I ask him.

"Are you kidding? I've been with you all day." He nudges against me as he says it.

I don't realize, until I turn to Kinlee and see the dumbfounded look on her face, that I'm grinning like an idiot. I hadn't realized how much things were changing between Connor and me, now that we're together on our own all day. Kinlee's still staring at me, her head tilted. I try to fight the flush spreading over my face, but it's no use.

So I stare back at Kinlee pointedly until she stops staring at us, silently begging her for once to not say exactly what's on her mind. She's got that mischievous look in her eyes and I'm sure she's going to ignore my plea, but thankfully, Raina calls us to order. Meredith, Dave and Joel rush over and join us as everyone settles down.

"Okay, okay," Raina calls out, raising her arms to get everyone's attention. "I'm sure all kinds of rumors have been flying since we called this meeting this morning, so let's get on with it and set the record straight."

A rise of murmurs waves over the crowd, until Raina starts talking over it and everyone goes still, except for some fanning themselves against the heat with folded papers or their hands.

"Unfortunately I do not have good news to share today. We all accept a certain degree of risk living here, and, despite our best efforts, sometimes those risks are realized."

Any remaining murmurs from the crowd is sucked right out. Tension seeps into the silence as we wait for the rest of it. I realize suddenly the strain behind Raina's eyes, and the stringy way her hair falls – she's exhausted.

"Today is one of those days. We've lost contact with Tad Martin, one of our brave pointpeople undercover in the Directorate, based in Quadrant Thirty-Four."

I straighten up. Thirty-Four? That's *my* Quad.

What was that name? Martin. Tad Martin. *Front-desk Tad.* Oh no.

I lean in to Connor. "I *met* him."

Connor whispers, "Shit."

I remember Tad's face as he handed me the coffee with that dumb note. Nervous and timid. Even without knowing why, I could see that he stood out among the others there. Not like Mara. She knew how to blend in.

Still. Tad was the first one to warn me. He tried to help. I might not be here without him.

Up at the front, Raina continues. "Our last contact with Tad was eight days ago. Tad was supposed to report back yesterday and never made check-in. Early this morning, we sent another of our points in the Quad to check on his personal quarters – which she took on at great personal risk. His things had been cleared out. She was able to remove some notebooks and our communication device from under the floorboards, but then she had to get out. I'll be honest, it does not look good."

My mind takes me back to the Med tent, to how awful and bloody it was when they dragged Benjamin in after the bomb. That same ruthless government probably has Tad, too?

No, this looks *terrible.*

Murmurs fill the crowd, and my mind starts spinning. I suddenly understand what it means for these people to be out there, to break in and out of the Quads. They routinely risk their lives to save people like me. I want to wrap my arms around Kinlee, around *everyone* in Intel & Recon, and squeeze them as hard as I can. I look over to her. While everyone else is murmuring anxiously to each other, Kinlee remains quiet and calm. She leans forward onto the table, her chin cradled in her hand, and glances back at me, eyebrows raised.

The crowd is getting louder. One voice raises, "It was the Licentia. We've got to end this."

What? I tug at Connor's sleeve. "Licentia isn't *real.*"

"Well, actually – " Connor starts, shaking his head. But he doesn't get the chance to finish. Another voice from the crowd responds to the first:

"No, this has the Directorate written all over it. Those damn bomb-dismantling units are meddling too much, and now they're onto us."

Is the Licentia *real?* My chest tightened at the thought of real terrorists residing within the Quad domes. But if they're the only ones in the Directorate willing to fight back, should an unchallenged Directorate frighten me more? I hardly know.

The rumbles of the crowd are rising, and another voice calls out over them. "It doesn't matter. We can't afford to put ourselves at further risk looking for him. He knew the risk he was taking on. We have to stick to the mission, or else his sacrifice is for nothing."

Another wave of arguing voices rises.

"Enough!" Raina hops onto the closest bench. "We are not going to lose our heads."

She waits for the voices to die down, sweat beading on her brow in the heat and her expression stern.

"Yes. It's *possible* the Licentia got him. It's also *possible* – and more likely – the Directorate got him. He could have been discovered by a citizen and subjected to vigilante justice. Or he could have run for it before they got to him. For all we know, he could be out in the Quad somewhere, hiding, waiting for us to do something. But we don't operate on 'possibles.' Intel is working around the clock to learn more about what happened. And yes, we do need to pursue this. Aside from saving Tad if we can, it could be a serious security issue."

My stomach knots. If Tad did manage to get away, I guess it's possible that he has secret hiding spots out there. Anything is *possible*. After all, I never would have thought it possible that the tunnels out into the woods existed. Or an entire world beyond the Quads. Or that I could be alive after my departure date. But the Quad I know? There's no way Tad is out there hiding. There's nowhere *to* hide.

"This is why we shouldn't have our own people in the Quads," another person shouts.

"This is why we need *more* people in the Quads!" another shouts back.

"What is taking so long with defusing the bombs? We need to attack already and take the Directorate down once and for all."

"We need to get the rest of our people out of there and stop meddling. They're going to find out, and we're going to have World War Four on our hands when they do."

Kinlee sighs and drops her head to the table. I wonder what she thinks about the contacts in the Quads, but maybe that's a question for later. I wouldn't be alive without them. I know that much.

All this chaos would never happen in the Quads. No matter how big the group, a single person speaks at a time. In the Quads, nothing ever happens to induce such panic in the first place. No one disagrees – the Directorate decides for us. Order is always maintained.

"We can't lose our heads," Raina scolds. "I know we all have opinions about how this camp should run, but this is no time for politics. We have a man in jeopardy, and we are going to get him back. The rest of this is going to have to wait."

The panic flattens out into silence.

Raina continues. "I'm not telling you this to scare you. We've got a lot more investigating to do to. In the meantime, everyone needs to be extra-sharp about security. We need you alert, should anything out of the ordinary happen."

She pauses and looks out at the crowd, which is frozen in silence. "Is that something we can manage?"

A murmur of agreement rises.

"Okay then. Meeting adjourned."

Raina turns and leaves. A muffle of voices and movement swell as everyone gets up.

Connor and I turn to Kinlee, and it's a matter of seconds before the other teens are doing the same.

She looks around at us. "What?"

"Tell us what's *really* up with all this," Ginnie prompts.

"Are you kidding? I have no idea," she shrugs.

"Come on, Kin. You work with them," Joel pushes.

"Yeah. And we have no idea." Kinlee's frowning now. "Not that I'd be able to tell you, even if we did. If I was allowed to, Mom would have said it already."

"Seriously?" Meredith rolls her eyes.

"Seriously," Kinlee snaps back, mocking her. "Why would we keep something like this from you?" She exhales in a sharp huff. "I gotta get back."

She pushes herself over the bench and heads off.

"She's been on edge the last couple of days," Dave says. "Guess now we know why."

I can't imagine what it would be like to carry something as heavy this around, and not be able to tell anyone.

"We should get back, too," Connor says.

"Right." Except I'm not really paying attention. I'm staring after Kinlee, a weight growing within me as I consider everything we just learned.

When I don't get up with Connor, he nudges me. "What's on your mind?"

"What if it's my fault?" The words tumble out of me before I've even realized that's what's bothering me.

Connor pauses, then gently runs a hand down my arm.

138

"How could this possibly be your fault?" he asks.

"Tad tried to help me after my departure failed. Our interaction wasn't exactly smooth."

I tell him how nervous Tad seemed, how he stood out like a sore thumb. And how terribly un-smooth I was when he passed me his message.

"And then I left it in the bathroom trash can. Where anyone could have dug it up. I wasn't thinking at all. What if…"

I can't bring myself to say it. I pause and look at Connor for his reaction. There is none.

"I mean, the *wastebasket*. Shit."

I run my hand through my hair, pushing it away from my face.

"You couldn't possibly have understood anything at that point, though," Connor says. "Sounds to me like he botched *his* job. Not you."

"Connor! The man is missing!"

Saying it out loud makes my shoulders tighten, as if I could brace against it.

"And that's awful. But getting people like you out safely is part of his job, right? Sounds like he caused a lot of confusion in what was already a dangerous situation. You're not a spy. You didn't even know we existed. How were you supposed to respond to that?"

It's an interesting point. Why *did* Tad make contact with me like that?

Life is different out there, he told me. I can still feel his fingers digging into my arm as he said it. And he was right – it's really different. But in the moment, it hadn't sounded like a good kind of different. It sounded like a warning.

But that can't be right – I must have been too scared, too confused, to understand him. He way trying to help. Wasn't he? Everyone from the Alliance has done nothing but help. But… well. Even then, Mara thought it was strange, the way he had spoken to me.

"I have to tell them what I know. It probably doesn't matter, but…" I don't know how to explain this weight that has settled into the pit of my stomach, or how it's not going to go away.

But Connor nods. "Go. I'll finish up at the farm."

"Thanks." I squeeze his arm and bolt after Kinlee. "Kin!" It's not easy to dart through everyone to catch up to her, and by the time reach her, my breaths are heavy.

"Seriously, I can't say anything else," she says as she turns to me.

"No, Kin, I met Tad. On my Departure Day. Maybe I can tell *you* something."

She raises an eyebrow and tilts her head. "Yeah, definitely. Mom and the others will want to talk to you. Follow me."

Kinlee leads me through the trees, and I start to realize each turn is marked with a small red dash of paint on its bark. But even with the marks, you'd have to already know where you were going to know which way to turn at each one.

"Is Intel hiding its location from the Directorate or from the camp?" It's a lame joke, but I'm nothing but nerves right now and the quiet is killing me. "Really. Where are you taking me?"

Kinlee smirks. "You know, the Directorate shut itself off gradually at first. It took a while for other countries to get concerned enough to respond. First they responded in small ways, like sanctions. Then, when the Directorate ignored that, everything escalated. Eventually it started a war."

We pass another red mark, and Kinlee makes an abrupt turn. I do my best to keep up.

"Sure. We got a version of that in lower grade History," I say. "Though in the Directorate's version, the other countries attacked the Directorate for protecting peaceful, painless life." Sarcasm leaks into my words as I quote the lies I was fed for so many years. It feels icky to say it out loud now, after so many weeks free of them.

Kinlee nods. "Uh-huh. So during the war, the Directorate put all these bunkers around its outer perimeter for border security. Their technology was a lot more advanced than the other countries. They obliterated us," Kinlee says. "Then they closed themselves off completely, and we had no way to stop it. But, they left the bunkers on the outside."

Kinlee comes to an abrupt stop, and I bump into her.

"Okay. And why am I getting this very delightful history lesson?" I say.

Kinlee stomps the ground. It doesn't make the muffled *thud* of soft earth. It makes the tinny *clang* of metal on metal.

"What the…?" I exclaim, jumping back.

Kinlee laughs as she presses her thumb to a scanner embedded on the corner of the trap door, and it pops open.

"Whoa," I say. It's the first decent tech I've seen since I got here.

Kinlee lifts the door. "Come on."

Then she swings in and starts the climb down.

I step to the edge and look in. The bunker below is deeper than I imagined, ending in a scuffed-up metal floor. It looks familiar, and my first arrival to the camp flashes back to me – this is the second ladder I climbed when I first got here that took me up to the camp. With my sprained ankle. My stomach churns at the memory. It's not so bad with two working legs, but all the same I take it slow, staring intently at my knuckles as they turn white, clenching each bar on the descent.

Kinlee gets down quickly, and by the time I've caught up, she's already getting Raina.

Unlike the rest of the camp – where we're practically living like people did a couple of hundred years ago – down here, everything looks state-of-the-art. It's floor-to-ceiling metal, and the entire wall to our left is covered in video feeds on large screens, showing various angles of the camp's perimeter. Three people man the desks in front of those screens, with more chairs pulled out near other disheveled desks.

Some of the feeds are surveilling something else, though. Perfectly lined sidewalks with perfectly manicured grass and perfectly spaced trees, with perfectly calm and content citizens walking past – the Directorate. On the wall opposite the screens, a large map is stretched out and marked up. A

141

series of bubbles, tightly organized, takes up almost half the map, each with a number, and other notes. I didn't realize there were so many Quads.

This is what Kinlee's up to while Connor and I are milking cows? Goofy, sarcastic Kinlee? It's like there's a totally different person hidden inside her that she doesn't show us.

I must look as nervous as I feel, because Kinlee cocks her head. "Relax. This is an interview, not an interrogation."

I try to smile. "Right."

"Maybe we should talk about something else," she says. Then her mouth twists into a mischievous grin. "Maybe we should talk about Connor."

"What! No. Why would we do that?"

"I don't know. Why *would* we do that?" She lifts one eyebrow suggestively.

"Damnit." What's the point. She already knows. "I hated him. When did he get *cute*?"

Kinlee snorts with laughter. "Better question: When are you going to stop being a chicken and do something about it?"

"What! No way." I think for a second. "What if he doesn't feel the same?"

"First of all, I have known him forever, and he does. You've done something to him. He's been so angry, for so long. Not that he doesn't have reasons to be angry. But since you got here, it's been fading. He's smiling more." A warm rush comes over me. "And second of all, so what if it turned out he didn't? Life would go on."

"But…" I don't know how to say the other thing holding me back. A cloud of dread that warns me to keep them all at arm's length, like I always have, to try not to make it any worse for anyone when my departure date finally catches up with me. Then I realize, it would be impossible to explain any kind of fear to Kinlee. "How are you so fearless?"

If Kinlee had a departure date, I don't think she would hesitate to get it diagnosed at all. She'd never have a fit of panic, run away, and then let it sit like a weight at the back of her mind for weeks.

She shrugs. "I have fears. But the more you get used to doing the thing you're afraid of, the less of a big deal it becomes. I do it all the time for Intel training. Then her face lights up and she jumps. "You should do Intel & Recon for your last rotation."

The idea alone shoots a shiver of fear through me. "That seems like a very bad idea."

"It's not," she says. Her eyes glint with excitement at the idea. "But suit yourself."

I'm still struggling to get my head around the idea of *me* working in a place like *this,* when Raina strides up, along with a large man in a soldier's uniform, and I remember why I'm here in the first place. They pull up chairs for all of us from a nearby table, and we sit.

"This is Grant," Raina says. "Tell us everything,"

I try. I give them every detail I can remember. Though it turns out my awareness for details on that particular day was terrible, with everything that was going on. They ask me a million questions on every point, parsing out some kind of meaning from it all that I can't see.

I start out talking too quickly, not quite saying what I mean. Their questions slow me down, though, and I start to understand what kind of information will help them. They don't care that Tad's gelled-back hair stood out from the other site workers; they write down every detail I can remember about what he was wearing.

When I get to the part about taking the note, they frown, and my cheeks flood with heat. "I'm so sorry. I didn't realize what I was doing. I was so stupid – "

Raina cuts me off, reaching out to give my arm a comforting squeeze. "Whatever is going on, Tad broke protocol a few times over that day. It's not your fault."

I let out a sigh of relief. The tight ball of nerves in my core settles.

Then, I tell them about the rest of my time at the crem site until I got in the car with Suits One and Two, and slump in my chair.

"So... what happens now?" I ask.

143

Raina and Grant lean in, frowning.

"Whatever happened, I don't think it had taken place yet. But I can see why he was an easy target," Raina says.

A target for who? For what? A new kind of uneasiness comes over me, inching up my spine.

Grant shakes his head. "Whatever the case, one thing is clear: Even if these behaviors somehow didn't contribute to his disappearance, wherever he is now, if he's alive, he is a security risk who can't be trusted to follow protocol and keep his mouth shut."

Raina nods. "Even just a few years ago, we would have insisted he should have more training before throwing him in like that."

The uneasiness creeps into my shoulders and clenches into them deep. This is bad. Even worse than it seemed before.

But there is nothing else I can do about it. Kinlee leads me back to the ladder.

"So what now?" I ask.

She shrugs. "We don't know yet. But this was good, Ev. This helped."

I still can't believe Kinlee is involved in all this. It's so different from the screwball who I've come to know this past month. Has it really only been a month? This place and its free, messy life already feel so natural. So necessary. Remembering the Quad is like remembering a dream – a bad dream, where the walls are too tight and it's hard to breathe.

We stare at each other solemnly. The Directorate has never felt so threatening, even when they were trying to correct my departure. That was simply a matter of maintaining order. But if they took Tad, this is something much worse.

I climb up the ladder and give Kinlee what I hope is an encouraging wave before shutting the hatch.

Chapter Twenty-Four

Evie

When I pull myself out at the top of the ladder, Connor is there.

"Hey!" I try not to sound too excited, but seeing him there, waiting for me, helps me shake off a little of my worry. "You're done at the farm already?"

"Already?" Connor frowns. "It's been a couple hours since you headed off with Kin."

"Oh. Wow." I guess we were talking for a while.

"So what happened?" he asks.

The nerves come back, tingling over my neck and knotting through my core.

"It's bad," I say. "I mean, really bad. They were really interested in what I had to say. I think it helped. But Tad's in serious trouble. I think we all might be."

How can a person just disappear? I look to Connor. His eyes are busy with thoughts, and his forehead is creased with concern. He reaches out and rubs the sides of my arms.

"You all right?" he asks.

He's peering into my eyes like he's going to find an answer in them.

"Yeah. I guess. I can't stop thinking about Tad. They said he wasn't following protocol. That if he's out there somewhere, captured, who knows what he's saying? And... I don't know. I saw him. I talked to him. What if I could have done something differently? What if he got caught, trying to help me, and it's all my fault? Maybe it was a mistake, trying to get me here."

Connor's hand runs down my arm and squeezes my hand.

His touch is like magic, quieting my thoughts.

"No way. If anything, he compromised *your* safety by breaking protocols. This isn't on you. You're perfect. You're right where you belong. Understood?"

He says it like it's a fact, as unchanging and obvious as any other piece of his ever-churning flow of information. I look at him, and his expression is so earnest and sweet. Could Kinlee really be right? Could he feel the same about me?

Connor blinks, and I realize how long I've been staring. His cheeks flush bright pink, and he shifts to pull his hand away. But I reflexively tighten against his pull – I'm not ready to let go yet. He gives in, his fingers relaxing as they intertwine with mine.

The rest of the afternoon passes in a haze. I've never felt like this before, giddy, but also calm, and, despite everything going on in the camp right now, safe. We wander the woods, something unspoken keeping us away from the camp. For once, Connor hardly says anything. We just coexist, enjoying the relative coolness of the shade of the trees' cover.

It's a feeling I have no context for. I can't remember my parents ever holding hands. Can the Directorate's algorithms calculate for this kind of connection? Or maybe they don't want to factor this in. The Directorate pairs for order and stability, but that isn't anywhere close to what Connor stirs up in me.

Order. Is it really worth everything the Directorate sacrifices to maintain it? My mind wanders to Gracelyn, and the carefully-planned, predictable path ahead of her, every step and detail a straight line, already assigned and carefully managed. There's an entire world out here she has no idea about. So many choices, and flavors, and surprises, that she'll never experience.

As it starts to get dark, my stomach rumbles.

Connor laughs, and I feel so giddy that I laugh too. "Guess we'd better head back," he says. "I know better than to mess with your stomach."

My heart sinks a little at this. I don't want to share him

with anyone yet. But he's right. Dinner time is coming, and people would worry if we didn't show up, especially considering the day's news. As we near the edge of the camp to meet the others, our hands drop apart and I try to tuck away the warmth that has been building up in me.

As it turns out, it's not too hard. The camp is quieter than usual tonight, tension settling over the scattered tables and dampening the mood. It tightens between my shoulders and in the pit of my stomach. Even Kinlee, who usually shows no sign of stress from her work, seems more tired than usual. It must be nuts in Intel right now. Still, she tries her best to brighten the mood.

I try to be like Kinlee and keep things light. Everyone at the table does. But the afternoon's announcement looms over us all the same. Arguments and heated discussions in hushed voices drift in from all the other tables. It's not just Tad. His disappearance has caused a rift through the camp.

The tension wedges between my shoulders and grips into me. Clashes like this never happened in the Quads – there wasn't anything to care about this deeply. And there certainly wasn't space for this kind of conflict amid our carefully-structured days. How can they look one another in the eye, sit at the same tables, continue to work together, while caught in such conflict?

"Do arguments like this happen a lot?" Even as I ask, I wonder if that would make it better or worse.

"No," says Ginnie, wide-eyed. "I've never seen this before, ever."

But Kinlee shrugs. "Oh come on. Adults fight all the time. These debates about how to run the camp are constant."

Ginnie's brows pinch together and her eyes widen.

"Okay fine. This one's a lot worse. But it's been building. It was kind of inevitable."

Connor puts on his thinking face, then nods in somber agreement.

"What do you mean?" I ask.

Kinlee shrugs. "The camp is kind of a misfit base, without a clear governing body. Officially, a lot of countries won't even acknowledge us anymore – they're too afraid of the backlash if the Directorate finds out, because no one can come close to matching their military power." She shifts, leaning into the table. "So we run on volunteers and under-the-table funds. It's a mix of a joint government espionage effort, and also a human rights effort. Some governments want to monitor the Directorate to make sure they don't become a threat to the rest of us again. Others want to gain intel to take it down. Some are more interested in taking out the Licentia cells so they don't expand to their own countries."

I still can't believe the Licentia are *real*. My mind flashes back to times when a loud noise or unexpected smoke rose from buildings in the Quad, any time a stretch of street was blocked off. Maintenance, the Directorate always said. But maybe it wasn't. It would never have occurred to me before that such destructive hate could really exist, and it scares me more than anything else I've learned since coming here.

But Licentia aside, Kinlee's breakdown explains a lot. Particularly, how low-tech this place is, other than the Intel bunker. But could the Alliance really take down the Directorate? What would happen to citizens like Gracelyn if they did?

Kinlee continues. "So sure, the camp is mostly peaceful and we work together on pre-agreed efforts that help us all meet our various goals. But we take some big risks here, and anyone willing to risk themselves by being here has strong opinions about what they think the priorities should be. Something like Tad going missing was bound to happen eventually. And we all have different things motivating how we think we should handle it. So of course it's chaos."

It's as if, in Kinlee's mind, the entire camp is a giant game of chess.

"It's kind of weird it hasn't happened earlier, when you start to think about it," Connor says.

Kinlee shrugs. "We haven't had anyone go missing before. Not like this, where we don't know what happened."

Dave sighs and sprawls out over the table in a dramatic

gesture. "Can we *not*? This day has already been tense enough without reliving the entire thing. Let's have some fun."

We all exchange looks. Kinlee jumps to her feet, her expression shifting into a troublesome grin.

"Fun? You want to have fun?" She leans forward to face Dave on the table and punches him playfully. "Isn't that all you do all day? Do you doofuses over in Food Prep even *work*?"

Dave grins. "Nope. That breakfast you wanted tomorrow? We thought about doing that. But we all agreed, it didn't sound *fun*, so we went swimming in the river instead."

Kinlee tries for another swat at him, but Dave catches her by the wrist. Kinlee lets out a giggling shriek as he tugs her onto him over the table and wraps his arms around her.

Their relationship is a strange push and pull of challenges, and I still don't really get it. But he definitely makes Kinlee happy. *Fun.* That's exactly it. They have fun together. We all do here. We didn't really do *fun* in the Directorate. We were content. We were healthy and safe. But fun?

Gracelyn. I had fun with her. Not like this, but more than anyone else in the Quad.

The memory of Gracelyn comes with a pang of sadness. I want her happy. I want her safe. It's become clear the Directorate is a dangerous place to be. Gracelyn, ever the perfect citizen, is about as safe as a person could be there. But I still worry about her. If only I could have brought her with me. If only –

"Ev?" Connor tilts his head, studying me. "What you thinking?"

I realize with a flood of embarrassment I've been staring at him. Shit.

"What? Nothing. Zoned out, I guess."

I'm not ready to share this new idea with anyone yet, but it charges through me, relentless as a heartbeat.

If only Gracelyn could be here, too.

It has to be possible – don't they bring people in from the Directorate all the time? I've just got to figure out how to do

149

it. My mind wanders to the giant map stretched across the wall of the Intel & Recon bunker. If there's a way to do it, that's where I'll find the answer, I'm sure of it.

"Hey Kin?" I'm calling out to her before I've even thought it through.

"Yeah?" she says. Dave is making a face at her, and she is giggling as she breaks away.

"I thought about it some more, and I'll do it. Tell Raina to sign me up for Intel & Recon next rotation."

She turns to me, eyes wide. "Really? It's going to be great, wait and see."

"Yeah. Great."

Gracelyn, out here, in the real world. The idea settles around my heart and grows roots. I'm not sure what comes next, but there's bound to be a way to do it. There has to be.

Chapter Twenty-Five

Gracelyn

I am starting to lose hope of finding anything more about Code Twenty-Seven. I have not found anything to explain the brief conversation between Gunders and Johnston.

What if there is nothing about it on the server at all? What if I misheard, or they had important additional information they didn't say out loud? If I keep this up, I am going to get caught, and my fear of the consequences grows each time. But it is too late now. If I let this go without understanding, questions about Evie will haunt me the rest of my life. I *have* to do this, so that everything can get back to normal again.

With all this sneaking around, I am realizing for the first time how carefully the Directorate monitors us in the Quad. Even our smallest actions are tracked and recorded and watched. It is in everything from the card swipe at the main entrance and again at my desk each morning and evening, all the way to the confusion in Mother's eyes when I leave for my day a few minutes early, and Hanna's side-eye glances.

It is hard to blame them – we have been taught to monitor one another like this. The expectation of our exacting schedules has been ingrained into us. Disrupting it triggers concern, and concern could lead to even more observation. And I don't dare risk being marked as noncompliant. So I have had to scale it back.

When I do slip in early, I turn on my computer and start sifting through hundreds of thousands of tedious corporate documents. I have never been more grateful for my photographic memory – without it, I would be lost.

This would all be easier if I could simply run a server-wide search for "Code Twenty-Seven." But I might as well stand up and announce it to everyone: *Hello. I am searching for what I assume is a highly-classified project I am not qualified to access. Could you hand it over, please?*

The search would surely raise a flag on the system, and Quinn would probably receive a notification of my suspicious actions, along with others even higher up the chain. Who knows where that would lead? Suspension? Complete removal from the Department? I'd lose my access to find these answers, and everything about the life I am trying to get back to would be ruined.

So no searches. Searching the folders one by one, if I get caught, I might be able to pretend I'm merely being over-ambitious. It would be odd, but it would not be the first time someone has gone to extremes to get ahead in this program. Even if they didn't believe me, at least they still would not know what I was really looking for.

My days have begun to feel like a side note, and the real reason behind everything has become the search. I have to hold myself back from going in early more frequently.

And then one morning something jumps out at me from the text. My heart pounds. It is not a mention of Code Twenty-Seven, but it is awfully strange.

It is old. And it is short. I read it slowly, making sure to capture every detail for later.

MEMO
September 9, 2231
FROM: Alan Gunders, Senior Associate
TO: Departure Management, Department Chair and Deputies

A significant aberration has been discovered with the time-release feature of the chemical compound in the departures serum. Although the serum works as intended for most citizens, there is a small minority for whom this process is not effective.

It is critical that we correct the issue before it becomes more widely discovered and disrupts citizen life.

So far, most of the very few victims of this failure are so stunned to find themselves still present upon waking that they do not take any action, and some did not wake until they are on their way to crematory. There was one incident where the victim went into a panic, and the spouse also became quite distressed. The victim was removed, and the spouse had to be heavily dosed with memory-altering medications. The greater challenge is keeping Departure Crews from spreading these stories to others, and keeping them unaware of the greater problem. Memory-altering medications are effective in most cases, but in one, an early departure was necessary.

We must act while we still have the advantage that the anomaly is unknown by the general public. The risk of exposure will only grow with time. Addressing this quickly is of the utmost importance.

I review the words again, sure I have missed something. But I haven't. *People are not departing when they are supposed to?*

For the thousandth time the shuffling from Evie's room that morning comes back to me, and this time the sound seems so much darker. My stomach knots. It makes perfect sense, in fact it is the first thing that *has* made sense in all of this. But if Evie was not departed when the Departure Crew arrived, what happened to her?

Don't be crazy, I scold myself. After all, this memo is over twenty years old. Surely they have solved it by now. Besides, they carried the body bag down the stairs and out to the van.

But…

I shake my head and try to think, my heart thudding in my ears.

"Good morning!"

A smooth, cheery voice comes out of nowhere. I shudder.

"Um, hi. Good morning," I stutter. I lean forward to tap away from the document still on my syncscreen, but a porcelain hand pulls mine away before I can. I look up and my stomach knots – it is Quinn.

Her eyes flit quickly over the memo on my screen, and my

face turns hot and red in spite of myself. I have never been a good liar.

Quinn taps to close the document, then looks back to me, her face expressionless but her eyes busy. "I think you'd better come with me."

Why did it have to be Quinn? I know the feelings I have been nursing for her are ridiculous, but at least right now I am in her favor, a promising future leader in the department. I cannot stand the idea of her writing me off as noncompliant.

Too late, Gracelyn. You should have thought of that before you started nosing around classified files.

How else could this have possibly ended? If Quinn had not caught me, someone else would have, eventually. And then they would have reported me to Quinn, and we would be back right here, with me following her to her office. A watchlizard skitters under a door as we pass it in the hall.

What will they do with me? Probation? Removal? Will I spend the rest of my days in a janitorial position, picking up litter around the parks? This will break Mother and Father's hearts. They have invested everything in me, in my future. I can feel it all disappearing, and I realize I can't make myself care like I know everyone else will. If I let myself get caught now, I might never find out what really happened to Evie. If she was alive on her Departure Day, she could still be alive now.

We reach the office, and Quinn gestures for me to enter. She follows in after me and closes the door.

***

I sit in one of the chairs across from Quinn's desk and stare at the floor. Instead of crossing the room to the other side, she pulls the other chair close, facing me.

Shame floods my cheeks, but under that, indignation simmers. I scold myself to keep it together, then force myself to look up and meet her gaze. She leans in, a brilliant red curl falling into her face.

"Why didn't you tell me?" she asks.

"I was – but – are you...?" I'm so confused by her question that I cannot piece a sentence together. It occurs to me I have no idea what she deduced from what she saw. Though I cannot see how this could possibly look like anything good.

I take a breath. "Tell you what?"

"That memo," she says, voice low. "You've been looking for something."

We stare at each other, in a standoff. Her eyes are clouded, mirroring the confusion I feel. My head rushes. Quinn is so close, I could brush my fingers over her leg if I were to only lean forward.

But no. I cannot let my feelings for her get in my head; there is too much at stake. Right now, Quinn is the Directorate, and the Directorate is a roadblock to the answers I need. I pull my hands in and rest them in my lap. I shake my head and press my lips together, unable to say anything.

She gives a tentative half-smile. "You're really going to tell me you haven't been looking for something?"

Evie. I crave to be able to talk to someone about everything that has happened. But that would ruin everything. *Stick to the plan.* I have lies prepared for this very moment. "No?" I just wish I was better at employing them.

Quinn leans forward, the crease in her forehead deepening. "Damnit, Gracelyn... tell me."

I look down at my hands, unable to speak and unable to resist.

A wall goes up behind Quinn's eyes, turning steely as she pulls back.

"Look. I don't want to play hardball with you, but I will if you make me. I saw what you were looking at. It's classified. And it's way out of your purview, both by department and position." Quinn taps her fingers against the arm of the chair. "I have every reason to report you. Depending on how I spin this, you could spend some time on probation. Or I could hold you back at entry level again next year. Or I could have you removed from the organization entirely. I like you,

155

Gracelyn. Don't make me do that. Tell me what's going on."

Her abrasiveness burns through me. But what to say? In my fear and confusion and the mounting pressure, I cannot think straight.

She reaches out and takes my hand. Despite everything, a thrill shoots up my arm.

"Trust me, Gracelyn. You might be surprised."

I almost give her the story I prepared, about curiosity and getting ahead. But it sounds so flimsy all of a sudden. A terrible pang of desperation trembles through my chest, and suddenly I cannot bear to keep carrying this secret alone. To my dismay, the truth starts to fall out of me.

"A few weeks ago, a man with a tag that said 'Gunders' from DMD said something to another employee. Johnston. He said something about a Code Twenty-Seven. And it happened on my sister's departure date."

Heat rises up my neck and into my cheeks. Even though I have been thinking it almost constantly for weeks, it still feels strange to say it out loud.

"And..." I am not really sure where to go from there. What is Quinn thinking? I can't meet her eyes. I must sound crazy. "Something *happened* that morning. Something not right."

She raises an eyebrow. "What happened?"

"I don't know what exactly, but I heard movement in her room. *Before* the Departure Crew got there. I would swear my life on it."

Quinn frowns. "What else?"

"There isn't much else." I shrug. "That memo is all I have found. It makes it sound like some people were not departing like they should. But it is from a long time ago."

It sounds ridiculous, now that I have said it out loud. Impossible. The Directorate does not make mistakes. My heart is racing so hard I can feel it in my wrists and behind my ears. What will Quinn do with me?

"I know it sounds like I'm crazy. I swear, I'm not," I say. The pounding of my pulse swallows me up and I can't think anymore. "I'm sorry. I will stop. I will talk to my mental health manager about it. Anything. Please don't make me stop working here."

My voice quivers, and I am afraid I am going to cry, so I stop talking. I do not know if I could really stop looking, but right now I am ready to say anything to make this moment end.

Quinn stares at me, her eyes busy and focused. She leans in close. My fingers tingle at her proximity.

"You're not crazy," she whispers.

I blink. She is staring at me, waiting for a reaction.

"What?"

"The memo. You read it right." She glances towards the door then leans in so that we are only inches apart. "I've been looking for things, too. And there's a lot more than this memo. You'd see for yourself in time. But you're risking too much, poking around the system in the open like this. Someone else is going to catch you. And that's not good for any of us."

I press my fingers to my temples. My thoughts rush and blur, making me dizzy.

"Wait. You mean…" I shake my head and try to clear my head. "You're not going to report me?"

"Shhhh," Quinn puts a hand on my leg to quiet me. My skin hums under her touch. "I'll need to put some kind of 'talk' between us on the record. The servers monitor everything that happens in the system, so don't poke around the files like that again. But I'll say that you didn't know what you were doing, you were looking for something else. It'll be on your record, but it will be minor, and it will be buried in accomplishments in a year or two. And hey, this is actually a good thing. Now we know we're looking for the same thing, we can work together."

I look up, hardly daring to believe what I'm hearing. "You're going to help me?"

A smile twitches at the edge of her mouth. "Of course I am."

Then she leans in and presses her lips to mine. Shock, relief and something new, something tingly and wonderful

157

floods me. I cannot move or breathe. All I can do is let it wash over me.

She pulls away. "We're going to help each other."

I do not know if it is the adrenaline from the fear, or the rush of total relief, or how soft and warm her lips were against mine, but this is the best thing I have ever felt in my life, a thousand times over.

For the first time since Evie departed, I do not feel wounded. I do not feel alone.

I feel *happy*.

It is such an intense relief to have escaped this close call. But even more, it is so nice to have someone on my side again, to not be carrying this terrible secret alone. Maybe now, with Quinn's help, I can find some real answers.

Chapter Twenty-Six

Evie

Kinlee's advice about Connor won't leave me alone, and finally, I decide to stop trying to play it cool and do what she suggested – go for it. That's what this new life I'm in is all about, right? So instead of slipping in at the edge of the group when I get to our table, I wedge in next to Connor.

"Hey there," he says. "Long time no see."

It's been maybe an hour. All I can muster in response is a giggle.

Shit, I'm no good at this. What am I doing? I look around, but Kinlee isn't here yet. Soon the food baskets begin to pass around.

"Is Kin stuck at Intel?" I ask. Their hours keep getting longer since the Tad announcement.

No one seems to know. We load up our plates and eat.

When Kinlee finally joins us, the sun is already down. Her steps drag, and her shoulders are hunched. At first I think it's just stress and tiredness, but then she slams her fist into the table so hard it makes the plates clatter and silences the entire table.

"You have a lot of nerve," she says, turning to me. Her cheeks are a hot red and her eyes simmer.

"Who, me?" My skin scrawls with pins and needles at the intensity of her glare. "What are you talking about?"

"Yeah. You, Directorate. And I'm *talking* about your departure. You know, death."

I flinch at the word.

"Yeah. You don't like that word, do you?"

"Kinlee, just – " I can feel myself retreating inwards,

trying to hide from her rage. I don't understand.

"Just nothing. I *cannot* believe you."

"Enough, Kin." Connor leaps to his feet. "What the hell is this about?"

Even in this moment of confusion and fear, I can't help the giddiness that flutters underneath it: he's standing up for me.

Kinlee takes a terrible pause. She stares at Connor with eyes so hot I'm surprised laser beams don't shoot out of them.

"She isn't diagnosing her departure. She's just waiting to see what happens to her."

Connor's frown deepens, then fades to blankness. His ears and neck go splotchy with red. He looks at me. "Is that true?"

In the confusion of the moment, no words will come to me, but his eyes flicker over my face and the truth reflects in his expression.

He shifts, turning on me, and echoes Kinlee: "What is wrong with you?"

"Stop yelling!" I whimper, staring down at the table. With all this talk about death, fear is welling up and blocking out everything else, and I can hardly think.

"No," Kinlee bites back. "This is a very yell-worthy situation. Do you understand what you're doing, Ev? Or haven't you even thought about it?"

A combustible churn of emotion explodes in my chest and turns my shame to fire.

"How'd you even find out about this?" I yell back. "Aren't a person's medical records private around here? Or is that another one of those *crazy* Directorate things?"

I fold my arms over my chest and narrow my eyes, daring Kinlee to defend herself.

"I can't see how this compares to throwing your entire life away, but it was an accident."

"An accident? Sure. You're in the Med cabin all the time, so you must have *accidentally* tripped over the file and it opened itself up to my most private information. Makes perfect sense."

Kinlee's nostrils flare. She leans forward over the table,

her fists pounding into it.

"*Or* How does this sound? I was helping Mom organize a campwide shipment to the outside world, and when Sue had absolutely nothing to add to it – no tests for analysis, for example – I put two and two together."

She glares at me. Connor glares at me. The rest of them all stare, wide-eyed and open-mouthed. Even some of the others sitting at the tables nearby are watching. My mind can't turn the hot wad of emotion pulsing through me into any more words, so I glare right back, fighting the quiver in my lip.

Connor is the one to break the silence. "What's it matter how she found out? I'm glad she did. Because shit, Evie, you *have* to know. You can't ignore facts just because you don't like them. I thought you were better than all this Directorate bullshit."

Slowly, I turn from Kinlee to him and fold my arms over my chest. "I *have* to? I thought you didn't dictate to people out here. You were all enlightened and special and free to make your own choices. Isn't that what makes you all *so much better* than me? Or is that only for choices you agree with?"

Connor flinches, as if I'd slapped him across the face. His jaw drops, and in a rare moment he seems to be speechless.

But Kinlee still has plenty left to say. "How about having some appreciation for those of us who saved your ass, and staying alive for a while?" She pushes the heel of her hand into her eye, and I realize she's fighting back tears.

Maybe there's something Kinlee is afraid of after all. But with all the yelling and the raging and anger pulsing through me, I can't find the empathy to process it, not now.

"Fuck you," I scream. "And *you*," I add, turning on Connor. "Hell. Fuck all of you!" I flail my arms at the group, turn away, and storm off towards the trees.

I march through the woods until the burning edge of my anger calms to a dull pulse. I've tried so hard to *avoid* thinking about diagnosing my departure ever since Sue brought it up. I'd almost managed it, too – pushing the idea far to the back of my mind, pushing the panic down to a dull weight. It wasn't great, but it was a lot better than the waves of terror that come over me whenever I consider what might be in store for me now that I'm past my departure date.

And I thought I was being brave because I was sitting next to a boy? Ugh.

I'm not stupid; I know Kinlee and Connor are right. But that's my head. In my heart, the idea of a bunch of medical tests terrifies me, let alone what those tests might tell me. I can't bear the idea of a countdown to death all over again, especially when this time it might be awful and painful and slow. No matter how I try to channel the passive acceptance I had in the Quad before my departure date, every time I think of it my hands start to shake. It's not the suffering that does it, I realize – I have too much to live for now, out here, in this new world. How could I face saying goodbye to it all?

Eventually the night turns cold, and it seems late enough to bet that if Kinlee isn't on shift, she's probably asleep by now. Even so, when I get home, I am relieved to find the cabin is empty.

Chapter Twenty-Seven

Evie

"You're late."

I'm already halfway through milking Lizzie when I hear Connor walk in behind me. After the fight, I couldn't sleep. And lying there in bed, staring at the upper bunk, wondering if Connor would come to wake me after all of that fighting last night, made me even angrier. So I got up.

"Sorry," he says. His voice is penitent and low, almost a whisper. "I got tied up."

I almost turn around, to try to read his face to see where we stand, but instead I tell myself I don't care – *I* decide where we stand.

"Don't tell it to me, tell it to Daisy," I nod to the cow next to me, who moos complacently. "And what is there to get tied up with before sunrise?"

"I brought you something."

Connor reaches around my shoulder and waves something at me – some kind of large round roll, from the looks of it.

"Not hungry," I say, shrugging away from him.

"Yeah, right," he says with a soft laugh. "Try it. One bite."

"I'm busy. There's milk to be… milked."

I don't care about his stupid roll, I tell myself. I've got work to do. Whatever.

"Just smell it," he says.

The roll creeps into my view again. And I can't help but breathe it in. It's *wonderful,* like nothing I've ever smelled before. This isn't normal bread; this is something totally new to me. It's sweet and rich, and my mouth begins to water. I turn and look at it for real. Steam wafts off it, and a thick white icing drips over its sides.

"What *is* that?" I ask.

Connor's eyes light up at my curiosity. "It's a cinnamon roll. Try it."

He hands it to me. I take its wrapping in both my hands – it's that big – and take a bite. Sweet cinnamon perfection explodes over my tongue.

"Oh!" The exclamation is muffled by the roll in my mouth, but I can't keep it in. "Shit, how is this so good!"

Connor perks up. "I was thinking. With all that careful monitoring for optimal health in the Directorate, the diet probably doesn't include much in the way of pastry. Thought it was time you tried one."

"Mmm," I mumble in agreement, my mouth too full to speak.

The food the Directorate gave us was all scientifically designed to keep our bodies in optimal health. Carefully-balanced nutrients and proteins. Minimal preservatives. No added sugars.

This cinnamon roll must be absolutely drowning in sugar.

The roll was huge, but it's already halfway gone. It's so good I want to swallow it whole. I want to eat only this for the rest of my life. I want to roll around in a pool of it.

"And," he sighs and looks down to the ground. "I'm sorry. Again."

I don't want to get into all of that. Especially while I'm eating this amazing thing. "Whatever."

"No, Evie." He steps around so he is in front of me, shoulder to shoulder with Lizzie. His eyes are pleading. "Really. I shouldn't have said those things last night. The Directorate makes me so angry, and I let that spill over to you. But you're so much more than where you came from. I guess I'm afraid to lose you like I lost my dad. And I'm so, so sorry. That's no excuse to yell at you, or to try to tell you what to do."

The anger within me is satisfied by his pleading tone. I take another bite of my roll.

"I know I'm impossible," he continues. "I know I get

myself wound up and say things I shouldn't. I'm working on it. I have no idea how hard it would be to make this adjustment between such different worlds. You're doing so amazingly that I forget that. But the last thing you need is more people telling you how to live."

He's right. It *has* been hard. A lot has changed. And so, so fast. Prime among those things, I'm not the scared, angry girl Kinlee led to this camp weeks ago. And I'm not afraid of a fight anymore. Maybe it's time I also stopped being so afraid of departure.

"But Evie, you have to forgive me. Or I mean," he sighs in frustration. "You don't *have* to, but I need you to. After this week, you're gone to another rotation, and I... I'm going to miss you around here. If I ruined it and we couldn't still hang out, I don't know what I'd do."

He shrugs as he says it, his cheeks coloring. *He'll miss me?* My heart swells with flutters. I look at him. His hair falls into his face in untamed waves, obscuring his eyes. But I can still see they are soft and pleading.

Damnit.

"I'll miss you too."

"Yeah?" He perks up, the beginning of a smile brightening his face.

"Shut up," I say, feeling the heat rushing to my face. "I didn't even say I forgive you yet."

"Well do you?"

I tilt my head back and sigh dramatically. "Yeah, fine. I forgive you."

"Can I have a bite of the cinnamon roll, then?" Connor asks.

"No way!" I pull back and take another large bite for myself. "You should've gotten your own!"

He reaches forward and skims some icing off of it with his finger, then licks it off. I shove the rest in my mouth before he can steal any more.

"Where did you *get* this thing?" I finish the roll and lick the extra icing off the wrapping.

Connor beams. "I traded for it. Some of us have hobbies,

like how you draw. Well, some people bake. They make things like the cinnamon rolls. Things they don't make for meals because we don't really need them."

"No. I definitely *need* that," I say, licking icing from my fingers.

He laughs.

He steps closer, and I can see a strand of his hair is caught in his eyelashes.

"You've got icing on your face."

His hand brushes over my cheek, a gesture that somehow feels like home in a way no place ever has. And then he licks the sweetness off his finger, his tongue trailing over his lips. My mind goes blank and I can't think straight. I lean forward and press my lips to his. His mouth presses back into mine softly, warm and sweet with icing.

And then I realize what I've done, and the bliss dissolves into panic. I pull away.

"Oh. Shit," I stutter. "Oh shit. I... I... I'm sorry, I..." I've got no excuse, I've got no words at all. "I'll go... I shouldn't have..."

All those years, I was so careful not to make connections I didn't have to, trying to respect their right to live without the pain of missing me after I was gone. And here I am, getting all involved. I don't even know what's wrong with me, or when I might depart. Connor doesn't deserve that kind of pain, especially after all he's already been through. Why didn't I think of this sooner? But somehow it didn't seem real. Not until right now.

I pull away to leave.

"Whoa, whoa, whoa." Connor reaches out and takes my hand. "What is this?"

"It's like Kinlee was saying last night. I'm still undiagnosed. I could still drop dead any minute. I can't go around putting that on people."

"What? You want to shut down and not even live, because the Directorate said it wasn't worth the pain? Evie. Life *is* pain. If that tradeoff isn't worth it to you, then you should go back to the Directorate right now, because that's not a life at all. But it's sure as hell worth it to me. If I'd been sure you wanted me to, I would have done this a long time ago."

And then he pulls me in for another kiss. It is long and soft, and for a moment I melt into him. But then I push away.

"That's not... I can't... That's easy for you to say – you don't even have a departure date. You don't know what it's like, having your entire life be a countdown. I'm like a bomb, Connor, and my timer's already run out. I could go off at any moment. Every connection I make before then, it's another hole of sadness that I make on my way out. What kind of mark is that to leave on the world?"

I push a tear away with the back of my hand. Connor takes a deep breath.

"Evie. I don't *care*. None of us do. Any one of us could go at any time. The idea that the Directorate can control that, it's part of their lies. Besides, you're telling me that you somehow insulated yourself from everyone, and no one in the Directorate misses you right now? I don't believe it. Impossible."

I shake my head. "I was careful. And no one wanted to take that on, anyway. People kept their distance."

"Not even your parents? Your sister?"

I shove the heel of my palm into my eye to rub away a tear. My face is probably all red and blotchy now, on top of everything else. "It's better this way, okay?"

He steps closer, and takes my hands in his. "We're all afraid of things. But you can't let that stop you from living."

I stare down at the zipper on his hoodie. "Yeah, right. No one here seems afraid of anything."

"Sure we are. You think I don't get scared of stuff? I get scared."

I peek up at him. "Yeah? Of what?"

He shifts uncomfortably and looks down to our entwined hands. "Well... okay. I'm pretty scared to leave here and go out into the real world."

"But you're dying to go see the world! It's basically all you talk about."

He sighs. "Yeah... But it's also pretty scary. I told you I

have to wait until I'm eighteen. But, the truth is, if I asked, I think Raina would let me go any time I wanted. I tell myself I'm not ready yet, but, well... I don't know if that's something you can be ready for. Maybe you just have to do it. I think maybe I've been hiding here."

His face is turning red and splotchy, and he still won't look at me.

"Well," I say, pulling him closer. "It's nice to know you're as human as the rest of us."

At that, he grins. Then, finally, he meets my eyes. They are dark and deep and solemn. "Listen, the point is this. I like you. A lot. You really think you can convince me that never being with you at all is better than being with you for a little while?" Connor steps forward and his chest presses right up against me. When he speaks again, it's a soft whisper. "Just shut up and stop ruining everything,"

When I look up, a goofy grin is lighting his entire face. He wraps his arms around me tight and kisses me again. Tingly threads of warmth like sunshine spread from my core out into my fingertips and out of the top of my head.

Maybe he's right, I can't keep everyone out anymore. Not out here. I relax and let it happen.

It's perfect.

Or, it should be perfect, except that I know he was right. And Kinlee was right. And I know what I have to do. Now, more than ever, I have to find a way to face my departure.

Chapter Twenty-Eight

Gracelyn

Hanna and I have only been at the office minutes when Quinn stops by my desk.

I didn't come in early today – I have not done that in over a week, ever since Quinn caught me.

"Good morning." She nods to Hanna before turning to me. "I'm afraid we need to go over yesterday's efforts in some detail. Let's grab a room."

As I get up, Quinn looks to Hanna. "Hanna, this would be tedious for you. No need to be in this one."

Hanna nods, her ponytail swinging, and turns back to her syncscreen with a smirk at the edge of her mouth, too caught up in her satisfaction at besting me to be suspicious.

"Coming," I say.

I follow Quinn back to a conference room, a giant ball of nerves. It's the first we'll be alone since she caught me. Since she *kissed* me. Suddenly I feel like my arms are too long, my legs are swinging funny.

But all that changes as soon as Quinn closes the meeting room door. She presses me against the wall by my waist and kisses me deeply. Everything stills.

"Good morning," she says into my ear.

"Good morning." My head is woozy with her scent.

"Sorry about that. It was the only thing I could think of to get us alone."

"What about the watchlizards?" I whisper, breathless.

The edge of her mouth twitches upward. "Don't worry about it. I did a security sweep." Then she kisses me again. Her hand brushes up my throat, and my skin tingles under her

169

touch.

"Hanna is going to get jealous if I am always getting all your attention. Even if she thinks it is because she is doing better."

"Then let her be jealous." Quinn pulls away, her mouth twisting into a crooked smile. I am inclined to agree. "But I didn't *only* bring you here for this." She presses her lips into mine one more time, then sits at the table. "Let's talk about that memo."

I am reluctant to leave her arms, but I hunger for answers at least as much. "Right."

I sit across from her and stretch out my legs until they are entangled with Quinn's. I want to be touching her all the time.

She leans over the table. "Tell me everything."

I do.

I tell her about Evie, and the strange sound I heard that morning. I tell her about how I tried to let it go, how I almost *did* let it go, until I heard Gunders and Johnston talking. And how after that, the not-knowing ate away at me, until the grief overcame my better sense.

"That is when you caught me. And I am so glad it was you who did."

She cocks an eyebrow. "Someone was going to. You were being sloppy."

"I know. And it probably would have gotten worse." I look down to my hands, fidgeting on the table.

Quinn nods. "We're going to find your sister. But you need to stop doing that and keep a low profile. The less attention we draw, the easier this will be."

"You really think she is out there somewhere?"

She looks at me, her mouth set with solemn determination. "I do. Don't you?"

"Yes," I breathe. My heart lights up like a switch has been turned on. I've hardly dared think it until now, but deep down I know Evie *is* out there somewhere. She has to be. "But how will we find her if we aren't looking?"

She leans in and kisses me. "Trust me. We are looking, but

170

we're doing it the smart way. And that starts with deflecting attention."

My skin tingles from her touch.

"How did you get involved in all this?" I ask her.

"It's hard to explain. I got fed up with all the ways the Directorate keeps us in line. Then I found some friends who felt the same way."

"In line?"

"The controls. All those little ways everything about this place is designed to keep us compliant."

Something inside me simmers, to hear it out loud. This is exactly what has been agitating within me since Evie's Departure Day.

"Over time, you start to see it in others, when they can see what you see about the world. That's how my friends found me – the ones who are going to help find your sister." She strokes my knee under the table. "And something changed in you."

"It's that obvious?" Panic pinches in my chest.

"You'd have to be looking for it," she says.

"So… you were looking?" I embarrass myself with the question and turn my eyes down to the table.

She leans forward to meet my gaze and pulls my hands into hers. "How could I not look at you?"

It's nice – more than nice, a relief – to have someone else who sees everything for what it is. Someone who believes me about Evie. Someone who feels the same wild, broken thing driving me to make these terrible choices.

"You said your friends are looking for the same things as I am. Who are they?"

Quinn raises an eyebrow. "You could meet them. If you want."

"Yes."

If Quinn and her friends are doing work that could help me find Evie, I need to be there, too. I need to help.

Quinn smiles. "Then I'll let you know when I can make it happen." Then she pulls me to her over the table and kisses me so hard that the sparks in my head cloud out everything else. When she pulls away, a small gasp escapes me.

I head back to my desk on wobbly legs, woozy on passion and anticipation. With Quinn by my side and taking control, I feel renewed conviction.

Evie is out there.

I am going to find her.

And I don't have to do it alone.

***

The controls.

With this little phrase Quinn blew a door open, one I am not sure I will ever be able to close again.

Now that this idea has a name in my mind, it's not just something that annoys me when it gets in my way. Now, I see the controls everywhere. Practically everything in the Quads is a construct to keep us in our place, so we fit neatly into the Directorate's big picture. The tight schedules, the carefully-monitored food, the little ways we watch and compete against one another – we're doing the Directorate's work for them.

I already know the lines I will be fed if I bring any of this up. How little the Directorate monitors us compared to what technology could allow. How these constructs are not there for control but to optimize our lives. How there is nothing stopping me from breaking these constructs – not really.

They wouldn't get it. It is all part of the illusion, like dogs kept in with an electric fence. What is it to the Directorate to leave us in an open field if there are reinforcements to shock us any time we stray too far?

So sure, the Directorate can point to things like low video surveillance and say we are free. But I know the truth – they don't need it. We are all surveilling one another.

Even now, Hanna is eying me warily from her desk space next to me.

"Are you okay?"

"I'm great. Why?"

"You look…" She frowns, but she doesn't finish her sentence.

We go to lunch. More controls – logging out of our Directorate-provided, Directorate-monitored desk screens. Tapping out with our digipads at the office entrance. Tapping in at the cafeteria food printer to receive our Directorate-assigned meals. Tapping into the lecture hall. With all our logging in and out all day, the Directorate could pull a minute-by-minute list of our actions any time they wanted.

It builds in me all day, counting the different ways the Directorate has a hold over my life. By afternoon lecture, my entire body is prickling with rage.

The projector screen reads in crisp black and white: *Design for Minimized Risk to General Population.*

The careful way they monitor our safety. Why haven't I seen it before? It's another excuse the Directorate uses to keep us pinned in.

The hall swells with electric hums as our digipads all push the same alert: *Lecture begins in 30 seconds.* We've all been trained to respond to cues like this our whole lives. The room quiets. On cue, Instructor Mathis polishes her glasses and takes the podium.

"Today we are discussing ways the Directorate manages risk to general population well-being through design elements for environment planning, with a focus on understanding why the Quadrant method optimizes the LQM mission of preserving life."

Instructor Mathis pauses and surveys the room.

Sure. *Optimizes life.* For who? To what end? It was only weeks ago, but I can't believe I ever bought into all this.

"Who can give me an example of the ways the Directorate's Quad construct optimizes daily life?"

Instructor Mathis waits for an answer, and several hands fly up, students eager to be recognized for their knowledge. Hanna is among them.

I slump in my chair and fold my arms over my chest.

She surveys the room, lips pursed, and lands on me.

"Henders," she says. "You have been quiet lately."

My hands clench against the arms of my seat.

A cool smile spreads over the instructor's face. "Do you have anything to contribute?" she prompts.

I don't know if it's her detached calm, or the subtle nudge to keep me compliant, or if it's just the wrong day, but something snaps inside me, and I am not willing to play along anymore.

I mimic her smile back to her and lean forward. "Of course. The provided transit ensures only properly-trained drivers are ever on the roads, and the low speeds reduce the risk of harm even if there was some kind of accident. The Quad domes keeps our day-to-day experience consistent and reinforces routines. The watchlizards wander through the Quads to keep an eye our well-being. But, Instructor Mathis," I tilt my head, the smile still stiff on my lips. "Did you mean to ask about safety, or compliance? Because we're told this is all done for our safety, but it also erodes our freedom."

Heat flashes over my skin as the students gasp and murmur. Hanna's hand flies over and grabs my wrist. Opposing forces rise in me like the wrong sides of a magnet: the thrill of letting out the terrible things I have pent up inside me, and the horror of what it could mean for me now that it is out.

Instructor Mathis folds her arms over her chest, her lips a tight line.

"You should know better," she scolds. "As we have studied, the Directorate's structure is not about serving the Directorate, but its citizens. Who can demonstrate this with an example?"

Eager hands fly up.

"I have one." I am on my feet before I know what I am doing. "The data-trail the digipads collect accounts for every minute of our day."

My head pulses. This isn't me, this isn't how I act and it damn sure isn't how I talk. My voice does not even sound like mine, angry and jagged. I sound like Evie.

Hanna squeezes my wrist so tight that my fingers start to lose feeling.

I tug my arm away from her. *What am I doing?* But the anger refuses to stay contained inside me anymore. The instructor shoots me a harsh glare, but then, thankfully, she continues, answering her own question with the appropriate lines.

Lines. That's exactly what it is. Half-truths reshaped to keep us going along.

Before I can stop to think, I am shouting.

"This is all as good as lies. The Directorate doesn't *care* about us. It cares about enforcing its order."

This time, Hanna leans away, as if to imply disassociation.

Instructor Mathis looks me over, a muscle in her cheek twitching. Then she nods. Two large men in black come in from the back. They wade down the aisles towards me and lift me from my seat by my arms.

"No!" I shriek. I try to tug away, but they only grip me harder.

As they carry me out, Instructor Mathis shakes her head. "Tsk, tsk. The stress of this program is too much for some."

The last thing I see before the doors of the lecture hall slide shut behind me is the students nodding in agreement, their faces smug with the satisfaction that they *can* handle it. Don't they see how they are being manipulated? As the doors settle back into place, a new question slams into my brain: *Why?* What's the Directorate's end game in all this? Because they must have one. And it's not the happiness of its citizens.

The idea makes my stomach churn. I go limp and let the guards carry me away, too caught up in these terrible new thoughts to keep fighting, and afraid that should I manage to find the answers, I might not have it in me to face them.

Chapter Twenty-Nine

Gracelyn

The guards take me to a small room down the hall and lock me in. In the silence, my thoughts rush at me in a panicked swarm – this is a disaster. I've all but guaranteed that I will be monitored very closely for the foreseeable future. How long will they hold me here, and what will they do to me? Have I just tossed away my future? How will I ever find out what happened to Evie now? How will I ever find out what the Directorate is up to? Under these terrible questions, a deep shame for my actions throbs.

Eventually, an alert on my digipad notifies me that my next appointment with Joyce has been brought forward to tomorrow. No doubt to discuss my outburst. The panic settles deeper into my stomach.

A quarter of an hour later, the door opens and the guard tells me to go home.

***

"Gracelyn. You're home early," Father calls from the living room. He sits on the couch, holding a syncscreen as if he were reading.

He's home early, too. They must have notified him about the lecture hall.

Dread rises in me and I remember the sneer on his face when he caught me in my sadness that first day in LQM. But my resentment is still hot, and I pull it around myself like armor.

"This is true," I say. I take off my coat and place it on my designated hook. Everything is designated, everything is labeled. The Directorate is everywhere, hovering around us and sucking up all the extra space.

I hear the click as Father repositions the screen into its holding pod in the wall.

"We got an alert from LQM's education department," he says.

"Oh."

"Come into the living room, Gracelyn."

I enter. We hardly use the living room now. We killed this room when we sat here all day after they took Evie away. It's not a living room anymore, it's a departure room. But we don't talk about it. Because we are good Directorate citizens, and that means everything is fine.

Mother is on the couch, her hands in her lap and her shoulders hunched. Her eyes are dazed and unfocused – she has taken more of those pills. I want to shake her until she is herself again. Father sits on the cushion next to her.

I stare at the tidy six inches of space between them and I wonder, have they ever felt anything like what I feel with Quinn? No, I don't need to wonder. I know they have not. Not even close.

"Have a seat, Gracelyn."

I sigh, and sit in a chair opposite them.

"We know this period has been, well, more challenging for you than for your peers," Mother says. "But this is too much. We thought – we hoped – you were keeping this under control."

More challenging. That is what we are going to call it? Because I call it *my sister departed.* Or rather, she didn't depart, and maybe something even worse happened to her – maybe she is still out there – but we are all supposed to pretend everything is fine.

Mother continues. "This phase of yours. It is beyond the normal emotional range."

"Beyond the normal emotional range?" I echo. What does that mean? Is the Directorate monitoring my brain's chemical levels? Now that I think of it, I would not be surprised.

Suddenly the digipad's cuff around my arm, which has always been a comfort and a resource, feels too tight. I want to rip it off and hurl it against the wall, but I know it won't allow me to remove it. "Well, I'm sorry that my emotions are not within regulations. Or whatever."

My voice is splintered with anger, and I know I'm teetering at the edge of what will be tolerated. I shuffle my feet and drop my gaze to the floor.

"Do not take that tone with your mother. She is not the one outside her bounds here," Father cuts in. "We all have your best interests at heart. You have a long and promising future ahead of you. We don't want your rash actions now to follow you for the next hundred years."

A hundred plus. One hundred and twenty-seven, to be exact. That is too many years of this Directorate bullshit. I shake my head – this isn't me, that's Evie again. But even Evie wouldn't dare say these things out loud like I did today. Her memory is melding and reshaping in my mind, becoming the things I wish I could be, and suddenly it feels like the real Evie is slipping away from me. The unanchored fear digs deeper into my core.

"Nobody wants that," Mother agrees. "But you've got to work with us, Gracelyn."

I slouch lower into my chair with a huff.

"What exactly *do* you want from me?" I snap. It's like no matter what I do or where I go, I am trapped in a too-tight box I cannot break free of. It is heavy, and it is exhausting me.

"That's *enough!*" Mother shoots to her feet, her face riddled with anger and her eyes sharp. It's satisfying, to see real emotion from her for once. Comforting. "You are acting just like your sis – "

The word hangs there, half-finished, as Mother tries to choke it back down.

"What's that?" I demand, rising to meet her. "Like my *sister*? I'm acting like Evie? Come on, you still remember how to say her name, don't you?" I pause. Instinctively I feel that this is the moment for the final blow, and I'm so angry and afraid at how far away Evie feels that I can find no reason to hold back. "Please tell me you weren't about to say I'm acting like my *dead sister* to get me back in line?"

"That is enough!" Father shouts, jumping to his feet.

"Which part is upsetting you?" I realize tears are dropping over my cheeks. "The part where I won't be manipulated, or the part where I mentioned your dead daughter? Do you remember her? Do you even care? *What is wrong with you people?*" I shriek.

I want to hurl the tablet across the room. I want to shatter the windows. Kick through the wall.

"Yes," Mother whimpers. "That."

Her eyes brim with tears. *Good.* I don't want to be alone in this horrible pain.

Father places a hand on her shoulder.

"Get it under control, Gracelyn," he barks. "Think of all those years of potential ahead of you. Don't throw them away."

"Yeah. All those precious *years*." And with that I'm out of things to say. I whip around and race upstairs to my room.

I slam the door behind me and the tears come immediately, hard and fierce, like I've never cried before. I can hardly believe what I've done. I feel as though I have been cut loose, untethered and teetering, at the edge of a cliff. Would I survive the fall?

If this is what it's like to let emotion in, I'm beginning to understand why so many don't mind opting out from it.

Chapter Thirty

Gracelyn

The next morning I am back in the MHM office, the plush cushions of the chair crowding around me.

"Well, Gracelyn? Anything to add since our last visit?"

Joyce presses her lips together, and it is clear she will not speak again until I do.

I am ready this time. I know what she wants, and I am prepared to deliver it. I nod slowly, looking down at my hands – a gesture I rehearsed in the mirror last night.

"I started feeling what you were talking about. Maybe I was already feeling it, and I was too afraid to admit it, even to myself."

Joyce leans forward. "And what is it you are feeling?"

"S-sadness."

"Mhm," she prompts.

"It's like..." my heart thumps in my throat. I try to swallow it down. "Part of me is missing. Like a puzzle. Like someone stole some of the pieces."

Uneasiness quivers through me – confessing these feelings out loud, it is putting me off-kilter in a way I didn't expect. I am already telling her more than I planned. *Shut up, shut up.* I can't afford to stray from what I rehearsed.

Joyce looks me over coolly, leaving it to me to fill the quiet.

To my dismay, I do.

"I feel so empty." Panic needles at me behind my ears. The words tumble out of me. "I can't sleep. I can't focus. I..."

My voice, thankfully, trails off in quivering stammers. I shake my head.

"I understand you had a tough time in lecture yesterday," she prompts.

There it is. The bomb I knew was coming. Her eyes are wide, as if hungry for me to have another outburst. A watchlizard skitters up the wall behind her, its bulbous lens head stretching out and peering around the room.

I panic, my mind racing with memories of Evie and flashes of LQM files and Quinn, and a surge of relief swells in anticipation of unloading it all.

Then my digipad beeps, and everything lurches to a halt.

Quinn invited you to a meeting at 11:30am.
Accept / Decline

A wave of excitement pulls me back to myself. Did Quinn find something? My mind rushes with the possibilities, and the pressure leaves my chest. I hastily accept without bothering to check my calendar for other appointments.

Joyce raps her knuckles sharply on the desk. "Your alerts should be silenced during appointments, Gracelyn. You know that."

What am I doing? I know better than this. I'm getting sloppy again, letting my emotions get in the way of my thinking.

"I'm sorry. I forgot." I hold the small button on the side to put my digipad into quiet mode.

I forgot. I never forget, not anything. And I have already said too much. I have been so consumed, and the weight of it all is clouding my thinking. I have to be more careful. Much more.

Joyce smiles. "Mistakes happen when emotions set in. That is why we are here. You were about to tell me more."

Her hands resettle on the table.

I let out a slow breath to calm myself and rest my hands in my lap. It's not too late to regain control.

"Actually, no, I don't think so," I reply. "It feels *so good* to tell all this to someone – someone I can *trust* – but I don't have anything more to say."

I smile what I hope is a sweet, sad, relieved smile, and press my lips together tight.

Joyce smiles back at me, and for a pause, the mellow, meditative sounds of the room build between us.

She breaks the wall first.

"Very well then. I am prescribing Amizol, to be taken with breakfast daily. This is a common aid for post-departure treatment to reduce inflated emotive responses. You will start seeing them dispensed with your food tomorrow, and these feelings should begin to dissolve within a few days."

She smiles again, like she is giving me a gift.

I know these pills. Mother's manic eyes widen at me inside my mind.

"We will have a follow-up in two weeks to see how that is doing for you."

Relief mingles with dread. I've managed to get myself out of trouble for now, but it's not over yet. Now I have to figure out a way to get rid of these pills, and how to act like they are working. If I don't start complying, or at least appear to, I will not be so lucky next time. Then who knows what will happen – maybe next time they will lock me in that tiny room for good.

And then I'll never find Evie.

Chapter Thirty-One

Evie

It's raining again. A cold rain that bites my skin with each drop and send shivers down my back with each roll of thunder. Even so, I can't make myself go inside.

I stand outside the Med cabin, staring at the doorknob, not ready to go in, but unwilling to let myself retreat. My pulse rises, and I catch myself wishing I could check my heart rate on my digipad. At least I've stopped trying to check my wrist from habit by now.

I don't understand what, exactly, I'm afraid of. Sue's tough, but she's hardly scary. And as for the tests themselves...well, she's right. And so are Kinlee and Connor. Knowing what's wrong with me can only help. This should be the opposite of scary. I should be afraid of *not* knowing.

Trying to rationalize with myself isn't helping, so I take a breath and force myself into the cabin before I can think myself out of it completely. I burst through the door, creating an instant puddle around me as my clothes drip onto the wooden panels.

"I'm ready now," I announce.

A chair scrapes on the floor as Sue turns and stares at me. She and Noah are hovering over the back desk – probably planning out tomorrow's schedule.

Sue lifts an eyebrow.

"To do your departure tests," I say, fumbling over the words to explain myself. "To find out what's wrong with me. I'll do it. I'm ready."

She and Noah exchange a look, and Sue comes to me at the front.

"Have a seat, Evie."

We both sit, facing each other, the desk between us.

"If you're ready, that's great. But I know you're used to being told what to do, and that's not how it is out here. I regret how forceful I was with you when we talked about this before. That wasn't fair to you. But going through these tests is going to take time. It's a commitment. What you learn could have major consequences for how you live and what comes next for you. If we're going to do this, you need to be sure it's what *you* want. Not what you think you have to do. Or what you think anyone else wants you to do." She pauses and gives me a pointed look. "I heard about the other night at dinner. Kinlee can be pushy, but that doesn't mean you should do what she says."

"Thank you." Sue is always looking out, always five steps ahead, always sharp. No one has ever looked out for me before – not like this, separating what they think I should do and what I want for myself. "But I do. I want this. I wasn't ready yet when you brought it up before. But I'm ready now. Or at least, I want to be ready. I don't know if I'll ever really be ready. But I'm done with going through life without questioning. I want to understand. I want to fight back."

Sue studies me for a moment. Then she smiles.

"Okay then. I'm proud of you. For whatever that's worth."

I'm surprised to find I actually think it's worth quite a lot.

Then, Sue is straight down to business, pulling out her clipboard.

"This would have been a little simpler to do while you were working here, but we'll make do. You're on farm duty, right?"

"Actually, I'm about to start in Intel & Recon."

"Oho, hot shot," she says. "Well, we'll have to squeeze this in between your shifts." She flips to her appointment log. "Come by around... three tomorrow. That works?"

I nod.

She scribbles on her pad.

"After that I'll need you here three or four more times. We got a lot of tests to run. Diagnosing a problem without symptoms is complicated, especially when it might be something no one but the Directorate considers a problem. We'll start with the tests we'll have to send out to a real lab, to get those going, and then move on to the stuff we can diagnose here. It's going to be a long few weeks. But, then we'll know a lot more."

"Thank you." It's all I can say.

Major things have shifted inside me these last few weeks. I've struggled with more things, been more uncomfortable, more scared, more uncertain, than the Directorate would ever have allowed me to feel in a lifetime. And happier, too.

And I'm better for it. These new challenges are stretching me in new directions, and I can feel myself reaching out to meet them like branches growing out from a tree.

Before, change was always scary, something to avoid. It was always bad. But now? I don't know. I think I might even kind of like it. Finding out what's wrong with me still scares me, but it also feels like a challenge. One I'm ready to face, finally.

I step back out into the rain, and this time, it actually feels good. Like the fear is dissolving and washing away.

Chapter Thirty-Two

Evie

When I get to the bunker for my new work assignment in Intel & Recon, Raina insists on pairing me with Kinlee. Kinlee hasn't talked to me since our shouting match at dinner last week.

I wanted to make up with her, but she's been impossible to catch up with, even in the cabin. I know the entire camp is doubling their efforts since Tad went missing – in Intel & Recon it might be *tripling* – but every day that passes that I don't see her, the more it feels like she's avoiding me.

I miss her. I know I've only known her about a month, but she's the best friend I've ever had, and fighting with her has my stomach in constant knots.

The only thing worse, it turns out, is forcing her to be around me when she so obviously doesn't want to be. Raina made her give me a tour of the bunker. But all I've seen so far is the back of her messy hair and the hallway.

"That's classified," she says, pointing to a closed door as we pass. "*That's* classified," she says, pointing to the next door. Kinlee's usual energy is restrained, and she skulks through the hall with her shoulders hunched. She won't look me in the eye.

If this is what my next few weeks working in Intel is like, I'd have had a better chance of finding a way to reach Gracelyn by joining the detonation crews on the Directorate's border. And without Kinlee to talk to, I'm missing Gracelyn more than ever right now.

"*That's* classified – "

"I get it. Spy stuff: classified. Kin, stop."

She turns around and faces me, staring down at my shoes.

"Kinlee," I plead. "Come on."

She folds her arms and looks at me. Her glare could turn a person to stone, but I'll take it.

I try to gather up something to say. Neither of us is exactly a glowing model of emotional intelligence, but one of us has to get this started. I swallow my nerves and give it a shot.

"You've got to understand, in the Quads, we hardly even *say* the word departure. Not even when we're preparing for one. It freaks people out. Including me."

Her gaze starts to drift away towards the wall. Not working...

"But that's not the point. The point is, you're right, okay? It's stupid not to diagnose my departure. I went to Sue. I start testing today."

She shifts her weight and cocks her head to the side. "Really?"

"Yeah."

The tension in her shoulders starts to ease.

I push it another step. "And... maybe you're sorry you exploded all over me instead of just talking to me?"

For a pause she stares at me, a crease forming in her forehead. The knots in my stomach double – ugh, I'm terrible at this. Maybe this was a mistake. Maybe I made it worse.

But then the edge of her mouth curls up in a smile.

"Yeah. Maybe I am." She shifts again, her arms relaxing. "I didn't mean for it to come out like that. I've just been so exhausted lately from all these shifts. I guess I freaked out a little."

A laugh escapes me. "A little?" She does look tired, even more than before. Her eyes are rimmed with dark circles, and her hair is even messier than normal – not just tousled, but unkempt.

"Well..." She shrugs.

"Do me and the entire world a favor. Never freak out a *lot*."

She shoves me, but she's grinning, and the light is back in her eyes. A weight dissolves from my shoulders – I have Kinlee back.

"Hey," she says, brightening. "You wanna see something cool?"

"Depends. Is it classified?"

She sighs, ignoring my jab. "Over here."

Then she turns around with a jump and leads me across the bunker's main open room, stopping in front of an elaborate machine.

"What is that?" I ask.

"It's an inking computer. You just enter in the image or letters you want, and it'll tattoo it onto your skin. It's what we use to falsify departure dates to agents going undercover in the Directorate.

"Whoa." I hadn't thought about it before. But of course they'd need to add departure dates before going in.

"This one affixes digipads," Kinlee says, moving on to the next table.

I look up, and I can hardly believe what I see. Past the machine, past Kinlee, amid the wall of screens in a darkened room behind them, is the view of a park. But it isn't just any park; it's *my* Quad's park, right down to the particular twists of the tree branches. I would know, I traced sketches of them on my syncscreen dozens and dozens of times.

I drift into the surveillance room. Each screen projects a different feed. And they're all familiar. *My* neighborhood, *my* school, *my* city center.

"It's my Quad," I say.

Something in my chest pinches.

"Oh – yeah," Kinlee says. "With the Tad situation playing out right now, most of the feeds are on Quad 34."

I stare up at the wall, my heart pounding. From inside the boxes of the screens, the Quad looks so small and far away. Is Gracelyn really in there? I step closer, squinting, as if she might pass on the screen. But the odds of that are too small to count. I shake my head and step away.

"Sorry – what else you were you going to show me?"

Kinlee shrugs. "Not much. Most of it really is classified. If you stick around and pass your training tests, they'll pull you in for more of it. I'd show you the tunnels, but you've already seen them."

She gestures to the corner, and I notice a large metal panel embedded into the floor.

"That's not – " I look closer. "That's how you got me here?"

Kinlee nods.

I turn back to the screens. "I didn't notice all this before."

"There was a lot going on."

"Right."

But it's more than that. Everything about the bunker looks different. Not as big, not as scary, as I remember from that night. I do a slow turn, taking it all in again, and landing on the hatch to the tunnels.

Suddenly, Gracelyn doesn't feel so far away anymore. In fact, she feels so close I could almost reach out and take her hand. With so much of the bunker off limits and everyone on high alert searching for Tad, it might be harder than I thought to get to her. But I'll find a way.

Chapter Thirty-Three

Evie

"Crap, I gotta go."

Kinlee and I spent the morning lost in the screens of security footage. The hours passed away in a zap.

Kinlee's been balancing her chair on its hind legs, and drops back to the ground.

"Right. Testing time. Hope you studied."

I laugh a little too hard at her terrible joke, releasing a ball of nerves gathering in my stomach.

"I wish it were that easy."

Since I talked to Sue, I've tried to avoid thinking about it. But now, my heart is beating a little harder.

In, two, three, four, five. I start my old breathing trick out of habit.

"It'll be fine. Wait and see. It's going to be a case of freckles or something."

I raise an eyebrow. "Freckles?"

She nods. "Can't have our perfect Directorate citizens' skin blemished, now can we?"

But what if it's something real? Something awful?

I muster a smile. "You're right. It's probably something dumb."

Maybe she can see the fear in my eyes, because suddenly she gets serious.

"And hey, Ev, this is good. This is brave."

"Right."

The walk to the Med cabin has never felt longer. When I get there, I stare at the door for a moment. Then I take a breath and go in.

Immediately, I feel like I'm intruding. The room is dark, the curtains pulled shut. Large equipment intrudes on much of the usually open space, and it's quiet except for a persistent mechanical beep.

As my eyes adjust, I realize that behind the wall of equipment, Rosie is in the patient bed at the back of the room. Why would they move her?

The door clicks shut behind me, and a figure rustles under the covers in response to the sound. It's Sue. She twists towards me, her face groggy.

"Sue?" A well of guilt and awkwardness rises over me. "I can come back later."

"Evie?" Sue jolts up and practically falls out of the bed. She looks at her watch. "Oh!"

She jumps to her feet and turns away, wiping at her face.

Since when was Sue out of sorts? Or off schedule? Behind her, Rosie's eyes are closed and her face is ghastly pale. She looks so tired. Fragile. Suddenly, my chest tightens with a panic I cannot explain.

"I can come back another time – " I start to close the door.

"No! Come in. In fact, you're late."

There she is. Sue's now back to her stern, commanding self, and it's dumb, but it makes me feel better. She opens the curtains at the front of the cabin, and the light helps disperse the mood.

"You're not getting away that easy. Sit."

She points to a chair by the desk and flips through her clipboard. I sit.

"We're going to have to cover everything from the most serious medical conditions, to cognitive and psychological conditions, to things the rest of the world would consider minor. There was one case where the worst thing we could find was a low IQ – at least, low by Directorate standards. Her departure date was unusually young, too. It's possible the Directorate's technology picked up something we couldn't, but if you ask me, they're screening for more than just health issues."

While Sue talks, she checks my blood pressure.

"What's that mean?" I ask.

Sue pauses to place the stethoscope on my chest and listen to my heart. It must be pounding.

"It means the Directorate may be using departure dates for more than avoiding suffering. To create a certain type of population. That there might be nothing wrong with you at all. In fact, if we do all our tests and don't find anything serious, we'll be one step closer to proving my theory."

There might not be *anything* wrong with me? I might just not be good enough for the Directorate? My fists clench as the anger kicks up within me. Knowing what this testing could mean, my resolve to see it through doubles in size.

Then we get started. We do a full body MRI scan and a series of ultrasounds, and then Sue sits me down while she takes vial after vial of blood. I ask questions about every step, and she answers them all.

"It's nice watching someone else get poked and prodded for once." Rosie's up. Her cheeks are pale and layered with a film of sweat. "She's going to tell you it's for your own good. Don't believe her. I haven't seen it help yet."

I know she's joking, but it's also the darkest I've heard her talk. I look at her closer. She seems thinner, but she was already so underweight it's hard to tell.

I try to play along. "All she's done so far is steal a bunch of my blood. Who knows what she's doing with it. Twisted."

Rosie starts to laugh, but it turns into a cough.

"That's enough," Sue says, making notes on her charts. "Both of you."

When we're done, I'm eager to get back into the sunshine and do some sketching before dinner. But Sue insists on parking me next to Rosie with juice and a cookie first.

"Fifteen minutes," she orders.

"I'm fine. You don't need to baby me." But I settle in and take a bite of the cookie. Chocolate chip. Not bad, as far as prescriptions go.

"We took a lot of blood. Take it easy a little longer."

"So bossy." Rosie rolls her eyes.

Sue reaches over and gently squeezes her arm. "You could

stand a little more rest too."

"Rest is all I do anymore." This time Rosie's tone has an edge to it.

A stiff silence falls over the room. Sue takes in a breath like she's about to say more, but the door flies open and Kinlee bursts in.

"Ev!" She skids across the floor. "All hands on deck. They know where Tad is."

Chapter Thirty-Four

Evie

I burst from my chair, cookie in hand, and race out of the door after Kinlee. Sue's protests are like background noise in the clamor of my mind.

They found him. It's all going to be okay now.

I chase Kinlee all the way back to the bunker and practically fly down the ladder.

Then we look around – only a few others are there, waiting in the main room. They look over to us as we join them.

"Welcome to the party," one of them says. "You're the first ones here."

"What do you mean?" Kinlee says, panting. "Everyone was rounding up when I left."

"Yeah. And everyone is either rounded, or rounding," the woman replies. "Leadership closed themselves into the strategy room as soon as they were done with Liz's debrief. Everyone else isn't here yet."

Kinlee frowns.

We hover around the main room, shifting our weight and pacing, arms folded in tight. The team grows as more agents join us. An hour passes.

"What could possibly take so long before they can even brief us?" Kinlee exclaims, kicking the wall.

No one answers. No one knows anything more than we do.

Finally the door opens. Raina comes out, along with the rest of the Intel & Recon leadership. They look somber and tired.

"We have news," Raina says. "Unfortunately I can share

very little with you right now. But yes, we have information regarding the whereabouts of Tad Martin."

A rise of chatter swells in response to this information.

"That's all I can say for now, even here." Raina continues, "This information is highly sensitive – and, in the wrong hands, dangerous. There are a number of questions still, and we don't want false information or speculation driving decisions, here or among the governments we work with."

The team grumbles. Next to me, Kinlee huffs.

"*But,*" Raina continues, raising her voice over them. "There is a great deal of work to do. I hope you've been getting your rest when you're off shift, because you won't be getting much now. We're ratcheting this up to full force, round the clock. Starting immediately. I've got assignments for now until night shift, at which time I will have assignments for the rest of the week."

Then Raina flips open her clip board and starts reading off names and stations. Kinlee and I are assigned to the security feeds. Again. After a while, monitoring the feeds gets boring, even with today's news. Meanwhile, outside the security room, the bunker is crowded and buzzing with activity.

I let out a huff. "Are they ever going to let us do real work?"

"This is real work," Kinlee says.

"You know what I mean. They're all doing something big out there," I say, gesturing to the other agents. "We're basically being babysat in here. I want to *help.*"

And all this security duty isn't helping me get any closer to Gracelyn. I already know what the Quad looks like. I need a way to *get* to her.

Kinlee shrugs. "You can't expect to catch up in a couple weeks. If you stick around, you'll do training and security clearances, and then you'll get to do more. And there's all sorts of advanced training you can do, too, depending on what specialization you want."

"Specialization? Like what?" I ask.

"Analysis. New tech. Undercover. Lots of things."

"Do you have one?"

Kinlee's face lights up. "Hey! You want action? I got an idea."

That's more like it. "What?"

"Not yet. You'll see. Whenever we're let off shift."

I sigh, and kill the time staring aimlessly around the room. I take in the monitors, the ceiling, the walls, the giant map of the tunnels at the far end of the room.

The tunnels.

Surely if they got me out through the tunnels, I can use them to get back in. I pick up my sketch pad, always with me, and flip to a fresh page. While Kinlee and I and three other agents keep an eye on the feeds, I keep my hands busy, starting a copy of the giant map on the wall.

Finally, something real to do.

My heart pounds. This could actually, really work. With each line I add to the sketch, Gracelyn feels a little bit closer.

I'm coming, Gracelyn. We're getting you out of there.

Chapter Thirty-Five

Evie

Hours later, when Raina finally sets us free, it's dark outside. My neck is stiff from twisting it towards the wall of screens for so long, and my fingers cramp from all the sketching. My eyes glazed over hours ago, and my body aches for rest. Even the brisk night air is not enough to shock the drowsiness from me.

"Perfect," Kinlee says, looking up to the stars. "Come on."

I squint at her moonlit figure. Is there something bulky under her jacket? I don't get a good enough look before she starts off deeper into the woods, away from the camp. And the beds.

"We only have six hours until we're back in there," I call after her. "Don't you want to sleep?"

Just the idea of what tomorrow will bring is enough to make my muscles ache with exhaustion and yearn to crash into my bunk.

"Absolutely not," she calls back. "And you won't either, when we get there."

That seems highly unlikely.

"But – " I start. Kinlee keeps marching into the dark. She's fading into it quickly. "Where are we *going*? Kin?"

"Come on," she calls. "I got something for you, and it isn't light."

I sigh, accept tomorrow's exhaustion, and chase after her. For once, I'm far too curious to worry about anything else.

Finally, Kinlee stops walking.

"You need to get rid of it," she declares, dropping to the

ground and untangling the bulk from her jacket.

"Get rid of *what*?" I plop next to her, trying to catch up to her train of thought.

She shoves the item to the ground and pushes it forward for me to see. I have to squint a moment in the darkness before the bulk takes shape.

"The inking machine?"

"For your arm," Kinlee says. "You gotta get rid of that stupid departure date."

"What?" It never occurred to me to do anything about it. It's been on my arm my whole life – it's defined my life. It's a part of me almost as much as my eye color or my freckles.

"You beat them, Ev. Those numbers are meaningless. Get rid of them."

"But... how?"

"Just cover it up with something else. Something happy."

"Ummm..." Still digesting the first part of this crazy idea, my mind goes blank.

"Come on, anything is better than a stupid reminder of your not-death. What do you like? An animal or a flower or a symbol?"

A flower? My hand traces to the chain on my throat, then to the charm on it.

"A rose."

"Perfect! The numbers can be a stem. Can you draw one to scan into the machine?"

"Actually, I think I can." I pull out my pad and frown at it considering. Soon my fingers are at work, and the rose starts to take shape. It's a simple design, just smooth clean lines, and I take extra care with the thorns – a reminder that everything beautiful also holds potential for pain. Then, I fill in the stem so it's dark, so it will stamp out my departure date completely. I wasn't sure about this, but as I finalize the drawing, my heart swells with warmth.

Kinlee loads up the design and aligns the projection with my arm.

"Wait!" I was so caught up in the sketch, I'm only now thinking about what I've signed on for. "Is this going to hurt?"

"Some," Kinlee says. Then she presses the start button and grabs onto my arm, stopping my cringe. "Deep breaths."

I gasp as the precision laser hits my forearm, but after the first cut, the shock subsides. It burns along my skin, but I accept it as the price for my change and watch the machine do its work. It's beautiful.

"Wow." The black lines are elegant and clean twisting down my forearm. It still stings, but somehow it doesn't bother me – a reminder of the control I'm taking for my own life. That the Directorate doesn't get to define me anymore. *I* do.

Kinlee was right. This is so much better than staring at those numbers for the rest of my life.

Kinlee pulls a roll of thin plastic from her bag and wraps it around my forearm, then tapes it down. "Leave it alone for a while," she says.

"But wait, we came all the way out here just for this?" I ask. We could have done this anywhere.

"Oh no, that's not the part we're out here for," Kinlee says.

The grin that spreads over her face is even more mischievous than normal. Then she looks up towards the trees.

Somehow, Kinlee has talked me into climbing a ladder up a very, very large tree, despite my still-stinging wrist. Even though she has strapped us into harnesses to protect us from falling, my heart pounds and my hands shake. When we reach the top platform, Kinlee stands up and points out over the branches.

"Check it out," she says.

From up here, the view grazes the tree line, allowing us to peek over it. Farther out past the forest, there's a broad concrete wall, and past the wall stretches a cluster of white domes.

"What is that?" I exclaim. But then I realize with a twist to my stomach, there's only one thing it could be. "Crap, it's the Directorate."

The Quad felt so big when I was inside it. But from out here, the Quads look tiny and crowded. And close. Too close for something that wants me dead. But even so, the feeling that I finally land on is comfort – Gracelyn's in there. Maybe she won't be so hard to get to after all.

"Thought you'd enjoy getting out of surveillance and staring at them from a different angle, for once," Kinlee says.

"The Directorate never showed us the Quads from the outside. It's so ugly and crammed."

"Yeah. Giant jail cells."

"And that's the wall the soldiers have been trying to break?"

Sue said there's been three more major injuries from the bombs since I left Med. She said it's happening more and more. As if someone has started watching.

Kinlee nods. "Doesn't look like much from here, but up close, it's huge. And it's got about any kind of tech weaponry on it you could imagine. Another soldier almost got killed today. Sue and Noah are miracle workers. But she won't ever walk again."

The mood turns abruptly somber, and for a pause, just we stare at the wall.

Then Kinlee snaps us out of it. "Okay, enough of that. We can go now."

I turn back towards the ladder.

"Oh no. We're taking the other way down," Kinlee says. She clips a new line to my harness and unclips me from the line that protected me up the ladder.

"The other way?" A quiver of fear runs over me from my toes to the top of my head.

Kinlee stands back. "Turn around, sit, and push off."

I turn where she points and squint into the darkness. The wire she attached me to disappears off into the trees.

"I'm sorry, you want me to *what*?"

"Let go and enjoy the ride," Kinlee says.

"Are you out of your mind?" It would actually explain a lot about Kinlee. "I already used up my stupid decision for the night on the tattoo."

"You wanted to know about training. You wanted to know about how I never seem afraid. It's stuff like this. It's not never being afraid, Ev. It's doing it anyway. You get used to that, and the fear isn't so big a deal anymore. You got rid of your departure number – you're not from the Directorate anymore. You're one of us. You don't have to be afraid. But it starts with *letting go*."

"It *ends* with letting go, I think you mean," I reply. "With this wire snapping and me dropping to the ground."

I cling to the tree's branch for support, my legs shaking so powerfully the leaves at the end of it tremble.

"That's never happened before."

"That doesn't mean it won't!"

"Eh. Sure it does. Close enough. What if I promise you? I swear this zip line will not kill you. You're harnessed in nice and secure, see?" She tugs on the clip connecting me to the wire. "It's fun, promise. There's nothing like it."

"No way."

"Okay then. Don't scream." And with that, Kinlee pushes me out, away from the relative safety of the tree.

I couldn't scream if I wanted to. My throat closes, and all I get out is a catching gasp as the descent begins. But then the panic passes, and I'm still here, flying through the night. Trees whoosh past me in a blur. Crisp wind blows around my head. The zip line hums and quivers, but it holds.

So this is what freedom feels like. I let out a joyful whoop before remembering Kinlee's warning and cutting it short. Stretch out my arms, no longer afraid, and let the brisk *whoosh* of the wind wash over me.

Just when I feel I could fly like this forever, I start to slow and the line lowers me to the ground. I unclip my harness from the line, my fingers shaky with adrenaline.

Seconds later, Kinlee soars down behind me, her cheeks glowing and rosy.

"Let's go again." I say it before she is even unhooked, revved up and ready.

"Another time," she says. "We should get back before we're caught."

Chapter Thirty-Six

Evie

Turns out we're too late for the not getting caught part.

As we approach our cabin, Raina is pacing outside the door. The adrenaline throbbing through me from our fun tangles up into a knot and weighs in the pit of my stomach.

When she sees us, she runs towards us and gives us each a big hug. "Thank goodness you're safe," she says.

"Geez, Mom. Overreact much?" Kinlee says.

But her tone sets Raina off. She pulls away with a frown on her face, her hands on her hips. "How could you break camp rules at a time like this?" she snaps.

"It's not like we left camp or anything," Kinlee says. "Who ratted on us?"

"No one 'ratted,' though I don't know how you could justify putting your colleagues in that position," Raina says. "I came looking for you. We needed your specialty."

My shoulders slump under the weight of remorse.

But Kinlee lights up. "Really! What can I do?"

Raina raises her eyebrows. "You think I'd trust an agent acting so reckless? I found someone else."

A scowl slowly takes shape over Kinlee's face. "But I need those training hours to make full agent."

"Not as badly as you needed to trespass on training grounds with an uncleared civilian, apparently," Raina snaps. "Go to bed."

I've seen Raina tense before, but I've never seen her so angry, so afraid. Guilt washes over me, chased by something even darker – a terrible feeling that the camp is in much worse trouble than we realized.

Raina turns away and heads back in the direction of the bunker. We stare after her, still shell-shocked.

"Well, I guess we should get some sleep," I say.

But when I look over to Kinlee, her face is red and blotchy, and tears are already escaping her eyes.

"Kin?"

But it's too late. Her eyes brim over.

"Let's get you inside." I get her as far as the bed, but instead of getting into it, she slumps to the ground and curls into a ball.

I plop down next to her and lean against the bedpost.

"It's gonna be okay, Kin."

"I know, I just…" Her shoulders shake with the sobs. "It's not just that. It doesn't *stop*, it keeps getting worse. I'm so angry. And so *tired*," she sniffles. She leans into me. "I've never seen her yell, not like that," she says.

"Yeah. She's been pretty on edge lately. I don't think it's just us. I think she's exhausted, too."

I realize as I say it just how little the word has meant to me until now. The Directorate never let us get even close to exhausted.

I rub my hand up and down Kinlee's back, the way Mother used to do when I was little, and got upset about my departure. I look down at the rose, now raw on my forearm under the plastic wrap. I've come so far from that rigid, insulated life.

But seeing Kinlee's pain right now, after weeks in flux and unpredictable shifts, maybe a *little* order can be a good thing.

Suddenly, I miss the clean, clockwork predictability of it all. I couldn't ever trade back the freedom or understanding I've gained, but it was all so simple and easy back then. I don't think anything is ever going to be that easy ever again.

That's when I remember Kinlee grew up right here in the camp. Has life always been this chaotic for her? That would have to catch up with her on occasions.

"I get it, Kin. I do."

It's kind of comforting to see Kinlee is as human as the rest of us, after all. At least every once in a while.

"I want to be a full agent so bad. And I'm so close," she says, banging a fist into the floor. "I passed all the skills tests. I have all my security clearances. I just need to get my hours in. I can't believe she's not giving me those hours. They *need* more agents, especially now."

I don't know what to say. She's right, they need as many people working on this as they can get.

"My dad was an undercover agent, did you know that?" she says, holding back sniffles.

"I didn't." She and Raina are both so independent and fearless, I never thought about where her father might be.

"He was on to something really big. Something related to departure dates. And then one time he didn't check in, and we never heard from him again."

"Wow." I don't know what to say. I keep rubbing her back.

"They don't even think it was the Directorate. Just a random Licentia attack."

"I'm so sorry." I think of Connor, and how his father died. This is just as heartbreaking. Is everyone here connected to this kind of awful death?

"At least he got to make a real mark on the world before he went – they're still working with the information he uncovered in Intel. That's all I want. To leave a mark. And if I can, finish what he started."

"You'll get there," I soothe. "The occasional chance to rest isn't going to kill you. Hell, it's good for you. We can't have our Intel team going around losing it all over the place. Dead giveaway, in the Directorate."

She chuckles through her tears. "Right."

We never turned the lights on, and in the quiet of the dark room, drowsiness sets in.

"Kinlee?" I ask.

"Mmm?" she responds.

"Thanks. For the tattoo and the zip line. Tonight was incredible."

"You bet your ass it was," she says.

Chapter Thirty-Seven

Gracelyn

Things have settled back to normal since my breakdown in the lecture hall. There were a few days of whispers and side-glances from the others, but eventually it all settled down into the usual routines, thankfully. Even Father stopped giving me that stern glare, after he eyed the little pill that started dispensing with my tray each morning. He even gave me a little approving nod.

I seem to be doing a sufficient job of acting like I am taking them, too. If only I could find a better place to hide them than my dresser drawer. It is only a matter of time before a watchlizard finds them.

"Gracelyn." Quinn's stern tone breaks my concentration. We're learning about matching couples this week, and I am surprised at how complex it is. "Come with me, please. We can still do better on some of these pairings you submitted."

Hanna sits straighter in her chair, but her head doesn't turn from her syncscreen.

"Right away." I log out of my station and follow Quinn back to her office.

As she closes the door, her demeanor transforms, and she blurts out her ulterior motive: "You wanted to meet my friends? It's happening tonight."

"Tonight?" Where could we possibly meet on a weeknight? "But what about curfew?"

Between fitness hour, dinner, commutes and curfew, time on weeknights is filled.

Quinn's hand goes straight from the door to my waist.

"Midnight. A place near the park." She kisses my neck.

"What, you afraid?"

I push away. "To break curfew? Absolutely I'm afraid."

Anything off-schedule raises a flag with the Directorate, but being out after curfew has to be one of the most suspect. The worst is always assumed.

She smiles. "I thought you wanted to be involved? This is a little out of the ordinary, but – "

"It's against the law." My cheeks grow hot.

She cocks an eyebrow at me. "Honey, what part of what we've done so far do you think *isn't* against the law?"

I cross my arms over my chest. She right, but this feels different. More dangerous.

"We're careful." She shrugs. "No one's been caught before – the Directorate really isn't as good at security as you'd think. Don't you want to find your sister?"

I want to do anything that could help Evie. But this? Even talking about it is enough to send needling pricks of anxiety down my neck.

"It's dangerous." I fight to match Quinn's casual tone, and not resort to hushed whispers.

"More dangerous than having public outbursts in the middle of lectures? You need an outlet for all this rage you've pent up," she says, stroking a finger down my arm. "Besides, it's not as bad as the Directorate wants you to believe. You'll see."

I narrow my eyes. "Mhm."

"I'd never ask you to do anything I thought would get you into trouble. Don't you trust me?" she urges. "I thought you'd do anything to find your sister?" She reaches around me again, and it's impossible to resist her embrace.

My heart tugs. She grins. She knows she has me.

I return to my desk and try to keep calm. But the rest of the day, I fluctuate between spasms of nerves and sweaty palms, between fits of terror and anticipation, as I digest the idea of breaking this big Directorate rule right under their noses. The day takes entirely too long to pass. By nighttime, I can hardly keep still.

Waiting in my room for Quinn to meet me, I am so nervous my breaths catch in my throat, and though I am sure Mother and Father have been asleep for hours, I force myself to place my feet down slowly with each step so the floor doesn't creak.

I can't believe I am doing this. But Evie would do it for me, no question about it. I have to find a way to be as brave as she would be. I owe her that much.

Finally Quinn appears in my window, perched on a branch of the tree that spreads between my room and Evie's. When she pushes it open, my pulse rises in my ears like a drum, bracing to be caught. But nothing happens.

"No alarm?" I can't believe that we are not immediately surrounded by guards.

"This disables it." Quinn says, smoothing out a metallic tape-like device she lined over the window's catch. "I told you, I know what I'm doing. Come on out."

She makes room for me on the branch. The night air brushes over my face. I take a deep breath, crawl over the window ledge legs first, and peer out.

"We're so high up," I gasp.

"Don't look," Quinn urges. "Don't think. Just slide onto the branch."

Don't think? Thoughts flood me like an attack, suggesting a hundred different ways this could go wrong – a broken ankle, a dislocated shoulder, even a scrape on my knee, and I am not only done for the night, but I have an injury that I cannot explain that would require medical attention. My knuckles turn white clinging against the sides of the window frame.

"Gracelyn, there's no time."

I can't panic. Not in front of Quinn, of all people. Not when Evie needs me. If Quinn says this is the best way to help, then this is what I have to do. I bite on my lip and try to follow Quinn's advice. I force my focus to the branch, and my skirt swooshes around me as I slide slowly onto it.

"Perfect," Quinn coaxes. "Now we just gotta get to the ground."

She swings down from the branch and steps to the next one down, then the next. I do my best to copy her, slowly lowering myself one shaky step at a time. When I drop from the final branch and fall to the ground, I have to clench my hands into fists to hide their shaking, and I hope Quinn does not hear my heaving, panicked breaths.

"Not bad, newbie," she says. As I brush myself off, she looks me over and chuckles. "What are you wearing? I told you to wear black so you'd he harder to see in the dark, not as a style tip."

I look her over, too, and realize her head-to-toe black is utilitarian. Heat flushes my face, and I am grateful for the night's cover – I am in a black dress from my events wardrobe.

"It's our first time out. I... wanted to look nice."

"Well you do," she says, pulling me in for a kiss. "But next time, fitness clothes. Now let's move."

Next time? Oh no, no, no, surely she doesn't expect me to do this more than once.

A sharp *click* breaks the night silence, followed by a sudden, prolonged *hiss*.

I gasp and drop to the ground, my skin prickling with anticipation and panic.

Quinn stands over me. "Well, we know your reflexes work. But calm down, it's just the night mist."

The night mist? I push myself up and look around. A vapor of moisture is rising from sprinklers all over the backyard. I take a shaky breath and chide myself for being so jumpy. Everyone knows the Quad is watered each night for climate control. I have just never seen it before.

"Let's go," Quinn urges.

"Wait," I say, struggling to will myself forward. "What about security? And the watchlizards?"

"I told you. I handled it. Security is easy. And for the watchlizards..." She lifts a small square device affixed to her hip. "This sends out a signal. Makes them redirect their commands to stay away. Okay? Now, come on."

It turns out Quinn was right. The Quad is monitored through the night, but the patterns the surveillance cars and cameras follow are predictable, like everything else in the Quads, and Quinn navigates us through them with ease.

My heart pounds and my breaths come quick, despite our slow, careful movements. I wonder what my heart rate monitor on my digipad reads right now – it must be a record high. I can feel my body straining and my stress levels rising. This is exactly what the Directorate doesn't want us to feel, and I am starting to understand why.

When we make it to the park, Quinn dives into a cluster of large bushes and disappears. In a rush of panic, I throw myself in after her and ram right into her back. Despite the bushes' full appearance, the middle is hollowed out. It is fairly spacious too – enough for five of us to all be crammed in together.

Three more people – a flare of panic creeps down my back. That's three more people who know I'm breaking the rules. Three more people who can get us caught. They turn to eye me as I squeeze in – maybe they're thinking the same thing about me. They are all in black, and their faces are covered – one of them wears a knit cap that pulls all the way over his face with only holes for eyes. Another peeks out with bright blue eyes from a scarf tied over her face and short pushed-back blonde hair. The third has a dark cap pulled low over his head, like Quinn, and a thick beard. This is not what I expected when Quinn said we were meeting friends.

"How could you, Q? We all agreed. No one new." The voice is muffled behind the man's knit mask.

"Relax, C. She can be trusted," Quinn says. Something prideful blossoms in my core at her confidence in me. "*G* has been helping. This is the one I told you about. The one whose sister was taken."

The others, previously busy settling in and keeping an eye out for surveillance through the branches, freeze and stare at me. They look at my done-up hair – now damp and mussed from the mist – and my nice dress, and I can feel their judgment scrawling over me.

"You really think she's Licentia material? She doesn't look like she can handle it."

"Licentia?" I exclaim. "But they're not – "

"Shhh!" they urge. Quinn elbows me. I huff.

Real. The Licentia aren't real.

Or at least, that is what the Directorate has always told us.

209

But here they are. Right in front of me. In the middle of the dark night, after curfew.

And so am I.

As far as anyone else could tell, I am practically one of them already.

All the stories I have been told about Licentia start coming back to me. Bloody stories. Violent stories. Stories so awful it was easy to believe they could not be real.

I look around at each of them, now eyeing me suspiciously, and I realize I have further proved that I do not belong here. But my embarrassment is no match for my alarm.

"Quinn, Licentia? You... you're all... *murderers.*"

C scoffs.

"No," Quinn stretches out her arms to halt them. "I promise, she's cool. She doesn't understand yet; she only knows what the Directorate tells her."

"Shit, Q," he says. "Get this under control."

Then she whispers to me.

"Yes, we're real. But we're not murderers. We just don't agree with how the Directorate controls our lives. We're fighting for change. The rest is more Directorate lies. Have there been times when things didn't go right? Yes. But we're not what they want you to believe we are. You've seen how much they lie to us, how much they keep from us. Don't let them control you. Give us a chance."

I don't know what to say. I cannot believe I have let this person I have hardly known a few weeks drag me out after curfew, and get me tangled up in all this. What now? If I leave, I am not even sure I could find my way back on my own, let alone get safely through all the night patrols. I tug at the hem of my dress.

Quinn continues. "I know this isn't what you expected. I'm sorry. I didn't know how to... I couldn't bear to keep hiding this part of me from you. And they really can help find out what happened to your sister."

Can they? My hands are fidgeting in my lap to combat my nerves. Quinn's bright gray eyes are dilated, her brows folded in pleading earnestness.

210

I cannot believe she has been hiding this secret from me. I cannot believe she brought me here. I can't believe she talked me into breaking out after curfew at all.

I lean away, and the branches of the bush jab into my back and neck. It's too late, I realize. If I leave now, between the security cars and the watchlizards and the climb back up into my room, I am bound to be caught. Whatever this is, there's no turning back now.

I feel confused. I feel betrayed. I feel reckless and unpredictable. What I imagine it must feel like to be Quinn.

And Quinn's right. We have hit a dead end, trying to find Evie. Maybe this is the only thing left.

"Okay," I whisper.

A smile breaks over Quinn's face. "Okay." She turns the rest of the group. "Okay."

C glares, but he doesn't argue. "I guess it's too late now anyway. She's here."

The others grudgingly scoot to make room for me, and I settle in next to Quinn, ignoring the knot of nerves tightening in my stomach.

Quinn has to break the silence. "G is the one who has been helping me dig up info on the research program."

The two figures who have not spoken straighten up a bit more and lean in, as if to get a better look.

C sighs. "We might as well get down to business. We don't have all night."

Tonight's business is a plan to get into the LQM storage building, on the Quad's outskirts. They say that if the secrets about this study on failed departures are anywhere, it will be there.

I did not even know the Directorate had storage buildings.

The plan is pretty simple – and, C says, keeping it simple is the best way to ensure it is successful. Quinn, C, another person they call P, and I will meet behind the building.

"I'm sorry, but is she really necessary?" C gives me a sharp glare.

"Yes," Quinn says. "She's the one who read the report. And she's got a photographic memory. She's the best one to know if we find something related to it, quickly."

We will break in, and then we will split up. Quinn and I will head to the top and work our way down; the other two will start at the bottom. We will meet in the middle, or if we do not find each other quickly, make our exit.

It will happen a week from today.

They fire questions at one another about timing, security, building layout, so fast that I cannot keep up. I listen, and hope they know what they are doing as much as they appear to.

Before we leave, C turns to me.

"Now give me your ID and digi account."

I lean away, jamming into the branches of the bush surrounding us. "No way. I don't even know your name."

With those two pieces of information he could get my name, my address, my data – my entire history.

"It's okay," Quinn says. "He needs to hack your profile. So it looks like you were in your room, asleep, this whole time."

"And again for next week, since she's apparently a part of that," C adds.

I hesitate, weighing my options, but Quinn hands him a scrap of paper. "It's all there."

I guess at this point there is no other choice. Why did I not think about my digipad's tracking before? I was so afraid of the immediate ways we could get caught that I failed to think ahead. That is not like me.

On the way back, even through the adrenaline and the mist's cool dampness, exhaustion seeps into my bones. At this point, there are only a couple hours left to sleep.

Climbing back up the tree to my room is harder than coming down, and pulling myself up makes my muscles burn. Before I slip back through my window, Quinn tugs on my hand.

"I'm sorry I didn't warn you. I was afraid you wouldn't come. I didn't know how to explain."

I study her. Her skin glows pale in the dark, and a bright ringlet escapes from the side of her hat. But is that fear clouding her eyes?

I know what I *should* do. Someone like Hanna, a good

Directorate citizen with a perfect record and a future to protect, would report this immediately, before they risked being associated with any of it.

But I am so tired of being perfect.

So tired of complying and scheduling and optimizing.

So tired of this cold, hard knot of fear in my stomach of what might have happened to Evie. I have to know. I have to help her, if I can.

How would I ever explain why I was breaking curfew myself anyway? I can already see the hurt, hardened expression in Father's eyes if I were to even try.

"You're probably right about that," I say. And then I lean over the branches and kiss her.

Nerves still swim through me, mixing with my drowsiness and making me feel out of control. *Out of control.* I have never felt so untethered in all my life. Like anything could happen. Like I might do anything. Like there are no safeguards left to hold me in place.

Quinn kisses me again. I plunge into her, and she reaches over the branches and tugs at my hair. Then I push away and climb back into my room.

"Here, for next time," Quinn says. She digs into her bag and hands me more of the silver tech-tape for the window, along with my own little watchlizard-repellant box.

"Thank you."

She flashes her gorgeous, crooked smile at me. Then she carefully pulls tonight's strip away from the ledge and closes my window.

So late past bedtime, I expect to fall into sleep right away, but I lie awake, my mind spinning, too stirred-up to rest. *The Licentia are real.* The Licentia are real, and I think I just joined their ranks. I hope C is hacking my vitals tracking in addition to my location log from tonight, because anyone who might be tracking my heart rate or adrenaline levels would know something is wrong, and that just like my data points, I have far surpassed the appropriate ranges of activity. I lie awake through the rest of the night in a state of shaken-up disorder.

Chapter Thirty-Eight

Evie

I wake up still slumped on the floor with Kinlee, both of us leaning into each other. Visions of last night still float through my mind – the rush of the air, Kinlee's wild giggle, the ominous glow of the Quads – and my arm hums with a slight sting under the wrappings from my new tattoo. I have never felt so alive.

I shuffle away from Kinlee and stretch. For once, it looks like a beautiful, temperate day outside. But *ouch*. Sleeping like that has left me stiff all over.

Kinlee starts to wake up, too.

"Shit, my neck," she grumbles. "Never let me sleep in this position again."

"Same," I say.

She shakes out her head, and suddenly, her expression turns from groggy to determined. She jumps to her feet. "I gotta get to the bunker," she says.

"I'll be there later," I say. "Testing again."

I was supposed to be there first thing this morning, and judging by the brilliant violet of the sunny sky pouring through the window, it's already second or third thing, by Sue's count. "Or, maybe I should reschedule and come to the bunker, too." After how shaken Raina was last night, and how exhausted they both are, I feel I should be doing a lot more.

"No way!" Kinlee looks exactly like Raina when she gets stern. "That's important too. Go."

I grab a few pieces of toast on my way to the Med cabin and keep moving, propelling myself forward as fast as my legs will let me, though I wish I could slow down and soak up this rare, gorgeous day. That's the thing about weather, I guess – it's only with the awful days you know how to enjoy the amazing ones. I never once thought about weather in the Quad.

"Sorry!" I burst through the door bracing for a scolding from Sue, but find only Noah's warm smile.

"Don't worry, Raina sent word you'd probably be late," he says.

"Is Sue already on rounds? I can come back – "

"No, no," Noah says. "She's with Rosie. I'm holding the fort today."

With Rosie? I look around.

"Hadn't they just moved Rosie in here?"

"Well. It was, um, too busy in here. She wasn't getting the rest she needed. And frankly, her condition changed again. She's better off in her own room, at this point. Have a seat, Ev."

I take the chair he pulls out for me next to the desk.

I remember how frail and depleted Rosie looked the last time I was here. A change from that has to be good, right?

"What do we have here?" Noah nods to my arm.

"Oh right." I hold out my arm to show him the rose, pride swelling in my chest. "Seemed like time to get rid of the departure date."

"Ah," he says with a nod. "Let me wrap it properly for you while it heals."

He replaces the wrapping with a proper bandage, and then we settle in for the business at hand.

"Testing today will be different from the last few times. We're assessing your brain today – psychological issues, learning disorders, that kind of stuff. No poking or prodding. Just you, me, and some puzzles."

He holds up a large ink blot. "What do you see?"

The next few hours are mental gymnastics. After the ink blots, he asks me questions about my life – challenges, behaviors, trends. Then I solve a series of written puzzles, and spend an unreasonable amount of time staring at a

215

blinking box on a screen, clicking a button when a dot is at the top. I read passages and he quizzes me on them. He calls out number sequences and has me repeat them back to him. By lunch time, my brain is fried.

"Well, Ev, no surprise, you're a very intelligent girl. But has anyone ever told you, you've got ADHD?"

Panic flutters through my chest. "What's that? Is it terminal?"

"No. It just means you think differently than a lot of other people. And between you and me, that can be a good thing."

He gives me that Noah smile, the one that always makes me feel a little better.

"Okay. But what is it?"

"It means you're spontaneous and creative. You're resilient. You're maybe not so attentive. Less able to keep focused on things. More likely to lose things. You get lost in your thoughts. It means you're a daydreamer, Ev."

I nod along as he talks – it resounds so deeply. Oh yes, these are all things the Directorate hated about me. How many times did I get caught drifting in class, doodling in the margin of my notes without realizing what I was doing, or confuse a homework assignment and do the wrong passage, even though it was right there, clear as day, in my digipad alerts?

Knowing this was all for a reason, having a name to call it, it's like a hole has been filled that I never knew I had.

He flips back through the notes of my chart. "I'm also seeing shortness of breath – when does that happen?"

"When something bad happens."

He nods. "Sounds like panic attacks to me."

"So… that's what's wrong with me? That's why the Directorate didn't want me?"

After all I've learned these past weeks, this shouldn't surprise me. But anger for the Directorate burns through me all over again, along with my relief. They end lives, separate families, over this?

"It's possible. There have certainly been cases where that's the best reason we could find for a departure, particularly in younger individuals like you. But we need to complete the rest of testing still, to know for sure there's nothing more serious we should be treating. Sounds like your coping methods for the panic attacks are working, so I'm not going to worry about that, but come to us if they get more serious. We can treat the ADHD if you want. But first I want you to learn about it. I'll request some books for you on the next supply run."

I leave for lunch feeling lighter, as if an invisible load has been removed. I grab a sandwich and run off towards the bunker, enjoying the light breeze in my hair.

But as Noah's news settles into me, a new knot of anxiety tangles through me. Everything I learn about the Directorate makes them seem more and more dangerous. If they're willing to kill their own citizens to keep control and ensure a certain type of population in the Quads, what else would they kill for? I assure myself that Gracelyn, ever the perfect citizen, couldn't possibly be in any immediate danger. But I can't shake the feeling that I've got to get her out of there, as soon as possible.

When I get to the bunker, it's stuffed full and bustling with tense energy, everyone crossing back and forth with grim expressions.

Kinlee is next to one of the large, usually quiet machines of the main room. Except now, it is humming and grunting and spitting out an endless stream of messages. Kinlee glances at each page and moves them into various stacks she's placed all around her on the table, the floor, and the machine itself.

"Crap. What'd I miss?"

"Hold on, it's coming too fast," Kinlee says. "Can't talk and read at the same time."

Even as she pauses to say this, more fresh papers begin to pile up. She shuffles through them.

"Mom!" she calls out, glancing past me. She waves, points at me, and goes back to filtering and stacking. Raina makes her way through the flow of traffic towards me. Her eyes are bloodshot and darkly-rimmed, her hair mussed and sticking out in spots.

"Glad you're here. I've got a big update for you and no time to sugarcoat."

She has that same tension in her eyes as last night, and my muscles tense, bracing for bad news.

She continues. "The big news the other day – we confirmed the Directorate has Tad. He's alive, and we know where they're keeping him. We were planning an extraction, but then last night we learned more. He wasn't *caught*. He turned on us. We're on full alert for our agents in the Directorate, getting all the info we can and checking in on our people. Reports are coming in from every Quad. Kinlee's sorting as they come in, and we could really use a runner to get them to the appropriate teams for briefing. She'll tell you where they need to go."

He turned on us.

Questions crowd my head in a rush, but already three more people are hovering around us, waiting for Raina's attention. Now isn't the time.

Kinlee hands me a stack. "Northeast Division," she says, pointing to one of the classified rooms at the far corner of the bunker. "Go."

A numbness sets in, like my emotions have switched off. How could he do it? I try to envision Tad running into Viv's office with that puppy-dog way of his and dumping the whole thing on her – how this other group is out there, and they're infiltrating the Directorate, and he's one of them. Seems more likely to land him in a mental health evaluation than it is to be taken seriously. Hell, *I* didn't take him seriously.

"Ev, Northwest Division. *Go.*"

Kinlee's words snap me back to the bunker.

"Right."

Even as I run, I sneak glances at the papers, trying to piece together more about what's going on. But it's impossible – they're written in an odd shorthand I can't decipher.

"Code, actually," Kinlee says.

We talk in snippets between paper runs, as she hands me the latest reports.

When I come back again I say, "Code? Seriously? Can you read it?"

And then I'm off again.

When I get back, she says, "Sure. But it's not helping right now. Southeast Division."

I make the run.

She continues, "Even if I hold a page long enough to decipher it, the information is too fragmented and out of context to mean anything. Southwest."

We continue on like this for a couple more hours before the pace starts to die down in the late afternoon, then stutters to a stop. Then we stumble towards the closest chairs and collapse.

"Geez, did every citizen of the Directorate send a report? How many agents are out there in the field?"

Kinlee has to think about that one. "I guess a couple in most Quads, plus some special hot sites, like where I got you out from."

I try to figure out how many Quads there are. Fifty? A hundred? More? I realize I have no idea. The Directorate kept each Quad isolated from the others.

"Yeah," Kinlee says. "Keeps you all in nice, easy-to-contain little bubbles. Literally. Something stirs up in one, most of the citizen body goes on like it never happened. Because for them, it didn't."

I remember what the Quads looked like from up in the trees when we zip-lined. Neat and contained – even from one another. It should make me angry, but thinking about it, how insulated and disconnected they are, just makes me sad.

Raina comes over to us. "Now that the field reports are in, there won't be much you can do for a while. Go to dinner," she says.

We get up – slowly, our muscles fighting back after the busy day.

"And Kin," Raina adds. Kinlee perks up. "If you want to check back in tonight – if you think you have learned your lesson – we can probably find something you can chip in on. For your training credits."

"Really?" Kinlee leaps in the air and tackles Raina in a hug. "Yes, yes, yes. Definitely learned my lesson." She pulls her expression into a sorry attempt at solemn.

Raina shakes her head. "I'll see you later then. Sorry Evie, you don't have the clearance for this. We might have something for you in the morning."

I am totally fine with this. My stomach is rumbling, my muscles are aching and my bed sounds like the most wonderful thing in the world right now.

Dinner is quiet, with so much of the Intel & Recon crew missing. Even the teens' table doesn't have the joyful chaos it did when I first got here, and we pass baskets of food without the usual banter. As the day winds down, a lazy sunset streaks a clear sky with fierce reds and mellow blues, and the air takes on a refreshing coolness.

Connor gestures towards the bandage on my wrist. "What happened there?"

"Kinlee." I grin, pulling it back for him to see.

He raises his eyebrows. "Nice."

As we eat, Raina comes out. She clears off the side of a table and climbs on top.

"I need everyone's attention for a minute."

I turn and look to Kinlee. *Is Raina really telling everyone about Tad? Now?* I thought they were trying to learn more first. Kinlee frowns and shrugs – *No idea.*

"I have an announcement, and it's not an easy one," Raina continues. "Our colleague and friend Rosie has passed away. She put up a hell of a fight, but the cancer was growing too fast. I'll let you know about memorial arrangements, but for now we all need to be supportive of her loved ones. Understandably, Sue is out of commission for the immediate future."

I drop my fork.
What?

Raina continues. "I hate to talk logistics at a time like this, but it's gotta be done. I know there are a number of beyond-the-norm strains on us, but for now go to Noah for anything medical, and be patient with him about anything that is not an emergency. They were overloaded in Medical even before this."

Raina steps down and heads straight back towards the bunker, pausing for sad glances with those she passes.

No one speaks.

Suddenly, the perfect weather today feels cruel. I hate this day and everything about it. I never want to have a day like this again.

It doesn't seem real. It *can't* be real. I saw Rosie a few days ago. Sue said this wouldn't happen. She wasn't going to let it.

Each new thought is like a wall slamming down in front of me.

I stand up. "I need to get out of here."

Connor stands too. "Want company?"

"Yeah."

In fact, I've never needed him more.

Chapter Thirty-Nine

Evie

"Are you okay?"

Connor asks it for the fifth or sixth time. But I can't find a way to answer.

I throw myself into the rhythm of my steps, wandering deeper into the woods. *Am* I okay? I hardly know, but if I open my mouth to say something, I will start crying, and I am afraid the tears will never stop. I am not ready for it yet.

"Evie. Evie! *Evie.*" He rushes out in front of me and embraces me, wrapping his arms over my own. When he draws back, he peers hard into my eyes through his shaggy hair. The tears start welling up. Despite the coolness of the evening air, my cheeks burn hot.

"Okay. Okay. Let's…" He rubs my arms. "Wanna sit in the barn? We're almost there anyway."

I nod. He squeezes me, then lets go to lead the way.

We settle into the hay near the cows. He wraps an arm around me.

"Okay," he says again, stroking my hair. As if saying it enough times can make it so. "Whenever you're ready."

We sit there a few more minutes, and the tears begin to fall. Where do I even start?

"She said she was going to live."

"What's that?"

"Sue. She said Rosie was going to live."

"Oh… Geez. She said that a lot. I think some part of her was trying to make herself believe it."

"But Sue's a doctor. Didn't she know? But it's not only that. It's… it's…"

222

I take a deep breath. All the crap from the last week swells within me, like it's going to choke me from the inside.

"Everything has gone so *wrong*. It's been totally nuts in Intel – all these shifts, and it's never predictable, and so much happens that I can't even talk about, and I hate that. And, shit, I'm so tired. And it's not only me – did you see Raina? And then Kinlee had a total meltdown last night, and – "

"Whoa, what? Kinlee?" Connor's frown lines grow deeper.

"Yeah. And now Rosie, and damnit, *Sue said she would live*. Like she said I would live. But we don't even know if I have something, other than this ADHD thing, something serious, and – "

"Hold on, you got a diagnosis? ADHD? Just a learning disorder! Evie, that's amazing news!"

"Yeah, I guess. But Noah said the rest of the tests still matter; they can't *know* if that's all it is for sure until they have them all back. Hell, even if it all comes back clean, they still can't be totally sure. Maybe the Directorate tech saw something we can't. And all I can do is wait, and hope Sue isn't lying to me like she lied to Rosie."

Suddenly I'm not sad anymore – the hot melting pot of emotion stirs and turns to a burning anger.

"I believed her. I *saw* Rosie was getting worse, but Sue said... Ugh, I am so stupid." I kick at the floor.

Connor runs his fingers slowly back and forth over my back, loosening my tense muscles.

"No. You're anything but stupid. You've never really seen death before. And you're right. It's awful. It never seems right or fair. It just happens."

Something in his voice catches, and I remember his dad. The mix of emotion stirs again, turning to stinging shame. How selfish am I being right now, acting like I'm the only one this affects? I lean over and wrap my arms around him, setting my head against his shoulder.

"Did you know Rosie well?"

"Not especially, but before the cancer, she was always all over the camp. Always in motion, always smiling, always joking. Sue's total opposite, in every way. But they hit it off from the start. Sue's always been... well, Sue. But Rosie wasn't fazed by it like most of us. Like they were made for each other." He sighs.

"Poor Sue."

For a moment we sit there, holding each other. Daisy moos from the other end of the barn. The more I think, the more hollowed-out I feel, like I could implode and break down into nothing. I can only imagine what Sue must be feeling right now. No one should have to feel like that.

Connor shouldn't.

But until the rest of my testing is finished – even if it all comes back negative, really – I could still end up just like Rosie. It's not fair.

I pull away.

"We should stop. At least until I know something more definitive. This isn't fair to you."

"Shit, Evie. This again? Now?"

He drops a fist to the ground. "I don't know how else to say it to you. It's not about avoiding pain. It's about taking your joy where you can find it." He's talking faster now, his muscles tensing in little twitches. "For me, that's with you. For however long you're here, whether that's another day or a hundred years."

He pulls away and stands up.

"I don't know how to make you believe me, but I can't keep having this same conversation over and over." He tugs at his hair in frustration.

I curl up in a ball. I hate it when we fight.

"Or *maybe*," he says, his voice getting louder. "This isn't really about that at all. Maybe you don't want to be with me anymore, and this is your easy pass to get out of it. After all, I've hardly seen you for weeks. And you've got a diagnosis now."

"No! Connor – " I bolt to my feet. "That's not it at all – it's just been so busy, and I just got my diagnosis today – it's the exact opposite. I love you. So much. I don't..."

As I realize what's blurted out of my mouth – *I love you* –

my stomach drops. Shit, I didn't mean to say that, not now, not with so much else to worry about. I reach for anything to say to blow past it. But how can I make him understand? Seventeen years in the Quad, and I had no one. Not like this. Or like Kinlee. It was all about keeping my distance, avoiding the terrible feelings of grief later. Sure, they can treat you to make the grief go away, but the ones who get to that point always seem broken, in a way. Like Mother, those last weeks before I left. "I feel this hole in me for Rosie, and I think of the hole I must have left in Gracelyn, and… and… I don't want to make any more holes. *Especially* not in you."

By the end I am crying so hard I am not sure the words come out right. My arms clutch around my middle and curl up in a ball, like maybe I can still hold myself together.

Connor's shoulders drop, relaxing, and his frown gives way to something gentler.

"Evie." He strokes his palms over the sides of my arms. "You aren't the hole. Rosie isn't the hole. My parents aren't the hole. Life. That's the damn hole. You're what fills it."

I'm not sure we're making sense anymore, but I get it anyway, and something sheds from around my heart.

He always has the words for everything, every idea, every situation. But right now, like so often, I have absolutely none. For a moment I stare at him. He baffles me daily, his mind so alive and crackling with questions, challenges, curiosity. And he thrills me. Does his brain never get tired?

His eyes are bright and his cheeks are flushed, his mouth set and determined, waiting for my pushback. I can hardly remember what it was like not to want him, not to have him on my side. I close the remaining space between us and press into him. He wraps around me, and he's right – it makes the hole feel a little smaller.

I give in, accept my fear and let it exist, like something separate from me. If he says he wants this, then who am I to say otherwise? I need it too badly myself to keep fighting it, to keep holding back from him. Once I am past the fear, my body wakes up with a hunger – a desperate need to feel *alive*.

I tilt my head up, and I kiss him, hard.

He pulls away. "Look if this is some tactic to distract me from – "

I kiss him again, softer, sweet, long.

He tips his chin so that our foreheads touch, his fingers tangling into my hair. "Then I am *completely* okay with it," he finishes, his breath a hot whisper on my cheek.

He leans in and kisses me back. His hand trails down my cheek and finds my neck, his thumb brushes over my jawline. Our kisses become more heated, and I press up against him.

I reach my arms around him, my hands settling over his hips, and pull him against me. His other hand finds my waist and wraps around me tight. Everything but his touch fades away, doesn't exist.

I slip my hands under his shirt and a thrill rushes through me as the warmth of his skin soaks into my fingers. It's like an addiction – suddenly, I want to be touching all of him. My body craves to be closer, closer than close, to wrap around every inch of him. My mind hums as if I'm on some kind of drug.

My fingers trail forward against the ridge of his jeans and settle at the button. I undo it.

Connor jumps back. The world forces its way back in with abrupt force.

"What is *that*?" Connor exclaims.

"Wh – what?" My head is still rushing. I take a breath and try to make myself focus. His hair is adorably tousled.

But he's frowning. Behind the anger, confusion and maybe even a little fear are etched over his face.

Maybe I should have left him alone after all. I reach for him. "What's wrong?"

He pulls away again. "Hold up. What exactly were you doing?"

What was I doing? I shake my head. "I… I don't know." I wasn't thinking at all, I realize. My entire face floods with heat.

"Was it… going where I think it was going? Because we've never even talked about that. I don't know if I'm ready for that. I haven't thought it through."

My face gets hotter as I begin to think again, and I realize, "Me neither."

My body is still humming with a craving for him, for his touch. I take another step back. "Shit. Oh, shit, shit, shit, shit."

I plop down onto the ground, wrap my arms around my knees, and tuck my head in against them. This was already the most terrible night. Now, I've made it my most embarrassing night, too.

"Aw, I'm sorry," Connor says, sighing. He refastens his jeans and sits down next to me. We're back where we started, in a huddle on the floor, and him comforting the crazy mess that I've become. "It's not a big deal. It's really not."

He's rubbing my back again, trying to comfort me. It's too much.

I can't keep up with this roller-coaster of emotions I'm riding tonight, all these things he draws out in me. It's a whole new level of living, and I don't know what to do with it.

"I want… you make me feel…" I sigh and bury my head between my arms. It's impossible. "I don't even know how to explain it. I want to be as close to you as I can get."

He leans into me and his lips press softly into my shoulder. "We're fine. Really. I was just surprised. It's… It's not that I don't, um, *want* to, ya know?"

"Really?" I lift my head back up and look to him.

He nods. "It just got… heated. I needed to think."

Of course he did. He always thinks. Leave it to me to forget to think.

"Besides," he says. "There's no rush, right? I mean. *I'm* not going anywhere."

My heart flutters. "Me neither." Definitely not.

He looks away and shifts his position.

"I wasn't ready for it, you know? I'm not exactly a hot commodity around here. I guess I thought maybe someday I'd grow out of all this gangliness and I'd move back to the real world, and *then*, maybe. But I never expected anyone… for *you*… to actually… I didn't think I needed to think about

227

it yet – not that I don't think about…" He sighs, tongue-tied.

I have never seen him at a loss for words before.

I remember what I thought of him the first time I met him – disheveled, obnoxious, awkward – and realize suddenly that must be how he sees himself. It makes my heart melt.

I wrap my arms around him. "Well, I do. You're amazing. I want you. Not in a few years, not when you've grown out of anything. Now."

He blushes, and I kiss his cheek.

"In a totally non-rushy, no-pressure kind of way."

He laughs and pulls me close. Then he turns to face me and reaches around my arm to brush his hand over my cheek.

His expression softens, then turns suddenly serious, and for a moment my chest flutters, wondering what I've done wrong now.

"I love you, too, by the way," he says, tilting his forehead against mine.

My heart swells until I'm sure it will burst. "I love you," I echo back. It feels good to say it again. To say it on its own, without the anger and confusion of earlier.

We sit there, trading soft kisses, long into the night.

Part of me is afraid to go back to camp. When we go back, everything else will come back with it. And everything else keeps going straight to shit. In fact, the worse things get, the more I start to believe something even worse is bound to happen, and soon.

Chapter Forty

Gracelyn

Work, and the rest of life, has fallen away into a blur. All I have been able to think about since my night out with Quinn has been the Licentia, and our plans to break out again. I spend the rest of my time bracing to get caught. Every time a watchlizard skitters by, or Father glances at me, or the instructor calls on me in class, I am sure I have been found out.

But nothing happens.

The day of our plan is normal, like any other day, except that I cannot seem to hold still. I bite my nails and tap my leg and hope I look like I am being productive. I hardly notice the light fading for curfew, and then suddenly it is time, and Quinn is waiting outside.

This time I place one of the strips on the window myself before we climb down the tree.

The trek to the DMD storage building is long, with all the dodging and hiding to get around security cars. I had no idea the Quad was so expansive – and the DMD building is far from the only structure the Directorate is hiding on the Quad's edge. There is a whole neighborhood of tall concrete blocks out here. What kinds of things would DMD have that would need to be stored all the way out here, hidden away on the outskirts of the Quad?

Quinn shrugs when I ask. "All sorts of stuff."

She slows as we near the buildings, but I do not see the two dark figures until we are almost on them.

"I told you I didn't want her here. She's too fresh," C says, popping up from behind a cluster of bushes along the building's side.

Quinn gestures to me, and we join them, ducking behind the bushes, our backs pressed against the rough bricks behind us. To C's other side is the scraggly-bearded man – P, I assume. C and P both wear knit masks that pull down over their faces.

"It's fine," Quinn whispers.

I hope so. My heart races, and I force myself to take slow, even breaths to fight it. Is this what Evie's attacks used to feel like? C is right, I have no business being here. I have never done anything even close to this before. Before all this stuff with Evie, I never broke a single rule. Not one my entire life. At least I wore more functional clothing this time – my black fitness leggings and a black turtleneck I used to wear to school.

"It'd better be fine," C says. He casts me one more glare. "A few more minutes before the security drive-by, and then we're heading in. Started to think we were going to have to go in without you."

Quinn shrugs, pulling her knit cap down to cover more of her hair. "We're here."

Like C said, a security vehicle drifts by minutes later. We duck back behind the bushes, and as soon as it passes, we rush to the door. P pulls out a large piece of tech and starts syncing it to the door's digipad reader. It hums, then the door clicks open.

"Don't they have security feeds in here?" I ask, pausing.

"That's part of what P is here for," C says. "He's re-routing last night's footage to the feeds. They won't see us."

I look to Quinn. She smiles. I guess it is okay.

"File room's this way," she says.

Inside, the building is as sparse as the outside. The large windows are filmed with dust and dirt. Does anyone ever come here?

As Quinn leads us through the halls, P lags behind, digging through his backpack, preparing, I suppose, for whatever is next. When we get to the archive room, he hacks a second digireader to get us in.

The archive room is gigantic – half an entire level of the building, at least. One part is filled with rows and rows of servers. Their hum is loud and persistent, dampened by the *shushing* of aggressively-circulating air.

But the other side… "Are those *drawers*?" I ask.

"Yeah. Paper documents. That's what we need," Quinn says. She is already pulling me towards them. "This is why we couldn't find anything on the system, even with hacking. It's not *on* the system."

"Hacking?"

"What, you think we can change your digipad's GPS, but we can't locate a few documents? When we kept hitting dead ends on the LQM server, I did a little extra digging."

As we turn into the rows, C and P stay behind, pulling something out from P's pack.

Trailing behind Quinn, I realize each drawer has years and initials labeled on them. Quinn stops us in front of a group labeled *DMD*.

"What year was that memo?" she prompts.

"2231."

We search until we find the right year and pull out the first drawer of the section.

A strange, musty smell wafts out of the drawer with the papers. When I pick them up to look closer at the dried ink upon them, they are chalky. Are all the drawers stuffed so full? So much waste.

But it does make the search go easier. We split the stack right down the middle and start flipping through them.

"It's not going to be here, though," I whisper.

"Why not?" Quinn asks.

"Why would they leave it all in paper for us to find here, when they have removed it from everything else?"

"*They* still need to be able to find it," Quinn says. "They don't want *us* to. That's why it's out here, under security, in a building they don't tell us about."

By that thinking, all of these documents must be very important. I consider a moment, then flip the papers faster. I capture every detail of every page I can run my eyes over –

memos, research, maps – for later perusal in my mind, hungry for any hint they might have to offer. I want to know as much about the Directorate's secrets as I can.

"Don't you have it yet?" C whisper-calls to us from down the way. "We're all set over here."

"Few more minutes," Quinn calls back.

"What are they doing?" I ask her.

"Nothing. Assessing some Directorate tech," she replies, studying the documents in front of her. "Find anything yet? We need to hurry."

We flip through the pages as fast as we can. Minutes tick away. C paces the hall between the door and the archive, stirring up my nerves.

"Finally!" I exclaim, jumping to my feet and waving a report over my head. I flip through the pages, hungry for answers.

Quinn jumps up. "Really?"

I glance over it to capture the full document in my memory, then hand it to her. "It even cites the memo."

Quinn studies the paper, then nods. "Amazing."

"Celebrate later. Let's go," C calls to us.

Quinn waves him off. I lean in, and we review it together. It opens with a short message, responding to the first memo and acknowledging the need for action. Then, it lays out a plan.

Except...

"Wait." I look over the details again. "There has to be more – it's a full twenty-eight months after the first memo. That's too long. There wasn't anything in your drawer?"

Quinn's eyes trace over the header, and then she shakes her head. "The Directorate can make things move really slow, when it wants to."

"But..." I sigh. Maybe I shouldn't be surprised at this point that the Directorate would care so little.

We flip through the next pages, too eager to wait until later. As I piece together the meaning from the verbose, bureaucratic language, my heart sinks. The extent of their plan to fix the serum was to get un-departed citizens out of the Quad as quickly as possible, collect a few data points for

232

research, and then… Dread clouds around me and I stop reading.

No.

Evie has to be out there, somewhere, no matter what a stupid report says happens to the bodies at the end.

"This is hardly a plan at all," I say. My nails dig into the palm of my hands.

Quinn flips through the next several pages. "Most of this is about cover-up. Protocols for Departure Crews and security requirements. I don't even see anything about what to *do* with the data once they have it. Bastards."

"There *has* to be more."

I pull open the next drawer and start flipping through the documents all over again, starting from the top.

"What are you doing? Q, what is she doing?" C snaps. "Time's up."

"Not until we find the rest of it." My shaky emotions are forcing a shrill note into my voice.

From the corner of my eye I can see Quinn gesture to C. She gets up off the floor and settles next to me. "I'm sorry. But this is it."

It *can't* be. I still don't know what happened to Evie, and my mind won't – can't – bear to accept the answer the report implies.

"We're outta here. Now," C urges.

Quinn grabs my arm and pulls me with her.

When we round the corner, P is waiting by a line of long, metallic constructs on the floor. The closest three are attached to a hodgepodge of wiring.

I halt to a stop. "What's that?" It's definitely not tech, not the kind we use in the Quads.

P pushes a button, and a timer lights up. "It's what's going to make this building disappear." He looks to C. "Eight minutes."

A slow heat creeps up my neck as the words sink in.

"Quinn?"

Her eyes flicker, but her expression hardens. Behind me, C scoffs.

"It's just a building, Gracelyn," Quinn says.

"But why?"

"Chaos, newbie," C says. "The Directorate keeps all its important documentation here. You think we're leaving it neat and tidy for them? Someone has to remind these guys, they can't control everything. That's all we're doing. They're the ones who stored the bombs here. They basically did it to themselves."

Why does the Directorate have bombs here?

I shake my head. That isn't the point.

"We can't do this. What if we need more information?" I exclaim.

"Are you kidding?" C says. "There's no coming back. Even with all our precautions, it'd be far too risky to return. This covers our tracks. No building, no trail. There's no time, we have to move."

A device in the tangle of wiring is already counting down: *7:41...7:40...7:39.*

A thundering pound-pound-pound floods my ears as I stare at the numbers. *This is not right. This is not what I agreed to.* Quinn pulls me by my arm to keep pace as we flee.

We are being less cautious now, racing through the maze of halls without checking them first. My mind is still back in the archive room with the ticking-down bomb, and it is not telling my feet what to do. Something catches, I jolt forward, and I'm already halfway to the floor before I realize I've tripped.

C and P keep hustling towards the exit.

Quinn tries to tug me up.

"Stop!" I tug my arm away. The disruption to the momentum of the moment allows the rest of me to catch up, and anger boils through my veins.

"Six fifty-two," she says. "We gotta keep going, honey."

Suddenly, the pet name feels ill-fit. I want to yell at her, but I cannot think straight in all this disorder.

"Is someone there?" A voice calls from down the middle hall. "Help! Please! Help!"

Shock tingles and bites down my arms as I skid to a halt

against Quinn's tugs, chased with panic and stinging rage. I look to Quinn. She opens her mouth, then hesitates.

"Please, help me," the voice begs.

Oh my God – secrets, bombs, and now people? What else is the Directorate "storing" in here?

I start towards the voice, but Quinn grabs my arm. "There's no time," she says.

I almost comply with her by habit, but guilt squeezes at my chest. I can't do it; I can't leave someone in here knowing what is about to happen. I yank away, turning to run towards the voice, not checking to see if she follows. After a pause, her footsteps echo behind me.

"Where are you?" I call out.

"Here!" the voice cries. "Thank you, thank you, thank you. I'm over here."

It isn't hard to find him. At the end of the hall is a series of cells, and inside one of them is a man. His black hair is tousled like he has just woken from nightmares, and his glasses are crooked, resting off-kilter over his pale, dirt-smudged cheeks.

He presses up against the bars. "Please, get me out of here."

"Six oh-six," Quinn breathes, catching up behind me. "Come *on*."

Every possible emotion melds together into a hot ball in my chest – fear and adrenaline, confusion and sadness, anger, and a burning sense of shame that we almost just ran off, knowing someone is here. What am I becoming?

"Hack this door," I order Quinn. "Then we can all go, like you want."

"I can't hack that – that's all P. And they're already out. We need to get out, too."

I ignore her and turn to the man in the cell. "What are you doing in there?" Of the thousand questions that demand answers right now, this is the one that makes it out of my mouth.

"I don't know," he stammers. "They promised me. I was going to be one of you. They were going to let me be part of

235

the Quads. But then they brought me here instead."

The words jam in my head. "But everyone is from the Quads. Wait – " I lean in. "Who are you?"

"Five thirty-eight," Quinn urges.

The man glances to her and then back to me. "What's going on?"

"Answer me, and maybe I'll tell you," I snap, pressing up against the bars.

"Please, get me out of here," he begs.

"Look, asshole." Quinn crashes up against the bars so she is inches from his face. "A bomb is going to go off in five minutes and," she checks her timer, "nineteen seconds. You can tell her what she wants to know, and we'll see about getting you out, or we can leave you here."

Words start to spill from him so fast they blend into each other. "My name is Tad. Tad Martin. I'm from outside the Quads."

"How did you get *in* the Quad?" My entire head buzzes with confused energy and heat. Then I realize I have more pressing questions. "My sister. Evie. Have you seen her?" I demand. "Green eyes. A little taller than me. Hair like this." I pull a few blonde locks forward from my ponytail to show him.

Tad looks at me closer and squints. "You two look exactly the same."

His recognition is like a bolt of lightning shooting through me. Is he saying what I think he's saying?

"Three minutes and – " Quinn continues her countdown, but I cut her off, interested in only one thing.

"Where is she?" I cry out. We've lost all pretense of keeping quiet now.

He jumps back a little at my sudden volume. "She's safe. She's with the camp."

"The camp?"

Everything stops, and for a moment these two words are the entire world. I don't know what the camp is, but if Evie is there, that means one amazing, wonderful thing: she's alive. *Evie is alive.*

All this time, all the risks I've taken, it's all worth it for this one little sentence. I *knew* I heard something. I knew she was alive. I'm not going crazy. And I still have my sister – somewhere out there. I feel like I'm floating.

But Tad is still speaking.

"The Alliance camp. It's a conglomeration of governments that – well, it was *started* by a few governments that – "

Quinn slams her fist into the bars of the cell door and it releases a sharp clang of metal slamming into metal. "We don't need a history lesson, tell her where it is and how to get to it."

His sharp blue eyes lock to mine, and through the blur of tears welling up, something shifts and softens in him.

"I shouldn't tell you this, and I already told the Directorate, so I don't know if you can even use it. But there's a network of tunnels."

"Tunnels?" My hands grip the cold metal bars.

He leans in too, pushing his glasses up on his nose.

"It's old, from the Third World War. The Directorate never sealed them up. I don't know if they use them still, or if they thought they might need to use them again someday, or – "

"Where's the tunnel?" Quinn demands.

Tad lets out a hard, short laugh. "It's everywhere. It runs under the entire Quad. Connecting the Quads. And out to the camp."

I blink at him, hardly believing this is all dropping in our laps. Forget the papers – this is what I need.

"How do we get to them?" Quinn, ever pragmatic.

Tad shrugs. "When they brought me here we came out at the park, but I can't remember exactly. It was a couple of years ago. It was the blue line. Follow the blue line."

"So you don't know," Quinn says. Her voice is cold.

A document pulls up in my mind from the documents I just scanned, falling in place like the last piece of a puzzle.

"It doesn't matter. I have the map." I jump and turn to Quinn, hardly believing it. "It was in the archives upstairs. It's in my head."

Quinn's eyes dilate. "Then we're done here." She grabs

my arm and pulls me towards the door.

"Wait! You can't leave me like this!" Tad slams his fits into the bars of the cell door, releasing a harsh clank.

"Quinn," I shriek. I tug against her grip, but her hold is too tight. "We've got to help – "

"No. We've got to get out of here."

Even as she pulls the door open, an earth-shattering *boom* quakes over the building and reverberates through my body, and the walls begin to crack. Quinn pushes me out so hard I almost fall to the ground, except that she keeps shoving, forcing me forward instead of down, until we are clear of the building and hidden in the brush behind it.

As the DMD storage building falls to pieces, she pulls me into her and kisses me hard, stealing my breath away a second time.

For a flash, I am high on the moment – the incredible good news about Evie, the cool night mist on my hot skin, the rush of the close brush with death – and tug at her shirt to pull her closer. Then I remember she made me party to a terrorist act, that she put my life at risk, that we left someone behind in there. I shove her away.

"You left him there. To die," I exclaim.

Quinn clasps a hand over my mouth.

"Shhh," she whispers. "Yes. I left him. Because it was him or us – him or *you*. And I chose you. I will always choose you."

Her eyes ignite with more than the reflection of the post-explosion flames, something beautiful and fierce, supernatural and heartless.

I will myself to be still. She takes her hand away.

"If you'd listened," I start. "If you'd let him out when I told you to – "

But she cuts me off: "Then he'd never have told us about your sister or the tunnels. And now, we'd have a prisoner on our hands. What would we do with him, Gracelyn? He can't stay in the Quad, and he can't go back where he came from, either. He's a traitor. And thanks to you, he knew our faces."

I have no answers. All I know is Quinn didn't tell me the

truth about tonight, she didn't listen to me, and now someone is dead. It isn't right, and Quinn's cool pragmatism about it sends quivers up my spine.

"Did you know they kept people in there? When you all decided to bring a bomb with you?"

Quinn purses her lips into a thin line. She looks me straight in the eye. "No."

"You did. You're murderers."

"Grow up, Gracelyn. Nothing is so black and white. We do what we have to. Someone has to fight back against all this."

Security car lights flash from the front of the building. They're gathering to investigate.

"I'll show you home," Quinn says.

"No. I can get there myself." At least, I think I can. What I can't bear is one more second with *her*.

I turn away before she can rebut me, and take off, running down the road.

Chapter Forty-One

Gracelyn

Evie is alive.

She is out there, somewhere, beyond the borders of the Directorate.

Weeks ago I would not have been able to believe that anything lay beyond the Quads. The idea would have been impossible, not even worth imagining. But since Evie departed, I have opened myself to all kinds of things. Knowing Evie is out there somewhere is a greater good than the troubles that come with discovering the Directorate's lies.

After this night's strange turn of events, emotions churn through me in extremes. Elation to know for sure that Evie is alive and safe. Confusion at the layers that keep peeling away from the Directorate. Anger at Quinn's deception and calculated coldness.

But mostly, relief.

Relief that I really heard what I thought I heard the morning of Evie's departure. Relief that all my risk and obsession was not for nothing, some imagined distraction, the manifestation of grief we are told so often to drug away.

The hardest part is over – I figured it out. I proved it. Now, I have to figure out what to do about it.

***

I lie in my bed and wait for morning, these thoughts and emotions racing through my mind in cycles. When my digipad's waking sequence initiates, I try to act as normal as I can. I get ready for work. I sit next to Hanna on the shuttlebus. I settle in at my desk. Even so, my cheeks are flushed with exhilaration. Which helps to distract from the circles under my eyes.

My mind still whirls.

I only manage a few minutes at my desk before I bolt to my feet again. Hanna starts at my abrupt movement.

"Sorry," I say. "Question for Quinn."

I make my way through the hall as calmly as I can, ignoring the friction as my need for answers chafes against my anger at her from last night. But I need her for this. Don't I? Or does dragging this relationship out for my own gain make me as bad as her?

I burst through her door, my mind too flooded with thoughts to wait.

"How are we going to get to Evie?" I demand.

Quinn is standing, leaning forward over her desk. She looks up, raising an eyebrow, and suddenly I realize there are voices in the background, coming from her speaker.

"Do you know how lucky you are that I'm on mute?" she says.

She presses a button on her digipad. "Something urgent has been brought to my attention. I'm going to have to sign off."

On the other end, a swell of voices begin to pardon her, but she hangs up, cutting them off.

She frowns, a line creasing in her forehead. Despite all that's happened, I have to fight an impulse to lean in and kiss it.

"I know you're wound up after last night, but that's all the more reason to be cautious. This isn't a time for action. It's a time for lying low."

How can I lie low when I know where Evie is? I don't know how to pretend things are the same as before. I hate how rational and detached Quinn is, and my anger from last night flares through me in hot threads. But I push it aside – there are more important things to deal with right now.

"Fine. I'll lie low. For a little bit. But since I have your attention now," I lean over the desk. "Let's figure how we get to Evie."

Quinn straightens, her mouth curling into that lovely, crooked smile.

"After last night, I wasn't sure you'd be up for that."

Up for getting to my sister? Seeing with my own eyes that she is really alive and safe?

I blink. "I am up for it." There is no other option.

"Well, great." She leans forward over the desk. As she draws in closer, I can see the fire igniting behind her eyes, and a warning tugs at my gut even as my heart flutters. "Can you imagine it? The looks on their faces?"

The powerful buzz that kept me up all night flickers. Who is she talking about?

"My sister?" Evie will be so proud when I tell all that I have done.

"No, the Directorate. All the citizens here who can't imagine any world outside this bubble. They won't believe it." Quinn's eyes dance, gazing off at something I cannot see. "They won't know what to do. None of them will. They'll have to understand, finally, there won't be any other choice."

"The Directorate?" Suddenly I feel dizzy, like the floor is shifting below my feet. "I want to *see* her, but Quinn, you can't be thinking of bringing Evie back here?"

The smile fades from Quinn's face. "That was the whole point from the beginning. Expose what the Directorate is doing. Your sister is the key. What did you think we were doing all this for?"

"But... They'd think she was one of you. They'd kill her." Her words stick in me like a jammed gear. I back away. "You don't care about Evie at all. To you, she's just a pawn for the Licentia."

Quinn slams her fist into the desk, her entire face igniting with anger.

"A pawn? Gracelyn, there is nothing more important than this. It's not about your sister. It's not about you, or me. This is about stopping it all. For good. Don't you get it yet? There is a whole world out there that they are hiding from us. They're holding an entire society hostage. We have to show everyone exactly what they are, what they're doing."

Her words pile up and bring my thoughts to a lurching halt.

Is this about something bigger? Should it be? I pause and try to wrap my mind around the possibility. The questions are too big, too hard. This is not what I wanted when I started down this path. Overwhelmed, everything in me wants to yield. To let Quinn take care of it all, like someone else always takes care of everything. To give in to her confidence and the force of her personality.

But even as I think about it, I see in my head how it would all play out. The Licentia thrusting Evie out among bustling midday crowds. The people staring, confused and unsure of what is happening, but afraid of the terrorists igniting chaos in the heart of their Quad.

Soon, the Directorate would swoop in, taking out as much of the Licentia as they could as they contain the situation. And then, if Evie hadn't been shot, they would take her away again, and this time there would be no getting away. I can hear myself scream as she is carried off, and feel the tears roll down my cheeks.

Maybe, if this would really change things, if letting Evie go would really save all the rest of them, I should try to accept that. But I can't, I can't, I can't.

And it wouldn't matter, even if I could. Because as soon as the Directorate had the scene contained, the lies would start. As they always have. The Directorate would do whatever was necessary to placate its citizens. There would be an explanation. A distraction. And then life would move forward. A few might question it all for a bit, but the tug of a content, easy life would ultimately lull them back into line – or they would be *put* back in line.

Because, I realize, here's the kicker: what most people want is not to trust their government. It's not to build a better world. All they want is to be comfortable. They want to carry on in this easy illusion the Directorate has created for them. As long as they have that to fall back on, no effort to shake them out of it will work. And with a sickening twist to my stomach, I realize that I am one of them. That I am not like Quinn. That despite all I have learned, all I want is to finish this, so my life

243

can go back to its safe clockwork routine again.

I look into Quinn's eyes, alight with her vision of chaos, and I know that she knows all these things. Somewhere, deep down. But she clings to her fight against the Directorate as tightly as the others cling to the comfort of order.

Clarity strikes in a bolt, and I see Quinn in a new light. Not the beautiful, ambitious professional I fell for, nor the heartless terrorist of last night. What I see now is a person who can't *not* fight, because it is the only way for her to bear this world she is stuck in. It isn't about changing this world. It is about the fight itself. It is a salve to her own particular type of suffering, as much as the Directorate's pills are for others.

I stumble back from the desk.

"Oh, Quinn." With each word I peel my spirit away from hers. "We can't. I can't."

Quinn shakes her head, her hands balling into fists on the desk. "Gracelyn. No. It's the only way. You need to see the big picture here."

"No. Quinn, it's over. All of it." I glance up to find Quinn's expression has fallen blank. We both know I'm talking about so much more than Evie.

"But no. We have to – "

"I don't have to. I can't." I turn to the door, but then stop, one last thing on my mind. "Look, I won't tell anyone about any of this, I swear. But you have to let me go. And unless I really was only ever a pawn to you, too, a way to get closer to Evie… If you care for me at all, you will not try to get to Evie without me. This ends here."

The light goes out of Quinn's eyes, always so brilliant and alive.

"Quinn?" I beg.

She nods.

I leave, my heart in shreds, wishing more than I have ever wished for anything that I could go back in time and stop all of this before it ever started, wishing I had simply believed Father's lie about what I heard on Evie's departure morning, and forgotten all about it.

Chapter Forty-Two

Evie

When I get to the bunker for evening shift, everyone is climbing out.

"Start rounding everyone up," Raina says. "We have news."

I consider telling her she looks awful, that she needs sleep, but I know she wouldn't listen. In fact I'm pretty sure I can't look much better – none of us do. It's been especially rough in Intel & Recon, with long shifts and late nights ever since we got the news about Tad. We need more people to pick up the long shifts and let others rest. But there is no one else. It's just us out here.

The camp is gathered in a matter of minutes. Everyone's been eager to know, well, anything at all.

I plop down at the teens' usual table near the back. And then the others start to join me.

Dave arrives looking sullen, Kinlee on his heels. She sits next to him on the bench and touches his arm, but he pulls away and turns his back on her. I look to her and tilt my head, questioning. I've never seen them like this. Kinlee shrugs. There's a bandage wrapped around her wrist.

"What did you do now?" I say, gesturing to her arm.

"Oh. Um, nothing." She pulls that arm under the table and turns back to Dave, who is still sulking.

Connor squeezes in next to me. "What's the deal?"

"No idea." Everyone in the bunker's been walking fast and talking low these past couple of days, and they don't tell me anything.

Raina steps to the front and signals for quiet. Then she nods to Kinlee.

"Guys, let's get out of here. I got things to tell you," Kinlee says.

"But don't we need to – " Ginnie starts.

"No," Kinlee cuts her off. "We're having our own talk."

My stomach knots – what wouldn't they be willing to tell us with everyone else?

As Raina calls out to quiet the crowd, Kinlee hops up and leads us towards the trees. We don't go far before Kinlee turns and stops abruptly, taking a big breath.

"The Directorate is coming," she says.

"Wait, what? Coming *here*?" Lucas exclaims.

We all exchange looks. Connor's hand presses into my back. What Kinlee is saying is crazy. She's always saying things that are crazy, but this feels different, and dangerously real. Dave folds his arms and stares down at the dirt.

"But... Why? How?" I ask. "I thought that wasn't supposed to be possible."

Kinlee sighs. "Look guys, Tad didn't just disappear. He turned himself in."

"Why would he do that?" Connor cuts in.

Guess working in Intel got me one piece of information before the rest of them.

Kinlee shrugs. "Our best guess? We think he liked it there. His rotation was coming up. Maybe he wanted to stay."

I remember his warning at the crem – that life wouldn't be the same out here. And that was true. But he said it like that was bad. Kinlee might be right.

"What the hell is wrong with him?" Connor says.

Kinlee shrugs. "What's the difference? He's a traitor. Forget him. The point is, we need to know what they know. And what they're going to do."

"So what are we doing? I prompt.

Kinlee pauses, shoving her hands in her pockets.

Dave stomps at the ground. "Damnit, Kinlee. Tell them."

"Okay, okay." She nods and squints her eyes shut, takes a deep breath. "I'm going undercover. Into the Quads." She is trying to be solemn for us, but when her eyes open, the excitement shines in them like a light behind curtains.

"No way. You have to be eighteen for that," Ginnie says. "They won't let you, Kin."

"They already let me," she says. "Look around. No one over eighteen is qualified. Anyone else with the training already went in. It's too risky for them to go again; they could be recognized. Besides, I'm eighteen in a few months."

I look down to the bandage wrapped carefully around her wrist. It wasn't tree-climbing this time. That's a departure number.

"But…" I protest. My mind is moving too fast, and I can't catch up. "Did you even finish your training?"

Kinlee shrugs. "We accelerated it a little. I finished last night."

That's why she's been extra busy. The realization makes my stomach hurt, like I've been punched in the gut.

"How long have you known?" I ask.

Kinlee's head droops. "For sure? This morning."

"No. How long did you know you might be going? How long have you been *accelerating* your *training*?" I want to yell, but the threat of tears chokes my voice back.

She kicks at the ground. "Not long. Couple of weeks."

Dave's sullenness settles into all of us.

"Oh come on," Kinlee says. "You all knew this is what I wanted. So it's a little early. It's important. Tad could be saying anything to them. We have to know."

"So they should get someone of age and properly trained out here and send *them*," Dave says.

Kinlee sighs. "We went over this."

"Not with us," Connor says. "I agree with Dave."

Kinlee sighs again. "Well, there's no time for that – we have to slip someone in now, while they're transferring soldier units between Quads for the attack. Besides, hardly anyone is interested in joining anymore. You think the camp is this small by choice? We're losing support. People are becoming more afraid of the Directorate, and fewer and fewer people are willing to take the risk."

Silence sets in. No one has any more arguments.

"When do you go?" I ask.

"In the morning."

She looks down and lets her hair fall over her face. I wonder if she is hiding sadness, or excitement.

I spring forward and wrap my arms around her. "I'm going to miss you. You're the best friend I've ever had."

"That's a little sad." Kinlee pats my back. "But, love you too."

"Damnit, Kin." Ginnie comes in for a hug too, catching me up in her arms too as she squeezes. Then Connor joins, and Lucas, and all the others, and soon even Dave is piled in, and it's all nine of us wrapped up with a Kinlee core.

"Guys. Come on," she protests. No one listens.

Soon after we hear the adults begin to protest, and it builds to tense arguing. After a while it dies down, and they disperse.

But we stay out there. All night. Taking in these last moments with Kinlee until dawn starts to lighten the sky and Raina comes.

"It's time."

Kinlee starts to get up, but I've got one last thing to say.

"Wait," I say, getting up with her.

She turns and waits.

My idea is half-baked, but I have to ask. "My sister, she's still in there, and she has no idea. She doesn't even know I'm alive. If I write her a note, maybe you could get it to her, somehow?"

Kinlee looks down and shakes her head. "I'm sorry, it's against the rules to make contact. You know I'm all for a little rule-breaking, but something like that, it's how people get killed. I don't know what Quad I'll end up in, anyway."

I nod, clenching my fists to fight back tears.

Kinlee takes my hand and squeezes. "It's for her safety, too."

I squeeze back. "It's okay."

And then Kinlee and Raina slip off towards the bunker for her gear, Dave following, and she never comes back.

Chapter Forty-Three

Evie

After Kinlee leaves, everything seems to go back to normal without her. Or at least, some new, awful kind of normal. The Alliance may be stepping up its game, but so is the Directorate. It seems like every day now there are new attacks on the Recon Crews on the Directorate's wall. Every day new injuries are coming in.

With Kinlee gone, I have even less to do in Intel & Recon. I finish my sketch of the tunnels map, and once that's done, I realize there isn't much here for me. Mostly I stand at the security monitors, alongside more seasoned pros who don't need me there. Really, I'm in the way.

I want to do something real. I want to *help*.

My mind keeps wandering to the Med cabin, and how swamped Noah must be in the midst of these attacks without Sue there. They were too busy even with both of them.

I miss the powdery slickness of the latex gloves and the sharp smell of the antiseptic and the hustle of moving from one patient to the next. I miss the feeling of knowing I lessened the pain in the world a little at the end of the day.

I've never gotten to choose for myself before. The Directorate always told us where to go, what to do, and what our contribution would be. To leave a post, especially to go and do something else that clicks better, feels selfish and wrong. But I don't listen to these feelings. It's more Directorate brainwashing, and I don't want any part of it anymore. I'm on the outside now, and I want to live like it.

"Raina?"

I squeeze my hands into fists in a fight against my nerves.

Breaking this to Raina feels like a betrayal, especially now, so soon after Kinlee left.

"Yeah, hon?"

I had to wait while she and an agent conferred in tense whispers, and now she's scribbling on her pad, her brow creased. Maybe I should go away and let her work. But she cocks her head to the side, waiting to listen.

"Well…" I'm not sure how to start. "Does Noah still need help in Med?"

"Yes. Noah could definitely use help." She's still writing.

"Because I was thinking I might be more helpful there."

"Oh." Raina puts down the pen and studies me. My stomach twists with nerves.

"Are you choosing your position then? It doesn't have to be, but I've been meaning to talk to you about that. It's just been so busy."

I felt useful in Med. Strong. Like I made a real difference.

"Yeah. I'm choosing."

Raina smiles. "Well congrats then, and thanks for your contribution. You are badly needed over there. I'll send word to Noah to expect you tomorrow."

That's it? I exhale, suddenly realizing I was holding my breath. I was worried for nothing. I feel like I've broken free.

***

The next day I'm settling into the old routines. It feels good to be in the Med cabin again, helping people and healing wounds. It's even busier than I expected, with new patients coming in frequently from the wall. Noah takes my training seriously – every patient is an opportunity to learn, and I stuff my head as full as I can with his lessons. I even get over my fear and help with those emergency surgeries for the soldiers.

At night, I pull out my finished map sketch and trace the blue line that still connects me to Gracelyn. Sneaking my way into the tunnels doesn't seem too hard. But once I'm back at the Quad, how will I get to Gracelyn without getting caught? No plan I can think of seems good enough.

A few days later, I am surprised to find Sue at her desk when I arrive. Her eyes are heavy and the lines around her mouth run deep. Even so, she gives me a half-smile.

"Life keeps going," she says. "Rosie would want me to keep going with it."

Having Sue back means we get lunch breaks back, too – at least if there are no new emergencies. I meet up with Connor, and we sprawl out in the woods, hiding from the tension of the camp. He talks, I draw. My sketch pad is the last safe place I've got left. When my mind gets too busy worrying about Kinlee, or when the Directorate will come for us, or how to get to Gracelyn, I draw. When my hand cramps, I roll over onto my back and watch the clouds drift.

"What's out there?" I ask.

"Aliens, probably," Connor says.

"Not in the sky, in the *world*."

"Oh. Well, a lot of things." He looks out to the fields. "I haven't seen any of it."

Right. He was born here. He seems like such a bottomless pit of knowledge, sometimes I forget that, really, he's about as sheltered as I am.

He must sense my disappointment, because he shifts closer and keeps talking.

"But I've heard a lot of things. Everyone here is from somewhere. And it's all different."

He tells me about Julie, who makes the cinnamon buns, and how her mother made raisin bread every morning when she was a girl. George, the lead farmer, grew up in a city so large he never found its ends, but knew he wanted to go somewhere with open spaces. Sue's from some small village no one knew, but went to her country's capital to become a doctor, and once she made it to the top ranks, she left it all to come out here.

"So many adventures," I say. "I hope I can find one someday."

"What do you think this is?" Connor asks. "Seems to me it's not so much *finding* an adventure. They're everywhere.

251

The hard part is choosing. Finding the right one."

I roll into his side, and he wraps his arm around me. Then he picks up my notepad and examines my work.

"Oh no, don't look," I say. "It's not finished."

If he flips through and finds the map sketch at the back, I'm in trouble. He lets me gently pull it away.

"You're getting really good," he says, glancing at the open page I was working on. "Is that you?"

"It's my sister."

He takes another look. "Wow. You look so much alike."

I try to hide the tears that come any time I think about her too much. That's why I had to draw her – she's on my mind all the time now, but it isn't so hard when I can focus on the curve of her nose or the way her hair falls over her shoulder, instead of how afraid I am for her.

Connor sits up, and I know he's studying my face, taking in the tiny shifts in expression I can't control.

"She's okay, I'm sure of it," he says.

I nod, blinking away tears.

"The Directorate is dangerous, but only to those in its way. It needs its citizens. And from what you've said, your sister sounds like an ideal citizen." The bitterness that used to seep through when he talked about people in the Directorate isn't there anymore. It's not some brain-washed Directorate citizen he's talking about, it's just my sister. He continues. "If anything, they probably give her extra protection."

"Yeah," I sigh.

He takes my hand and kisses it.

Everything he says makes sense, but I can't shake the feeling that Gracelyn is in danger. She might be a valuable asset to the Directorate now, but if she lets a single toe out of line, what then? She doesn't even have to know she's doing it. One mistake and everything could turn.

It wasn't fair to ask Kinlee to get a message to Gracelyn. But I have to get to her somehow. And the way things have escalating lately, it feels like I'm running out of time.

"Hey!" Connor says, suddenly bright. "What are you doing tonight?"

"Nothing." I blink back the wetness building in my eyes and smile at him, willing thoughts of Gracelyn away.

"Perfect. Let's go out."

"Isn't that what we're doing now?"

"Well yeah, but let's do something special. I'll think of something fun to do. We need some fun."

He pulls in closer and holds me, pressing his face into my hair with sudden earnestness. I'm still holding his other hand, and suddenly I realize I'm squeezing it too hard. Because, sure, we seem to be safe for now, but how much longer can this last? Every day the world feels like it turns more and more upside down.

"Okay. Great."

"Excellent," he says. "I got planning to do. See you tonight."

He hops to his feet and swoops in for a kiss on my head before racing off. After he's gone, I stay in the woods a little longer, sprawled out on my stomach, tracing over the lines of the tunnels again, straining to think of a plan to get to Gracelyn. The rules say I can't, but if I have learned anything since I escaped the Directorate, it's that the rules can be broken. There has to be a way.

Chapter Forty-Four

Evie

Though the rest of the day is busy, the anticipation makes the afternoon creep by. Dinner is no longer the camp-wide gathering it used to be, so when I don't see Connor around, I fill a plate and retreat to my cabin.

I'm eager for our night to begin, but I figure I've got until dark, which gives me some time. I pull out my pad and start sketching to kill the time and keep my mind busy, and next thing I know a hard *rap* at the window jolts me from a heavy focus.

Connor is pressed up against the panes. I cross the room and open it, letting in a gust of air that makes me shiver – another cold front is setting in.

"Give me a heart attack, why don't you," I say.

It's almost completely dark in here now – it's a wonder I could see what I was drawing at all.

"Sorry," Connor says. But his eyes glimmer with excitement.

"Why'd you come to the window?"

"I dunno," he says. "Seemed romantic. But I guess that sort of sensitive gesture is lost on you."

"Yep." It's a total lie. I love it. I have a feeling the goofy smile that's stuck on my face gives me away, too, and I'm not even trying to hide it. "I'll meet you around the front, doofus."

He beats me to the door and holds it open for me.

"Wow, look at you," I say. He's wearing the nicest top he owns, one he never wears to work with the animals, and a pair of trousers I've never even seen before. He looks good.

Under his arm is a bundled-up blanket and a basket.

I'm in my normal regulation clothes. "Guess I didn't get the memo about the dressing up."

He smiles. "You kidding? You look perfect."

I can't help it. I blush. "Well. What now?"

"Follow me," he says.

I grab an extra layer and let him lead me away, out through the trees and into the field. He shakes out some blankets and lays them out, then gestures to me to take a seat.

"No offence, but isn't this exactly what we do all the time?" I ask, teasing.

"No. Because usually, it isn't nighttime." He jumps down beside me and lies down. "Come here."

I lie down next to him.

And he's right. I've never seen anything like *this* before.

I've seen the stars plenty of times since I arrived at the camp, through the trees, but I've never had a clear, open view. I've never stopped to stare up at them. Out here, with no lights or trees, they expand far and deep. The longer I look, the more I see, and it's like they go on forever.

Then a familiar sweet aroma fills the air. He hands me a cinnamon bun.

"This night is the best of all the nights," I say, taking a bite.

"It's that easy, huh?" he teases.

"Yes it is. Cinnamon roll. Stars. You. Best night."

I couldn't begin to express it, but it's not just him, or the treat, or even the stars. It's the way the chilled air nips at my nose. It's the quiet after a busy day of meaningful work. It's the freedom that allows all of these things to simply be. Even with the Alliance, I have never felt so free as I do in this moment. Things have never felt so effortless and beautiful.

For a few minutes we simply lie there, eating our rolls and watching the stars, pressed together at our shoulders. When I have licked the last of the icing off my fingers, I roll onto my side and kiss him on the cheek.

"Thank you."

He shrugs. "It seemed wrong for you not to see this. Who

255

knows how much longer we'll be here, between the dwindling support and the threat of the Directorate all rising. It felt important."

I nod into his shoulder. "It's unforgettable. All of this is."

He kisses my forehead, then my cheek, then the tip of my nose. He rolls onto his side and pulls me into him, and his lips find mine. In the midst of the beauty of the field, it's like there's no one else in the world.

His kisses are eager and hungry, a trail of warmth over my mouth and along my jaw and down my neck. I kiss him back, over his neck and his ear, his shoulder, my hands running across his back and over his sides. My fingers hook into the belt loops of his trousers.

I want him. I want him like I've never wanted anything before. And this time I'm ready for it.

"Wait." I sit up. I glance up to him and try to give him a smile, to let him know nothing is wrong. One hand stays tangled in his belt loop, the other fumbles into my pocket and pulls out the small square of foil. I hold it up.

He smirks and sits up, too, digging into his own pocket. He pulls out a condom in the same wrapping as mine.

For a pause we simply smile at each other, and my head is giddy with the implications. "I took mine when Noah was putting the equipment away this afternoon," I say. "How'd *you* get one?"

He laughs. "I asked."

I laugh back.

"But only if you're sure you really want to," he says. "It's totally fine if we... you know. Just lie in the grass and watch the stars or something. Or go back to the cabins, we can totally go back and – "

He's rambling now, unsure of himself in a way I've ever seen. I press my fingers to his lips to quiet him.

"I'm sure." A big goofy smile is plastered across my face and I can't get it under control. "Are... are *you* sure? You really want to do... *this*. With *me*? Even though we still can't be totally sure what might wrong with me?"

I realize he's got the same smile on his face, too.

"*With you?*" He rolls his eyes and reaches out to take my hand. "Always you. Yeah, I'm sure."

For a moment we stare at each other, hands entwined, eyes locked, those awful goofy smiles on our faces.

Then he leans close, presses against me, and when he whispers to me, I can feel his breath on my cheek. "So…?"

I look around. The night is still and peaceful, not a sound except the crickets, no one in sight and everyone tucked into their beds back at the camp. Overhead the stars twinkle into oblivion. Part of me still can't believe I get to *choose* all of this – choose Connor, choose this night, choose what happens next. The alternative of what my life would have been in the Directorate hovers at the edges, and the darkness of that life – an assigned life with an assigned mate and the cold, loveless life of orders and limits that goes with it – makes this one feel so much brighter. Overwhelmingly so.

But I have it. And I'm not about to let it go to waste.

I grin, and rip the side of the wrapping on my little square package.

Connor pulls me in close.

We stretch out between the blankets again. We are clumsy and fumbling and shy, a little scared even, but we go slow, and we figure it out. The night air is crisp against my skin, but Connor hovers close over me, and the heat of his body soaks into me and keeps me warm.

Afterwards, not ready to lose the closeness of our skins brushing against each other, we wrap the blankets around us and stare at the stars.

Lying here out in the middle of nowhere with this odd boy, I am happier than I have ever been. Like I am glowing from the inside out.

Happier, in fact, than I could ever have been in the Quads, even if I'd had a normal, long life there. Real happiness – this kind of happiness – doesn't happen in such a controlled life. You have to pay for this kind of happiness with risk and work and unknowns.

And suddenly an understanding explodes over me: how incredibly lucky I am to have had this second chance, how many odds were stacked against me. Even if it does come with cancer or some other terrible disease, I have lived so much more in my short time out here than I could in an entire lifetime in the Quads.

I can hardly imagine accepting that life now: a life without risk, without choice, without friendships. Without Connor. He's nodding off beside me, snoring slightly, his mouth agape.

I've found my place in the world, and this is it. Not here at the camp, but with these people, this way of life.

And that's when I realize: I can't wait any longer. It's time to stop daydreaming about getting Gracelyn here, and take action. *Now*. Before I lose my chance altogether. The reality of what I need to do sinks into my stomach like an anchor.

"I have to go back."

Connor rolls over to face me, his eyes still hazy with sleep. "Hmm? We will. In the morning. They won't even know we left."

"No. I have to go back to the Quad."

"Back to the…" Connor jerks up as my words hit him. "Evie. No. You can't. Why would you ever want to?"

"It's not – "

"Is it because of tonight? Evie, we won't have to do anything. Ever. I'll leave you completely alone if you want, but please – "

"What? No! It's not like that. Well. It's kind of because of tonight, but not the way you're thinking." I'm struggling over the words, not sure how to explain the feelings churning through me. "It's not you. You're wonderful. And that's the thing."

"But Evie – " He frowns, and I can see a rant coming on.

"Stop, Connor. Listen."

"Sorry." His face is flushed.

"It's this life. It's so different. It's so messy and chaotic and filled with these highs and lows and pain. But it's beautiful. It's not just better than in the Quad. It's… I don't know, it's important. I've only been here a little while, and it's already changed me. It's a real life out here, my own decisions, and not a series of Directorate-mandated tasks. Like I'm finally living in full color. I don't know how to explain. It's wild and free and cinnamon buns and… and…" I reach out and trace my hand over his naked shoulder. "Nights under the stars."

His arm wraps around me in reciprocation. "So then stay. Stay. Why would you want to leave it if you love it so much?"

I have to break his gaze and look away, down to the quilt's pattern below us. "I'm not leaving. But Gracelyn. I have to get her out of there."

The silence grows thick between us like a wall. I look to him, to see what he's thinking.

His face is a mix of anger and confusion.

"It can't be done. How do you think you would even get there?"

"The tunnels," I start. I take a deep breath. It's time for the truth. "There's a map of them in the bunker. I drew a copy of it."

He pulls away. "Shit, Evie. You've been *plotting* this? How long have you been thinking about it?"

I drop my gaze to the ground. "I don't know. A few weeks."

His expression hardens, and his voice turns rough. "You can't. I love you. I want you to be happy, to have everything. But you can't go back."

A defensive burst of anger flares in me. What was I thinking, telling him this? "You could never understand. You can't even remember that all those Directorate citizens are real people, too."

He freezes and studies me, a crease deepening in his brow. For a moment I think we're about to have another blowout argument, and tighten my fists at my sides. But then the tension in his shoulders melts away.

"Oh, Ev. No. If I've learned anything from you, it's that the people in the Directorate deserve as much freedom and compassion and opportunity as the rest of us – nothing in all this is their fault. But think about it. As soon as anyone sees you, you're as good as dead. And then they'll come for the camp, this entire way of life you say you love so much. And in the process you end any possibility of life for others like you, who are immune to the serum. All of that, for a single person. I know she's your sister, Ev, but no one person is worth destroying all of this."

He fastens his trousers then picks up his shirt.

My anger still burns in me. I didn't expect him to drop everything and go with me this minute. Or even to understand it, really. I didn't expect anything at all. Truth is, I didn't think, I just said it, because it was true, and I felt so close to him in that moment, and I thought I could count on him. I clench my jaw and take a breath. Tug on my clothes and hunch over, closing myself off from him before speaking again.

"I just thought... I don't know. Intel manages to get back and forth from the Quads, and pass messages back and forth, without ever being detected. But there's *no possible way* I could manage to get my sister out without the Directorate destroying the world? That's the *one* thing that can't be done? I don't believe it. It's too important. So I'm going to find a way."

Maybe it's the way my voice is straining, giving away the tears I'm fighting back, but he doesn't push it any further. He just wraps an arm around me, and together we walk back to the cabins.

Chapter Forty-Five

Gracelyn

After my confrontation with Quinn, everything settles into a dark haze. The world is exactly the same as before. Except now, everything feels hollow. I know too much, and I wish I could drill it out of my head and go back to how it used to be.

"You must have messed up big time," Hanna says. "It's like you barely exist to Quinn anymore."

She leans in, waiting for me to tell the full story. But I lock my gaze to my screen. For days I have sat here like this, rotating through our lecture documents on the screen, while in my mind I pull out the papers from the archive building – the ones I scanned as I searched for more information related to the memo – and meticulously review page after page, searching for anything that might help.

Hanna sighs and turns back to her work.

A lot of the archived papers are meaningless. Memos. Forms. Business as usual. But other pieces are strange. Some of it makes my gut twist into knots. What is the Directorate doing with full genetic analyses of citizens? Why are traits being flagged that have nothing to do with a person's health – things like mental capacity, inclinations for special talents, personality type? Is the Directorate using departure dates to select the genetic traits it wants to propagate? Did Evie just inherit the wrong set of genetic code?

My digipad beeps. A reminder for my mental health appointment. It is time to see Joyce again. I push up from my desk with a sigh and start the walk to the MHM building.

***

My eyes lock with Joyce's as I settle into the usual plush cream chair across her desk as we size each other up. No more pretension of us as friends, or equals, or anything more than opponents.

With a smile curling at the edge of her mouth, she splays my latest performance marks out on the desk.

"What happened, Gracelyn?"

I could hardly explain even if I wanted to. It's not just Evie, anymore. It's everything I've come to know about the Directorate as the outer sheen has peeled away and exposed the rot underneath. It's losing my faith in Quinn and her plotting with the Licentia, knowing I can't do anything to stop it. It's the sheer dullness that my life has become without it.

I loved my old careful, ordered life, and that has been stolen from me. I want it back desperately, and I hate myself for it.

"Did you take the pills I prescribed?"

Joyce leans forward over the desk, her brows folded in a shape mimicking concern. As if she really believes she helps people. As if she could really help me.

I shrug, staring down at my shoes.

She nods. "I'm going to prescribe you more. Take them this time. And you know what? No more follow-ups."

I am so taken off guard by this I look up to her.

She purses her lips, almost disguising a pleased smile at getting a reaction from me. "Either you take the pills and get back to life, or they're going to put you away. If these visits were going to do you any good, they would have already."

She turns away from me to type on her screen, dismissing me.

As I stand up, she adds over her shoulder, "It's not too late to get back on track, Gracelyn. But it will be soon."

***

Joyce's threat itches at my ears the rest of the afternoon, making it impossible to continue my mental search of the archive's documents.

On the shuttlebus home, Hanna talks at me the whole ride

– she has really warmed up to Quinn, now that she is the favorite by default. It makes me cringe. I tune her out, staring aimlessly at the people getting on and off. At least, until I am distracted by a woman a few rows ahead of us who keeps turning around and staring at me. Her short blonde hair and bright blue eyes are familiar, but I can't place her. The way she looks at me makes the back of my neck prickle.

When I get off at my neighborhood's stop, so does the blonde woman. Out of the corner of my eye I see following behind me as the others disperse towards their homes. I try to hurry, but she closes in and grabs my arm, forcing me around to face her.

"Don't do anything," she orders. "Stay calm and nothing bad needs to happen."

My head thunders with a pounding pulse. Though her grip is hard on my arm and her eyes are sharp, the woman's expression is smiling and friendly. From a distance, no one would notice anything out of the ordinary. It is only in her glare that I recognize who she is – it is the woman from my first night out with Quinn, the one with the scarf over her face. She's Licentia.

"You think you can get out that easy?" she says, her mouth stretched in a smiling grimace. "Quinn might think you're okay to go back to your little life and pretend nothing happened, but you know what I think? I think you look like a rat. So do C and P. So we'll be watching you. One false move, and you'll find out for yourself how murderous we can be. And don't forget, we can see everything."

She shoves me as she lets go of my arm and steps away. "And have a *great* evening," she calls back for all to hear, the tight smile on her face broadening.

I stare after her, too scared to think, my hands shaking.

I never wanted this. All I wanted was to understand what happened to Evie. The Directorate was right about one thing, at least – chasing emotions does nothing but hurt you. When I regain my composure, I run home, not caring who observes my reckless hurry. I go straight upstairs to my room and stare out of the window, searching for other familiar faces. They

263

have my digipad codes. They know where I am every second. They have every bit as much information about my life as the Directorate does. What am I going to do?

The next morning, another small blue pill dispenses onto my plate with breakfast, staring up at me next to my protein. I snatch it off my plate before Mother or Father can see, and shove it into my pocket.

I can feel myself running out of time. Am I still going to be able to find Evie, all on my own? Do I still have the guts do see this through? I do not know if I have it in me. But I also know that if I don't, I will feel like this forever.

Chapter Forty-Six

Evie

"Evie."

The voice is sharp, cutting through my dreams into consciousness. I bolt upright and look towards it.

"Raina?" Raina is never harsh. Never demanding. Something is wrong. From outside, the night swells with voices and loud shuffling. I rub my eyes.

"The Directorate is coming," she answers. "We have to go."

I bolt from the bed and pull my clothes on. "Oh shit."

As I shake off the haze of sleep, I look out of the window to see the whole camp is bustling, loading up packs and taking count in groups.

"Grab what you can," Raina says. "Thirty seconds. Then you're outta here."

I lie down flat on the ground, pull out my drawing pad and pencils from under the bed, and shove them into my backpack on the dresser, then add a few sweatshirts and whatever other clothes I can grab.

"Ready."

Raina nods. "I need you to find Sue and stay with her. She was out by the Med tent."

That's when I realize Raina is not packing anything for herself.

"Aren't you coming?"

"Not yet. Soon. A few of us have to stay behind. Stay in touch with the contacts inside."

Her hair sticks out in funny directions and her shirt is crumpled. A solemn ache hides behind her eyes. I can't remember the last time I saw her sleep. Or even come inside the cabin. I don't say anything. I get it – this is what she has to do: to deal with the risk Kinlee is up against, and the rest of them. She has to be there. Surely someone on her team knows when to stop listening to her and get her out.

She hands me a folded-up map. "Just in case. I marked the best way to safety."

I take it from her and stick it in my back pocket.

As I head to the door, Raina pulls me in for a tight squeeze. "I love you, Evie. Good luck."

No "*Be careful*," no "*Stay safe*." That's not how we do things. We just love, and we do it fiercely.

I squeeze her back. "Thank you. For everything."

There is far too much to thank Raina for, and nowhere near enough time, so I don't try. I just cling to her tight for an extra moment, trying to convey all the ways she has not only saved my life, but transformed me.

Then I shift my pack higher on my shoulder and set out into the crowd, currents of fear and confusion pulling me in like an undertow. I have never seen anything like it, and could never imagine such a scene. It's impossible to believe the camp is over, even as I watch it break apart before my eyes.

"Evie!"

A hand closes around my wrist as I look towards the voice. Connor's bright eyes meet mine, and my core goes still despite the swirl of activity around us. His pupils are dilated, and little tense lines gather around the edges of his eyes.

"This way," he says. I'm grateful to be able to follow instead of finding my way alone through the madness.

He leads me past the camp behind the trees, pulling me close. He brings his hand to my cheek.

"Are you all right?" he asks.

"Yeah," I say. "Are you?"

"Yeah. But…" He shakes his head, glancing out towards the chaos.

"Where are you going to go?" I ask him.

"I don't know. You?"

I shrug. "Wherever Sue is going. Raina gave me a map. You should come with me and follow Sue."

266

I take his hand and hold it tight. He squeezes it back, hard. Wherever we're going, we're going there together.

I try to smile, though whether it's to assure Connor it will be okay, or myself, I couldn't say. I look out at the camp and realize this is goodbye.

Goodbye to first friends.

Goodbye to first jobs.

Goodbye to where I learned about choice and pain, and how much more I could be.

"Guess I don't get to know for sure all that's wrong with me, after all." I'm not sure why this is the part that comes out. Maybe because it doesn't hurt as much as the other things.

Connor squeezes my hand again. "You can start over with the testing. Wherever we end up, maybe they'll have better tech for it, anyway."

"Yeah."

Goodbye to my last thread of connection back to the Quads. Goodbye to submission. Goodbye to departures.

Goodbye to Gracelyn.

As this last fact hits me, it is as if I've fallen and knocked the wind out of myself.

No.

I can't let this be goodbye, not to her. Even if the camp is destroyed, I still have to get her into this world – she has to experience all this freedom and choice and love for herself.

"I have to go back."

"Did you forget something? Because I don't – "

"No. Back to my Quad."

Connor's expression darkens into a frown. "Evie, I know you wanted to get your sister, but surely now…"

I wait, but his words drift off.

I shake my head. "It's even more important now. This is my last chance."

This is something I have to do. I just have to.

Connor studies me, and I stare back at him.

"It's okay, Connor. Get somewhere safe. I'll find you, I swear."

267

I start to let go of his hand, but he holds onto me tighter.

"Are you kidding? You shouldn't have to do this alone. I'm helping."

"But the evacuation," I say. I tug on the straps of my backpack, fighting the impulse to swallow him in a giant hug. "By the time I get back, everyone will probably be gone. You should stay with them."

He shrugs. "I wanted to go out on my own and see the world. Might as well start now."

I leap into him and wrap my arms around him tight, before realizing there isn't any time.

My drawing pad is in my backpack, which means I have my map of the tunnels with me. I can figure out the rest on the way.

"I have to get to that tunnel under the bunker," I say.

"Then let's get to the tunnel."

Still holding hands, we head back into the chaos. My heart pounds and my chest tightens, and I am afraid that my old breathing problem will come back, but I don't dare slow down. Slow down, and I lose Connor, or we get caught, or we get carried away by the wild current of the people running in every direction.

It quietens again as we head into the woods towards the bunker. We break into a run. When I reach it, I throw back the trap door, and a cacophony of voices rises from within.

"Are they *all* in there?" I exclaim. "Shit." It scares me all over again, thinking of the Intel & Recon crew disintegrating into chaos like the rest of the camp.

And if there's that many of them down there rushing around, I'll never make it to the tunnel before one of them sees me.

But I can't turn away from Gracelyn without trying. I *will* make it, because there is no other choice. We make our way down the ladder as quietly and as quickly as possible. At the bottom, I press up against the wall and watch the chaos of the bunker while I wait for Connor to reach the ground too.

Agents stand at each and every station, and more are rushing back and forth, carrying thick folders of papers and wearing tense frowns.

Thankfully, I don't see Raina anywhere. She must be in one of the inner rooms.

Connor lands beside me.

"Wow," he says.

"Yeah."

"Well... what's the plan?" he asks.

"Um. Look like we're supposed to be here?" It's not great, but it's the best I've got. "People are used to seeing me in here. Everyone is so rushed and distracted, maybe they'll forget I left. Or assume I came back to help." Guilt tugs at me – that's probably what I should be doing.

"All right," he says. His shoulders hunch in, betraying the false confidence in his voice. "Which way?"

"Come on."

I lead the way towards the surveillance room, trying to keep us near the back wall, out of the main flow of the traffic.

"Hey." A large muscled man calls out as he approaches us, and I freeze in my tracks. It's Grant, the man who interviewed me with Raina about Tad. "You authorized to be here?"

My mind goes blank with panic.

What would Kinlee do? I try to project confidence.

"I've been working here a few weeks now, don't you recognize me? Raina said she needed all hands on deck."

It's a risk, using Raina's name. It helps my story sound more believable, but if he calls to her to verify, I'm done. He studies me, then nods.

Relief rushes over me.

But then he turns to Connor. "And you?"

"I... "

Shit. I was hoping that would be enough.

Connor looks to me, squeezes my hand, and then releases it. *Go.*

"Like I told her, I won't leave without her."

"Teens," the man says, shaking his head. "No way kid, back up top."

Connor gives me a slight nod, grinning ear to ear. "Make me."

269

And then he darts off into the whoosh of agents dashing around the main space. The man rushes after him, leaving me free to keep going.

Thank you, Connor.

There's no time to worry about what will happen to him next – probably get tossed back out to the chaos above, to get out with the others. Where will he go? How will I find him? My heart aches to think of it, but I can't let his gift go to waste. I've got to get to the tunnel.

I slip into surveillance, and find the room full, but quiet. Every station is manned, agents standing and watching each and every screen with intensity. Some are on the Quads, but most now show the camp's perimeter. All at once, the gravity of the situation hits home. This time, it's not a question of *if* something is out there. It's a question of *when* it will come for us. A quiver of fear shoots up my spine. It makes me want to turn back. It also makes it all the more important that I go.

There's the trap door to the tunnel, right in the middle of the floor, and all the agents' backs are turned to it. Can I be quiet enough? I try to hold my breath, but my lungs are working too fast. Adrenaline throbs in my wrists and twitches in my neck.

I'll never make it while I'm so on edge. I lean against the back wall and close my eyes. Breathe in and count like Father taught me – *In, two, three, four, five. Out, two, three, four, five. In…. Out…. In….*

I move, carefully and slowly, towards the trap door in the floor. None of the agents so much as shift their feet. I kneel down and glance over again. They are so focused on watching for the Directorate out there that I am not sure they are even blinking, but they still haven't noticed me.

I slip my fingers under the metal lip and *slowly, slowly, slowly* lift it, just enough to slip through. My hands are slippery on the metal ladder, and I have to hook around it with my elbow to steady myself as I slip the door back into place. I breathe deeply and try to keep my cool.

Once the door is set, I pause to catch my breath, hardly believing I made it.

Gracelyn, I'm coming.

Chapter Forty-Seven

Gracelyn

"Gracelyn. Gracelyn. *Gracelyn*." The last one is accompanied by a sharp tug on my arm. I turn to see Hanna at my side.

"Yes?"

"Didn't you hear the announcement?" she shouts. "We're being attacked! There was a bomb!"

I become aware of a loud voice blasting through the speakers: "*An unscheduled curfew is enacted, effective immediately. Return to your home, where we will deliver additional instructions.*"

Lost in my shuffling through the files from the archive, I guess I pushed its repetitive rhythm out of my mind, along with everything else.

I look up towards the speaker and stare at the red flashing light.

"We have to *go*," Hanna says, pulling me towards the door.

I follow her as the crowds file into the streets, all of us bumping into one another in the chaos. Transport employees in yellow vests wave us into lines, where shuttle after shuttle is lined up along the curb, heading to every corner of the Quad, waiting for us to board them.

There was a bomb? I look around and find there is smoke rising from the other end of the Quad, near the archive buildings.

People shove and yell, confused and anxious to get home. The order of the day-to-day is the thing the Directorate protects at the expense of all else. If they are willing to put it at risk, the threat must be really serious.

Hanna and I shove our way onto a shuttle. Through the window I see even more citizens hustling down the sidewalks, hunched and afraid, determined get home, where the Directorate promises they will be safe.

Once we are home, an announcement pushes out on universal livecast, a voice booming over the speakers. The voice is friendly and familiar, paternal and comforting. Father turns on the big broadcast screen in the living room and we all watch together as the recording delivers the news: the Directorate has been bombed by an unknown outside rebel group.

Mother gasps. Father wraps an arm around her.

"Remain in your homes," the voice orders, *"and the Directorate will notify you when it is safe."*

I stand up, arms folded over my chest. I think of Evie and everyone else who must be out there, and my mind reels. This can't be right. Why would they attack us? Why now? All that has happened crashes through my head like dominoes, small flashes of sounds and touches and scenes: waking up to the strange shuffle in Evie's room; the warmth of Quinn's kiss; Joyce's hungry eyes leaning in for my confession; the night mist on my skin; the little blue pills piling up in my pockets and drawers; Tad's panicked eyes through the bars of his cell, pleading to be let free. *I told them everything.*

I gasp, echoing Mother.

The Directorate didn't know there was a group out there watching them. Not until Tad. And they gained more by staying off the Directorate's radar. Why would they attack?

My head rushes as the truth strikes: we're not being attacked. The Licentia did this. And now the Directorate is using it to attack this new enemy Tad has led them to.

I don't have all the pieces to prove it. Only everything I have learned these past weeks. And every particle of my being knows it is true.

And I know one more thing: I have to get to Evie and warn her, or at least see her and know that she'll be okay. I didn't go through all of this – the sneaking around, the days and days of research, the late nights, the roller-coaster of Quinn – to spend the rest of my life wondering all over again if Evie is alive out there somewhere, or not. It would end me.

In my mind, I pull up the color-coded map of Tad's tunnels that I stored in my memory from the archives.

I have to get to the tunnels.

Chapter Forty-Eight

Gracelyn

I stand as calmly as I can through the rest of the livecast, my fingernails digging into the flesh of my palms at my sides. When it is done, Mother and Father huddle on the couch next to each other. They look to me as if they expect me to join them. To sit and wait for the voice to come back and tell us everything will be okay.

I excuse myself to my room.

The tunnel, the tunnel, the tunnel. It bounces through my mind like a rolling echo. I shut my eyes and focus on the map. The entrance into the tunnels is in the park.

Digging into my drawer, I pull out one of the metallic security tapes Quinn gave me, and use it to slip out of the window. Then I make for the park, trying to stay close to the bushes.

The streets are abandoned except for the circling security vehicles. But this time, the light of midday is bright, and security isn't following its usual, predictable patterns.

Stop. This is crazy. You're going crazy.

My joints lock, my hands shake. I am bound to get caught. Or worse, I could run into the Licentia.

But this is the one last thing I absolutely have to do. If I do not, all the rest of it was for nothing – I would be right back where I started, wondering if Evie is alive or dead, and bound to spiral out again.

I can't spiral out again. I have to find a way back on track, back to my promising future. This one last reckless thing. Then I'll let it go. I'll go back to what I used to be.

I urge myself onward, waiting for the open moments and

274

sprinting to the next row of bushes. By the time I make it to the park, my chest is contracting like I am being squeezed by a giant fist. I launch into the hollowed-out bushes the Licentia hid in, and peer out at the open grass. The door into the tunnels below must be out there somewhere.

I have to find it. I *will* find it, I command myself. I figured out everything else to get to this point, and I will do this, too. Except, Quinn did all the stealth. All I did was snoop through some files.

This demands stealth.

I strain my eyes, as if the ground will give up its secrets if I stare at it with enough willpower. If the map is right, it should be in the open stretch of grass beyond these bushes. But I can't crawl along the grass sticking my hands into the dirt every few feet – I'll be caught.

Wait – is that a *ledge* in the grass?

I squint and lean forward, trying to suppress the charge of hope that pulses over me. But it is. There is a small but definite rise in the grass, a hard line that pops ever so slightly higher than the rest around it, over by a tree in the middle of the park.

The Directorate doesn't do uneven ridges.

A prickle rises up my neck. *Why is it open?* The question nags at my mind, but I can't worry about that now. Right now, I am simply grateful to have found it.

But in the middle of the park, I'll be vulnerable to any passing security car, from any angle. Once I get my chance, I'll have to move fast.

As the security cars make rounds, I miss my first opening, too scared to venture out. And then I miss my second. I'm wasting time. But I don't know how to get to the ledge without being caught.

Another explosion rumbles from the Quad center, shaking the ground.

There is no time to be afraid. The security cars slam to a stop, then turn towards the rising smoke. As they disappear, I race towards the ledge, slide to it on my knees and dig my fingers into the ground around it. Sure enough, my fingers don't press into dirt, but a smooth metal ledge. I pull it up and slip in, relief rushing around me with the darkness as I clasp to the rungs of a cool metal ladder.

I have to tug the ledge extra-hard to get it properly into place, so it will not stick up again for someone else to find. The force of the effort throws me off balance, and a bolt of panic cuts through me. I cling to the ladder's rungs, listening to my involuntary gasp echo down the tunnel.

I shut my eyes and focus on the pounding of my heart. It doesn't help, but my fear of remaining on the ladder wins over my fear of climbing down it, and I manage to make my way, bar by bar, until I am on the ground.

The tunnels are dark, and a mildewy stink fills the air. A series of colored lines trace the top of the wall, and the air is charged with an uncomfortable quiet.

Where do I go from here? Panic prickles in my fingertips, but I close my eyes and force myself steady – *think*.

The blue line. That's what Tad said.

I find it along the wall's stripes and hustle down the paths as fast as I can without breaking the quiet. There could be others down here, especially if the Directorate is launching an attack. Dirt sticks to the bright clean canvas of my shoes, but I will worry about that later.

The tunnels are dark, and I soon feel lost and disorientated. In the Quad, signs tell you where you are and where to go at every corner. But down here, fear clouds my mind and I question each turn. Studying the lines of a map is one thing, but actually being in these awful tunnels, all alone, in the dark, is another completely.

I reach an intersection and halt to think. This was a stupid idea. Desperation fills my chest like lead. I'm never going to make it. I'm never going to see Evie again.

Chapter Forty-Nine

Evie

Breathe in, two, three, four, five. Out, two, three, four, five...

I lean forward over my knees, fighting to get my breaths under control as I wander the tunnel's paths.

These attacks don't bother me the way they used to. I used to think it meant that I was weak and broken – a reminder of my early departure date and why it was assigned. But somewhere in these past weeks it has taken on a new meaning. It isn't about my limitations anymore. It's about knowing I have something worth fighting for. Being scared? That's no big deal. But giving in, not fighting through it? That would be.

My breathing steadies, and I straighten up.

How far is it back to the Quad? I should have brought some food. Or at least some water. Though how I would have gotten either, in the chaos of the camp's retreat, I don't know. What I do know is, I've been running for a *long* time. I have to be getting close by now. Don't I?

A shuffle from around the next corner stops me in my tracks. Then my mind catches up and I press against the wall, hoping the dark will hide me.

Who else would be down here? I strain for any sign of further movement. I almost convince myself it wasn't real, but then I hear it again – the soft sound of steps in the dirt. And it's closer now, just around the next corner.

My stomach churns with dread and I ball my hands into fists. But it isn't a Directorate guard that steps into the dim light of the intersection. It's a woman. She looks a few years older than me, with bold red hair, and skin so pale it almost

277

glows in the dark. She turns, and our eyes lock.

Crap. My body freezes in panic.

She gasps.

But then she studies my face, and steps closer.

"Gracelyn?" she says. "No wait – Are you *Evie*?"

I gawk, too shocked to respond.

"You are. You have to be," she continues. "You look exactly like your sister."

I blink, pressing back into the wall behind me. "Is Gracelyn here?"

"No." Something flickers behind her eyes. She shifts into a softer posture. "But come with me. I'll take you to her."

My heart leaps – I can't believe my good luck. I step forward to go with her, but then something about the intensity behind her eyes makes me hesitate. Maybe I *shouldn't* believe luck this good, and especially from anyone from the Directorate. Maybe it's not luck at all, or at least, not the good kind.

"How do you know Gracelyn?"

The woman's eyes narrow at the edge, then she forces a smile.

"I'm Quinn – I know Gracelyn from work. LQM."

I frown. "And what is an upstanding employee of LQM doing down here, in secret underground tunnels?"

Quinn huffs and rolls her eyes. "There isn't time to explain, just *come with me*."

She lunges forward, grabs my wrist, and pulls.

I pull back, trying to free myself of her. "No way."

"But you have to." Quinn tugs my arm again, her grip digging into my skin. "Don't you get it? *You* can expose the Directorate. *You* can be their undoing. But you have to come with me."

"What?" Surely I'm misunderstanding her. No one would ask what I think she is asking – and definitely no one who Gracelyn would trust.

She tugs at me again. "We have to show them all, or they'll never understand."

"No." I yank my arm and finally break free from her grip.

278

Her face scrunches into a terrible grimace. "Yes."

Then her hand flies at me in a fist. Pain bursts over my face and my vision clouds with a flash of darkness.

Before I can regain my bearings, she grabs me again and tugs me forward.

Chapter Fifty

Gracelyn

A murmur of voices echoes towards me from down the tunnels. I freeze, straining to listen over the rising pound of my heartbeat, but it is impossible to understand them through the tunnel's reverberations.

Wait, was that my *name?* I listen harder, but I can't tell anything more. I could have sworn...

I move towards the voices, my hands shaking. As I get closer, both voices become clearer, and both are familiar to me. My heart skips and thuds.

I round the corner in time to see Quinn slug Evie in her face.

Evie. She's alive. She's here.

For a moment I am so overwhelmed that I am frozen. Relief bursts through me. Then it is followed by terrible understanding that drops over me like a bucket of cold water.

Of course.

Of course it was Quinn who went through the hatch in the park before me. No one else knew about it. She must have crawled over every inch of that park looking for the trap door. Or maybe the Licentia has tech for that, too. They're probably using the tunnels for the attack.

Of course she broke her promise to me and came after Evie. She is only repeating what I should have already learned to expect from her.

But it stings all the same, even more because of the shame and guilt that come with it. I should have known. I should have stopped it, somehow.

I can stop it now.

"Hey!"

Rage simmers over my skin. Before I know what I am doing, I charge forward and throw my fist at Quinn, connecting with her cheekbone. She sneers, the hit having little effect on her, though bolts of pain shoot down my fingers and wrist. Helpless anger explodes through me.

"You promised!" My voice hits a shrill register I don't recognize as my own.

"Promised?" Quinn scoffs. "Hardly. Make me the bad guy if you must, but the bottom line is, some of us are willing to do what it takes, and some don't have it in them, when it comes down to it."

"*Shut. Up.*" I swing my other fist at her, hardly caring if I injure myself again. After sixteen years of being careful, of being protected, of being cautious and precariously staying within all the lines, I can't contain the tension of these past weeks any longer. Then my hit lands and the pain explodes, and a whimper escapes me. I recoil in on myself, giving in to the pain.

"Gracelyn?" Evie asks.

She frowns, rubbing her cheek where Quinn made contact. But she is real, she is alive, and *she is here*.

I bound to her and wrap my arms around her, still unable to fully believe, even as I squeeze her tight, that I really found her.

Everything is going to be okay now.

Chapter Fifty-One

Evie

Before I can process what is happening, arms fly around my neck so tight they constrict my breathing.

"Gracelyn?" A lump tightens in my throat.

Did I really find her? Did this half-baked plan actually work? But it is, it's her. I'd know this smooth blonde hair, the sound of her voice, the specific way her arms wrap around me, anywhere.

I squeeze her back, and I don't know if I can ever let go. There is so much I have to tell her. But even more importantly, we have to get out of here.

And did Gracelyn, my sweet little sister who has nothing but love for anyone, just throw a punch?

The pain in her hands must be horrible, for someone who has never felt any. The searing ache of that twisted ankle the first time I was in these tunnels will never fade in my memory.

I take her hands in mine. "Are you okay?"

Her expression is shaky, and her gaze drops down to her hands. Her fingers are swelling.

"Oh no," she says. She pulls them back and shakes out her hands as if she can fling the pain away.

"It's okay, Gracelyn," I tell her. "Gracelyn? *Gracelyn.*"

She looks at me.

What I find in her expression holds so much more than the pain of her fingers. The thrill of finding her gets buried beneath confusion and concern. The soft warmth of her eyes has been crowded out by an uncertain edginess, her smile replaced with a grimace. What's happened to her since I left?

It's only been weeks, but she seems older. Harder. I've never seen her scowl like that, not ever.

"Well, shit."

A new voice joins the commotion. A voice that feels a lot like home. As I turn to look, a whoosh of dark hair races between us, and clocks Quinn in the head. This time, Quinn crumples to the ground, unconscious.

"*Kinlee?*"

I knew she was somewhere in the Directorate, but the odds of her actually being *here*, *now* – of seeing her again *ever* – were so small that her seemingly magic appearance raises goose bumps over my arms.

"It's Kate now," she says. The Directorate uniform she's wearing seems stiff and out of place on her. Her hair, straightened and pinned back in a tight ponytail, is the tidiest I've ever seen it. She frowns. "You were supposed to get out, not come back. One of you idiots tripped an alarm. You have no idea how hard it was to convince them I should go ahead to investigate, before they sent in a whole unit."

I know I should care about what she's saying, but I'm still trying to get past the fact that she's there. Hell, I'm still trying to catch up with the fact that I found Gracelyn.

"But what… I thought you were in a different Quad."

"They're rounding up everyone to attack the Alliance. Please tell me you're the only dummy who hasn't evacuated by now."

"I am the only dummy," I say. "And Kin, this is my sister. Gracelyn."

She glances over to Gracelyn, who stares back, eyes wide. "You two look exactly the same, you know that?"

Chapter Fifty-Two

Gracelyn

I stare at the girl in the Directorate uniform. The badge on the lapel reads *Quad Fifty-Eight*. It looks stiff and tight over her restless shoulders. And she can *fight*.

And somehow, Evie knows her.

Kate-Kinlee turns to me. "Not bad, by the way. But don't close your fist like that when you punch."

I blink. "Oh."

Snap out of it. I'd set out to find Evie, and here she is. This should make it all better. So what is wrong with me?

This new Evie is different from the one who departed from the Quad.

Evie was the bold one, always, but the anger that fueled her seems to have dissolved, and a different kind of energy fills her now. She looks free. She looks strong. Despite her intense expression right now, she looks happy.

Evie, happy. Have I ever seen that before? Not like this, not this contentedness that seems to be anchored from her core. There never seemed to be time for *happy* in Evie's limited years.

Kate-Kinlee checks her digipad. "I can't stall them long. You're sure everyone else – "

"Everyone is safe," Evie says. "Even the Intel crew was finalizing their precautions when I snuck out. That was at least an hour ago. Probably more." She rubs sweat off her forehead with her sleeve.

"Snuck out?" Kate-Kinlee grins. "Look at you. But seriously. You gotta get out. Now-ish."

"That's what I was trying to find you for," I exclaim,

butting in. "You've got to get out. This Tad guy told the Directorate everything. They're coming for you."

Kate-Kinlee turns to me, one eyebrow raised. "How do *you* know that?"

"It doesn't matter now. You have to get somewhere safe," I say.

"I had to find you first," Evie says, reaching out to me. "Gracelyn, you've got to come with me."

I almost take her hand, but then her words register: *Go with her?* Something slams down around me. That wasn't the plan. The air feels suddenly cold and clingy with dampness.

I stumble back.

"What?"

Chapter Fifty-Three

Evie

Gracelyn pulls away, and the entire world stalls to a standstill.

Come with me. It's like the words are still hanging in the air, creating a wall between us.

Her brow pulls together into a frown. She shakes her head. Suddenly it's like the earth is teetering below me. My mind reaches for the right words, but like so often, now that I need them most, I can't find them.

"Please. You have to. The Directorate – there's an entire world out there, you have no idea – I know it's different for you in here, that the system *works* for you…" Gracelyn's eyes break with mine and her gaze drops to the floor. Again I reach for her and again she pulls away. "But there's so much more."

I want to explain the *more* to her, but how can I explain stars? How can I explain love? How can I explain freedom? The idea would only frighten her, now.

But it's too late. She takes another step back. She's already frightened.

"Please, Gracelyn…"

She has to understand. She has to come. She just has to.

Chapter Fifty-Four

Gracelyn

Go with her? The idea feels impossible, like breaking through a wall. Evie's stare presses into me, her eyes wide with the weight of all she's promising. But I struggle to come to terms with the idea, and find it is an unwelcome one, jarring and invasive.

"I can't."

Regret pools around the edges of my words.

Evie's eyes flicker with confusion. "You can. Just follow me. That's all you have to do."

Oh, how to explain.

I thought, because I had strayed so far, I had cut my ties to the Quads. But leave? I realize now it's not a tie, but an elastic band, and I have stretched this mess as far as I am able. Any further, and I will snap apart. What lies beyond that to put me back together? I don't know. It's not enough.

This wasn't the plan.

There is no option left but to let go. To give in to the band's tug and allow it pull me back in. Back to where I belong.

Go with her? Evie might as well ask me to leap off a cliff.

As this truth sinks in, my hands begin to shake. My fingers throb from the punches I threw at Quinn, and all I want is to curl up on the ground and wait to be cared for.

I want to go with Evie. I do. But I look in her eyes and I see the resilience that made her into this person before me now, and I cannot find it in myself. What seems to have made her stronger in these past weeks has almost broken me apart. It *will* break me, if I don't let go of it.

"No," I whisper.

And it is as if I have smashed everything into pieces.

The pain spreads over Evie's face slowly, in waves, knocking away her smile, wrinkling her forehead, extinguishing the light from her eyes.

Joyce's word – *grief.* It comes to my mind as the familiar, ugly darkness spreads through me again. It is so much worse than the first time, when I thought Evie was departed, a pain that seeps into my core in a way I am sure will scar and reshape me permanently. Because this time, it did not just *happen*. This time, I have failed her.

Evie reaches out her hand one more time, and her eyes beg me to take it.

Instead, I shrink away, unable to look her in the eye. Even with the Licentia still to face back home, this is far more terrifying – something that shakes me to the core and threatens everything I know.

"I'm sorry," I whisper.

Chapter Fifty-Five

Evie

Gracelyn steps back, tears brimming, and pulls her wounded hands close to her chest. As if I might pull at her again. As if I might *hurt* her.

And that look in her eyes. Like I've betrayed her. It's a look I never expected, not from Gracelyn. Never in a million years.

No.

Her word hangs in the air between us, stiff and final and shattering.

"Please, Gracelyn. You've got to. There is so much more than the Directorate out there. You can't begin to imagine. There's a whole world. And it's incredible."

I scramble to find the right words, the ones that will convince her. I realize now I wasn't prepared to explain. I thought that somehow, she'd understand, like she has always understood me. But of course she can't – she hasn't had all these weeks to live it like I have. And I am pathetically unprepared to show it to her.

I've lost her, I realize. *I've failed her.*

In a single, slow split, my heart breaks.

Kinlee's digipad buzzes. She checks it, then looks to me. "Time's up."

As if the sound of the alert broke a spell, Gracelyn draws back, still shaking her head. Then she turns and runs, stumbling down the tunnel, back towards the Quad.

Chapter Fifty-Six

Evie

All I can do is stare as Gracelyn disappears into the tunnel's darkness. I don't know how I can ever learn to accept Gracelyn's choice.

But that's what I wanted for her, after all, isn't it? Choice?

"Evie, *now,* damnit!" Kinlee isn't asking. She's ordering.

And she's right. Gracelyn's gone. I can't accept it, but somehow, I'll have to. That's one thing I have learned these past weeks: life goes on. Even when you think it can't. I don't need to accept it right now. Right now, all I have to do is run.

"What about you?" I ask.

"You know I'm staying," she says.

"But what will you report back to the Directorate?"

Kinlee – Kate – nudges Quinn's limp body, still unconscious. "Looks to me like a lone Licentia was stirring up trouble. But how about that, I caught her. I'll probably get a promotion soon, high performer like that. Now *go.*"

She shoves me, and I let the momentum carries me down the tunnel towards the camp.

I run as hard as I can, run from the limits, the fears, the heartbreak of Gracelyn's choice. Run for Connor, for nights in the stars, for zip lines and cinnamon rolls and possibility so open and bright it's blinding. I run until my lungs burn and the pounding in my head forces out all thought, until the immediacy of my body's strain drowns out everything else.

Chapter Fifty-Seven

Gracelyn

My breaths heave like I have never experienced before. I fixate on the force of the *in* and *out* of the air in my chest and follow the blue line back towards comfort and safety, blurry through my tears.

With each step, a tearing pain shoots through me, as if my heart was splitting. A pain so deep and all-consuming it blocks out the throbbing of my swelling fingers. All else falls away, and I am left with only a desperate need for the pain to end. As I reach the ladder, I collapse against it. Something like a sob escapes me.

"You made the right choice, Gracelyn."

The unexpected voice makes me jump. It's distorted by the echo of the tunnels… and yet it is familiar – the voice of the loudspeaker announcements that ring through the Quads, and the Directorate orders that feed through the screen in my living room. A voice that trails from down the hall at the office and reverberates through my house.

I turn to it to find a glint of glasses over a dark moustache, hovering in the darkness of the cover near the ladder. Finally, it all comes together, that strange sense of recognition this voice has always given me.

"Father! What are you – "

He shakes his head. "No more questions, Gracelyn. You're done with that now. Aren't you?"

He's not wrong. I am so tired. All my questions led to was problems, which led to pain. I only have a few left in me now.

"You knew, didn't you? This whole time."

"Of course."

"And Evie? You knew she was alive? That she was out here?"

Father blinks. "I knew about the failed departures. They don't trouble me with the details of whom or when."

The details. I let it slide, too defeated to fight back anymore after all that's happened.

"Are you in charge of it all? The Quad? The Directorate?"

"Not alone. A group of us."

It sinks in slowly: a prism shifting to expose new colors of light, a truth that was there all along, hidden from sight.

"How can you do it? How can you toy with an entire society's gene pool?" I want to lash out, but I find I am too tired.

Father's mouth twitches at the edge. "You're a smart girl, to figure that out. But you know why you're so smart? Haven't you figured out where that perfect memory comes from? The work we do here to advance humanity."

"Advance humanity? You're manipulating us all. Manipulating our genetics."

"We prefer the word 'optimizing,'" Father says, his expression still blank. "Don't you want to be as smart and healthy as possible? Don't you want to live longer? You don't get a photographic memory and a hundred-and-forty-year lifespan by accident. You are old enough to understand that all things come at a price. We make the hard choices necessary so that citizens like you can benefit."

"What about the others?" I reply. "What about citizens like Evie? It's not right."

Father shakes his head.

"'Right'? 'Wrong'? These are children's words, Gracelyn," he replies. "You're grown up now. There is what serves the greater population and what does not. There is strong and there is weak. The Directorate is strong. Its people are strong. I tried to tell you. All of this fighting and questioning, it isn't good for you. You see that now, don't you?"

I do.

292

What was it all for? Evie was fine – more than fine – this whole time. And I am so tired. I press my forehead against the cool metal of the ladder.

"How did you know?" I ask.

His glasses glint as his head tilts. "Do you really think we could allow citizens to break into the tunnels without supervision? Or sneak out at night? Or search our database?"

No, I realize. The full force of my stupidity wrenches through my chest. Of course not.

"We allow those who need it an outlet when we can afford to. In fact, I appreciated your help settling the Martin boy situation. Ugly work, but it needed to be done." He pauses, assessing me. "But that's over now. Isn't it?"

There is nothing left to do, and all I want is to go back to how it was before. I nod, tears dropping from my cheek.

"Then let me make it better."

He stretches out his hand. In his palm rests something small and round. *A pill.* Joyce promised they would bring me peace. I pick it up and stare at it.

"The Licentia. They have been following me."

Father shakes his head. "We took advantage of their attack today to do a little tidying up. You won't see them again."

As I consider, the pain is chased by something new – a collapse. A stillness. A giving way. And with it, relief.

Why keep fighting?

The question hovers in my mind, and nothing rises up against it. There is nothing left to fight for, if I am choosing to stay. And I have made my choice.

I thrust the pill into my mouth, and even as I swallow it, a sense of peace settles over me. The first peace I've had since I heard Evie stirring through the wall that morning. Was it only weeks ago? It feels like a lifetime.

"Good girl," Father says.

With slow, mechanical movements, I pull myself up the ladder, Father behind me. I step out from the darkness and back into the life of order and predictability waiting for me above.

Chapter Fifty-Eight

Evie

I trace the blue line through the tunnels all the way back to the camp. Between burning breaths, I choke on sobs that are hard and relentless.

Why wouldn't Gracelyn come? How could she possibly choose the Directorate after all they have done?

It doesn't matter why. She did.

I reach the ladder. As I climb up, I flash back to the fear I felt the first time I climbed through its portal, and the life I did not yet know waited for me on the other side.

I open the hatch, half-expecting to find the frenzy of activity I left behind – maybe even for Raina to be there, waiting to scold me for my foolishness, or Connor, pacing anxiously in wait. But the bunker is dark and abandoned. The machines are sleeping, not a single sheet of paper left to hint at the life that filled this place only hours ago. Where did they go? How far have they gotten?

I dig Raina's now-crinkled map out of my pocket and trace the pen-lined path she drew on it towards safety.

I'll find Connor. And Raina, if I can. And a whole new life.

And then… Well, I have no idea what comes after that. It's all open and unknown.

And for now, that's okay.

Fantastic Books
Great Authors

darkstroke is
an imprint of
Crooked Cat Books

- Gripping Thrillers
- Cosy Mysteries
- Romantic Chick-Lit
- Fascinating Historicals
- Exciting Fantasy
- Young Adult Adventures
- Non-Fiction

Discover us online
www.darkstroke.com

Find us on instagram:
www.instagram.com/darkstrokebooks

29479510R00169